H...

"Fabulously entertaining—a great romance in an inventive, believable steampunk world!"
—Stephanie Laurens, *New York Times* bestselling author of *The Capture of the Earl of Glencrae*

"*Heart of Brass* is riveting! I couldn't put it down. I can't wait for the next book. Kate Cross is fabulous!"
—Victoria Alexander, #1 *New York Times* bestselling author of *My Wicked Little Lies*

"A delightfully adventurous steampunk filled with riveting action, wicked spies, steamy romance, and an all-star cast. Lush world building transports us to an exciting time where carriages and automatons are beheld side by side. . . . I recommend Kate Cross's newest steampunk series if you enjoy strong protagonists, witty dialogue, delish romance, and exciting adventure."
— Smexy Books Romance Reviews

"An engrossing and enjoyable read."
—That's What I'm Talking About

"A great tale that deftly blends a solid mystery, enemy spy–versus–spy espionage excitement, and a potentially lethal romance."   —Genre Go Round Reviews

"A very developed, complicated book."
—Fiction Vixen Book Reviews

"A fascinating steampunk spy novel complete with a heartwarming reunion."   —Dark Faerie Tales

"Rip-roaring . . . [a] thrilling tale set in steam-powered London. Cross layers her exciting romantic tale with mystery, treachery, and even a serial killer. Riveting from beginning to end, this book is an exceptional launch to a series."   —*RT Book Reviews* (4½ stars)

Touch of Steel

A NOVEL OF THE CLOCKWORK AGENTS

KATE CROSS

A SIGNET ECLIPSE BOOK

SIGNET ECLIPSE
Published by New American Library, a division of
Penguin Group (USA) Inc., 375 Hudson Street,
New York, New York 10014, USA
Penguin Group (Canada), 90 Eglinton Avenue East, Suite 700, Toronto,
Ontario M4P 2Y3, Canada (a division of Pearson Penguin Canada Inc.)
Penguin Books Ltd., 80 Strand, London WC2R 0RL, England
Penguin Ireland, 25 St. Stephen's Green, Dublin 2,
Ireland (a division of Penguin Books Ltd.)
Penguin Group (Australia), 250 Camberwell Road, Camberwell, Victoria 3124,
Australia (a division of Pearson Australia Group Pty. Ltd.)
Penguin Books India Pvt. Ltd., 11 Community Centre, Panchsheel Park,
New Delhi - 110 017, India
Penguin Group (NZ), 67 Apollo Drive, Rosedale, Auckland 0632,
New Zealand (a division of Pearson New Zealand Ltd.)
Penguin Books (South Africa) (Pty.) Ltd., 24 Sturdee Avenue,
Rosebank, Johannesburg 2196, South Africa

Penguin Books Ltd., Registered Offices:
80 Strand, London WC2R 0RL, England

First published by Signet Eclipse, an imprint of New American Library,
a division of Penguin Group (USA) Inc.

First Printing, December 2012
10 9 8 7 6 5 4 3 2 1

Copyright © Kathryn Smith, 2012
All rights reserved. No part of this book may be reproduced, scanned, or dis-
tributed in any printed or electronic form without permission. Please do not
participate in or encourage piracy of copyrighted materials in violation of the
author's rights. Purchase only authorized editions.

SIGNET ECLIPSE and logo are trademarks of Penguin Group (USA) Inc.

Printed in the United States of America

PUBLISHER'S NOTE
This is a work of fiction. Names, characters, places, and incidents either are the
product of the author's imagination or are used fictitiously, and any resemblance to actual persons, living or dead, business establishments, events, or
locales is entirely coincidental.

   The publisher does not have any control over and does not assume any responsibility for author or third-party Web sites or their content.

If you purchased this book without a cover you should be aware that this book
is stolen property. It was reported as "unsold and destroyed" to the publisher
and neither the author nor the publisher has received any payment for this
"stripped book."

This book is for the steampunk community, not only for all the enthusiasm and support I've been given but for being the most incredibly wonderful group of people I've ever met.

It's also for Steve, for teaching me that friendship is the ackbone of a successful marriage. You're my BFF, babe.

3 1133 07066 0610

Chapter 1

The only sound louder than the breath panting from her lungs was that of blood dripping onto the toe of her boot.

Claire Brooks crouched behind the grimy chimney stack and pressed her hand to her side. Wet seeped through the boning of her corset and the thin wool of her coat, warming her chilled fingers.

Her lungs burned and her gun hand was cramped, but she refused to set down her pistol. She refused to give up the chase. It would take more than a hole in her side to stop her now.

Across the roof, she heard Howard scurrying away like the rat he was. He could not escape, not when she had already chased him across five countries. Robert's death could not go unavenged.

Gritting her teeth against the ungodly burning in her side, she braced her shoulder against the sooty brick and leaned hard as she dug her boot heel into the rough stone. She pushed herself to her feet, biting her lip to keep from crying out.

She lifted her gun, blinked the sweat out of her eyes, took aim and fired. The dark figure running toward the edge of the roof ducked as the aetheric blast sent bits of brick scattering near his shoulder.

Damn it. A miss. If her vision weren't so blurry from sweat trickling into her eyes, she would have gotten him.

Still clutching her side—blood soaking her fingers now—she ran after him, every strike of her heels a new lesson in pain.

You're not going to die just yet, she told herself. *Not until you know for certain you're going to take that bastard with you. He dies first.*

She thought of Robert, of how there hadn't been enough of him left for her to have a proper funeral for him, how he'd been betrayed by the organization to which he had pledged his life. The thought of seeing him again, whether in heaven or hell, wasn't what pushed her forward. What kept her running despite the sheer agony of it was that she had sworn to send Howard to his judgment first.

Moonlight cut through the clouds as Howard leaped from the edge of the roof to the next. Claire didn't hesitate, her stride easily bridging the narrow gap between buildings. A shot whizzed past her ear, and she pitched herself downward. She hit the roof hard, falling to her knees.

"Arrhh!" Lights danced before her eyes as agony ripped through her. Bile rose in her throat as darkness threatened to claim her. Ignoring the smell of burned hair, she swallowed and staggered to her feet. Howard was putting too much distance between them; he was already at the opposite side.

She raised her pistol and fired again. The sound cracked the night like the lash of a whip. Howard made a guttural cry. She'd hit the bastard. A grim smile tugged on her lips as she forced her legs to move faster. Her battered knees protested, but they did as she willed. Howard had stumbled when she shot him, and she was closing the gap between them.

This time he hesitated at the edge of the roof. He clutched his shoulder as he turned his head to look at her over his shoulder. Smoke drifted upward from between his fingers, the fabric of his coat smoldering from the blast. His face was different than the last time she had seen him, but then his face was different every time. He was a master of disguise, and Claire doubted that even the higher-ups at the Company knew his true countenance. When she killed him, she would peel back the layers of his disguise and see the real him for herself.

He raised his hand—she had winged his gun arm— and waved before dropping over the ledge.

Claire froze, but only for a second. *What the hell?* She ran to the edge, her gaze searching the distance between the ledge and the next building. There was no sign of him. Realization crashed through her skull just as something closed around her ankle. She looked down.

How could she be so stupid?

Stanton Howard grinned up at her from where he hung on a crude rope ladder. Just a split second before he yanked her off balance, she realized it was his hand wrapped around her leg. She raised her gun, but it was too late—she was already plummeting toward the alley below.

She twisted her body so that her back was to the ground, raised the gun at the man climbing back to the roof and fired. He jerked, and—

She hit with teeth-jarring force. Pain embraced her entire body, and everything went black.

She woke up to the low murmur of nearby voices. Fog swam thick in her brain, and her limbs were heavy— almost as heavy as her tongue felt in her mouth.

Not dead then.

A dull, faint ache radiated across the back of her skull. Her back was sore and her side burned, but none of these complaints bothered her as much as not knowing the location of her gun.

Opium. They had given her opium—whoever "they" were. They had drugged her and taken her weapon—her clothes, too. Damn it, that meant she was in a hospital.

Why wasn't she dead? Howard couldn't have allowed her to live out of the kindness of his traitorous heart. She remembered falling toward the street . . . a carriage stopping below her . . . men with guns appearing just as she yanked her body around. That carriage had stopped her fall. It had saved her.

Opening her eye took every ounce of strength she

possessed. The room was a blur of motion and colors, and her lids felt as though they'd been lined with sand.

"She's waking up." The voice was female, the accent a strange, melodic mix of Irish and that of some exotic land.

Slowly, her eyes righted themselves and began to focus. Claire blinked. Standing before her were a dusky-skinned woman so strikingly beautiful she probably had very few female friends and a tall, stern-looking man with a very British nose. The two of them looked very official, but neither of them had the constabulary look.

"How do you feel?" the woman inquired.

"Like I was shot and fell off a roof," Claire replied. The words came out as "thot" and "rooth."

The woman actually smiled a little. "I imagine so." She came closer to the side of the bed. Claire watched warily as she poured a glass of water from a pitcher on the tray of a small, squat automaton, its engine whirling with a sound much like a kitten's purr. Then she bent at the waist and wound a large key on the side of the bed. A few seconds later the bed gave a tiny but still-painful lurch. Slowly, as the mechanism ground into use, gears churning and clicking, the upper part of the bed rose, until Claire was almost upright. There was an audible "click," and then all went still.

The cool lip of the cup pressed against Claire's parched lips. "Drink," the woman instructed.

Claire did not need to be told twice. She gulped greedily, closing her eyes in pleasure as the cold water ran over her thick tongue and down her parched throat.

She couldn't remember the last time she'd tasted anything so delicious.

And then she realized it wasn't the opium that made it impossible to lift her arms—her wrists were strapped to the bed frame.

When the cup ran dry, the woman refilled it and held it for her once again. This time as she drank, Claire allowed her gaze to roam around the sterile ward. Her heart threatened to pound, but she kept herself calm. She'd been in worse situations before.

There were two other patients in the room. One was a man several beds away. His face was a mask of bandages, and one of his legs was encased in a brass boot that extended above his knee. Wait. That wasn't a boot at all. That was his leg! The prosthesis looked like a boot, but the knee was reticulated, not encased in brass like the rest. That there was no flesh beneath it was the only way Claire could tell that it was a false limb.

It was impossible to determine whether the other occupant was male or female. Its entire length was wrapped like an Egyptian mummy she'd once seen on display. Carrying fluids in and out, tubes and wires ran out of the body, stimulating the muscles with a low aetheric pulse so that they moved and twitched beneath the bandages. Metal braces kept the body still, and a large bellows above the bed kept the person breathing.

It was a terrifying sight. Surely death would be preferable.

Obviously neither of these patients was the reason

for the heavily armed guard at the door. There was no chance of either of them escaping any time soon. And if the guard was there for their protection, he would be watching the door, not the patients.

Damn. The weapon in his hands—a Baker scatter rifle—was used to kill rather than simply injure or maim. It was very effective as well, the casings of the bullets designed to fragment and burrow once inside the body like little metal predators.

That gun was meant for her.

"Who are you?" she asked the woman.

"I'm Dr. Evelyn Stone." The doctor took the cup and set it on the bedside table. The automaton had shuffled off to assist a nurse tending to the "mummy." "You are a very fortunate woman. If that carriage hadn't broken your fall, you might have ended up in far worse shape than you are now."

Yes, like the person four beds away. "Where am I?" And where the hell was her gun?

It was the man who answered. "You're in Warden custody, Miss Brooks."

The Wardens. Hell's bells. She wished Howard had killed her. Claire kept her face blank—it wasn't difficult, given the heaviness of her muscles. Opiates were the very devil as far as she was concerned. She'd rather have pain than helpless oblivion. "Is that supposed to frighten me?"

The man stared down his imperious nose at her. He embodied everything pretentious and controlling the Wardens of the Realm stood for with their empire and monarchy. "If you are not afraid, you are clearly less intelligent than most Company agents. I wouldn't aspire to such a claim."

Arrogant British bastard. What did he know of fear? He probably spent his days behind a desk; the most worrisome thing he ever had to face was his undoubtedly bitter wife.

"If you wanted me dead, I'd be dead," she responded, words slurring around her lazy tongue. "That means you've actually deluded yourself into thinking you'll get information out of me. Which one of us is lacking in intelligence now, Mr. Idiot?"

A dull flush flooded his muttonchop-covered cheeks. He looked as though he had scrub brushes bolted to the side of his face, the things were so bushy. "I would be happy to put you in an interrogation chair." Yes, he looked as though the idea of putting her in what was essentially a torture device pleased him greatly. "Whether or not you cooperate is entirely up to you, Miss Brooks, just as whether or not you live or die is up to me."

Dr. Stone shot him a dark look, her striking features downright intimidating. "You mean it's up to the director, Ashford."

"Yes, well . . ." He sniffed. "She's not here right now, is she? And during her absence and Wolfred's leave, I am acting director."

Aw, hell. She had to go and piss on the boots of a man filled to the brim with his own importance. Being locked up or killed was not going to help her find Howard. Time was already against her. He was undoubtedly on his way north by now. Every moment put more distance between them. At least she knew where he was headed.

She had not come this far to let him slip away. She could not let Robert's death go unanswered. He was all the family she had left, and now she was alone in the world. She had no one to lean on. No one to tell her when she was wrong or when she had gone too far—when she was too reckless for sense. Not that Robert had been around when she could have benefited from any of those things. Still, just knowing he'd been out there, that she wasn't alone in the world, had been enough most times.

"What do you want from me?" she asked, lifting her gaze past that beak of a nose. There was no use in wallowing in self-pity. This vulture would use it against her if he thought he could. He'd probably peck out her liver while he was at it.

Cold eyes brightened with a malicious gleam. If she had full control of her limbs, she'd stab him in the neck with his own cravat pin. "I want to know why you're in London. I want to know whatever Company secrets you have in that pretty little head of yours. I want the names of every enemy agent here on British soil."

And she wanted her brother back. "I can't give you all of that."

"You'll give me something or I'll see you hang."

Dr. Stone grabbed him by the arm. "I'll report you."

He shook her off. "What will it be, Miss Brooks?"

She had to get out of there and soon. This bastard wasn't about to let her go. She needed an ally—someone who knew her, who could provide a little protection until she could figure out how to escape. Her luck hadn't quite forsaken her, not yet.

"I want something in return."

He made a scoffing noise. "You're not in any position to bargain, girlie."

Claire clenched her jaw. "Then you may as well hang me, *laddie*." She affected a bad British accent on the word. "Then you can explain to your director how the Wardens missed out on capturing Stanton Howard."

What color the man had in his pasty cheeks drained. "Stanton Howard?"

She grinned. "Prepared to bargain now?"

He cleared his throat, glaring at her as though she were a bug he'd dearly like to grind beneath his heel. "What do you want?"

There was only one person she could trust in all of London. "Lucas Grey," she replied. "I want to talk to Lucas Grey."

"You look like shite."

Alastair Payne, Earl of Wolfred, wiped the dirt from his hands with the remains of an old shirt. Smears of oil and dirt stained the once-pristine linen. He'd been working on the Velocycle for a good three-quarters of an hour before his oldest friend, Lucas Grey, showed up, and now the machine was in top condition.

"I've been back in the country for a fortnight, and already you're trying to woo me with your considerable charm." A sardonic smile curved his lips. "Really, Luke. People will talk."

Many men would bristle at the affront to their mas-
culinity, but Luke merely chuckled. "What I lack in tact
I have an abundance of in sincerity. Arden's worried
about you."

It was a cheap shot, and they both knew it. Alastair
no longer considered himself in love with Arden, but
she was still a dear friend. In fact, she and Luke were
possibly his only true friends. Because of that bond, he
knew that Arden wasn't the only one of the two of
them who was worried.

"I'm fine."

"No pain?"

As though on cue, his left leg twinged—a bone-deep
ache, though there wasn't any bone left to cause discomfort, just metal beneath the flesh. "None. Evie says
I simply need to regain a stone or two and I'll be right
as rain." He'd been putting his body through its paces
in an attempt to regain the strength he'd lost after being
left for dead in Spain. He would be strong again. Stronger.

And he would be more careful as to whom he offered his heart.

"Good." Luke's pale gaze was sharp as it met his.
"And mentally? Are you recovered there as well?"

Had it been anyone else, Alastair would have told
him to bugger off, but Luke was no stranger to the ef-
fects a life of intrigue and deceit could have on a man's
mind. "Better than I ought to be, I'm told."

Luke frowned, dark brows pulling low over pale
blue eyes. "According to whom?"

"Evie." He tossed the soiled rag of a shirt onto a

nearby workbench. "She seems to think I'm afraid to admit how deeply the attack affected me."

His friend regarded him for a moment, his sharp face as unreadable as a blank slate. "Are you?"

"No." Alastair settled his hands on his hips. "This concern for my welfare is appreciated, believe me, but I'm getting a little tired of everyone thinking I'm headed for a cell in Bedlam. I've had people try to kill me before."

Luke's expression didn't change. "This is the first time it was someone you fancied yourself in love with."

"I didn't love her," he scoffed. No, but he had liked her awfully well.

"Fine. You cared for her, and you believed she cared about you, right up until the moment she led you into a trap that resulted in your being stabbed, crushed beneath a carriage and left for dead. I don't understand how you can be all right with that, either. I wouldn't be."

"You seemed fine enough when your former mistress tried to kill you," Alastair shot back. It had been little more than a year since Rani Ogitani revealed herself as a traitor and almost got Luke and his wife, Arden, killed. At the time, Alastair had been in love with Arden, and part of him wouldn't have minded comforting his friend's widow. After all, they'd believed Luke to be dead for seven years before that.

Well, Alastair had believed him dead. Arden had never given up hope. She had never stopped loving a man who really had no idea how lucky he was to have her. Luke knew now, though. The forced amnesia that had kept him from his wife hadn't completely gone away, but Luke hadn't needed his memories to fall in love with Arden again.

Luke scowled. He was devilishly good at scowling. "I never loved her, and she never pretended to love me."

"I guess that makes you a better judge of character than I am," he said, sounding like a peevish five-year-old, "because I thought Sascha's affection for me was genuine." Right up until she stuck a dagger in his side. Fortunately, she missed all the important bits. She hadn't expressed even a hint of remorse when she limped away from the carriage, leaving him pinned beneath it, her betrayal cutting far deeper than any blade could.

The thing that cut deepest, however, was the realization that he'd allowed himself to be played like a fool, like a boy right out of the nursery.

Luke's scowl deepened. "This isn't about me. It's about you, you great ginger arse."

"I told you, I'm *fine*." And he was, for the most part. "Are you too thickheaded to understand that?"

"You're the one who's mentally impaired if you think I believe that load of horse shite. You're not fine, Alastair. No one in your situation would be fine."

Alastair paused, on the verge of telling his oldest friend to go straight to hell with hopes of being buggered by the very devil. Luke was only concerned for his well-being, so why was he denying what the other man so clearly understood? What was he trying to prove by lying?

"You're right," he admitted. "I'm not fine, but I will be, and I don't want to talk about it. I don't want to discuss her or what she did—not until I can do so without blaming myself for being such a naive fool. That said, will you please leave it alone?" Or would he not be satisfied until Alastair laid himself flayed open before him, whining about how he'd thought himself so smooth, seducing the German girl into gathering information for him, only to realize too late that she was a Company sympathizer set up to seduce him, and the lover of the same man he'd been sent to investigate?

Luke's mouth tilted. "Not another word. Show me what you've done to this great hulking beast." He gestured at Alastair's custom-built Velocycle, which was equipped with concealed weapons such as aether pistols and a tracking mechanism that allowed him to "call" the machine to him by simply pressing a button.

Grateful for the change of topic, Alastair showed him the modifications he'd made, such as a small aether cannon over the back wheel for firing upon pursuers. "I put a new engine in her. She'll top fifty now."

"Miles?" At his nod, Luke whistled. "I'll have to get you to take a look at my machine. You've always been the more mechanically inclined of the two of us."

Yes, for all the good it had done him. "Bring it over some afternoon. I'll take a look." He pointed out the other improvements he'd made—mostly cosmetic. Tinkering on the Velocycle had kept his mind occupied, giving him something to think about other than having been made an arse of by a woman he'd entertained a future with. Though, when he first met Sascha, she'd simply been a substitute for the woman he couldn't have—Arden. That only added insult to injury—that he'd been completely taken in by a woman he'd seen only as a diversion.

A bell rang as Luke studied the Velocycle. It was for the handset and mouthpiece that provided communication between the building that stored his engine-based vehicles and the main house. He grabbed the handset on the second bell. "Yes, what is it?"

His housekeeper's voice filled his ear. "Begging your pardon, my lord, but there's a young girl here who says she has a message for Lord Huntley's ears alone."

It had to be W.O.R. business. Only the Wardens of the Realm would send a verbal message. Notes were too easily found and read. Verbal messages could be turned into lies if the messenger was set upon. Verbal messages could be taken to a person's grave.

"Send the girl out, Mrs. Grue."

"Of course, sir. Right away."

Alastair hung up and turned to Luke, who stood beside the Velocycle, watching him. "Something wrong?"

"There's a messenger here for you."

Luke frowned. "Warden?"

"I assume so. Are you on assignment?"

His friend shook his dark head. "I meant it when I gave my and Arden's resignations. I haven't done any work for the W.O.R. other than consulting on Company operative interrogations."

"It must be important for them to track you down here." They hadn't bothered with Alastair much at all since his return, but he had no desire to seem petty, so he kept that to himself. Plus he'd wager Ashford—the bird-beaked ponce—was enjoying his position as acting director too much to risk Alastair's taking it from him.

"It had best be." Luke wore a dark expression that would make even Alastair think twice about engaging him. The man's skeleton was entirely augmented with gregorite—the hardest metal known to man—and he'd been trained to kill by both the Wardens and that organization's enemy agency, the Company.

The rivalry, for lack of a better word, between the W.O.R. and the Company went back to the years leading up to the war with America. The Company had started in Boston, but quickly spread its tentacles around the world, gathering up those who wished to bring down the British Empire—and its friends. They'd started as rebels—idealists—but now had their own agenda for world domination, their goals long since bastardized and twisted.

At least that was how most Wardens viewed them. Alastair reckoned Company agents saw themselves as the heroes in their intrigues, just as any Warden might regard him/herself. Sometimes he thought right and wrong amounted to little more than point of view.

A few moments later there came a knock upon the door. Alastair opened it to find a young girl of perhaps twelve standing at the threshold. "Lord Wolfred?" she inquired. "I'm Betsey Meekins. I've a message for Lord Huntley."

Her no-nonsense, very-adult tone made him smile.

"Come in, Miss Meekins." He stepped back so she might enter the building. She crossed the threshold as regally as a queen and walked directly up to Luke, who was easily a full foot taller than she.

Betsey offered her hand, which Luke took, a vaguely amused expression replacing his scowl. "Pleased to make your acquaintance, Miss Meekins. What is the message?"

She glanced over her shoulder at Alastair. "They didn't say anything about having an audience, my lord."

"I assure you Lord Wolfred is trustworthy, and he can be privy to anything you wish to tell me."

She shrugged as she turned back to him. "So long as you'll take responsibility for him. I'm to tell you that a Miss Claire Brooks from America is in the infirmary and will speak only to you."

Color leached from Luke's lean cheeks. "Claire Brooks. Are you certain?"

The girl nodded. "I'm never uncertain, sir."

Alastair would have chuckled at her youthful arrogance were it not for the expression on his friend's face. Luke looked as though he'd seen a ghost.

"Tell the acting director, Ashford, I'll be there shortly." Luke took a coin from his pocket and handed it to the girl. "Run along now. There's a good girl."

Betsey curtsied to them both and quickly took her leave. Alastair waited until the door had shut and she would have to be out of earshot before he asked, "Now it's my turn to ask whether or not *you* are fine."

Luke chuckled with little humor. "I don't think so,

my friend. Not at all. I'm off to the Wardens, and you are coming with me."

"Good lord, man. What the devil for?" Luke had never asked for him to accompany him anywhere that he could remember.

"So you can plead my case to Arden when my past bites me on the arse."

Understanding dawned. "So Claire Brooks . . . ?" Alastair raised his brow suggestively.

His friend rubbed a hand over his brow. "Is a Company agent. And my former lover."

Chapter 2

If she could lure the guard to her bedside, Claire might be able to overpower him long enough to use his own weapon against him. Unfortunately, she was wearing nothing but a flimsy chemise, and her injuries would make escape a slow and arduous task.

"You wouldn't make it out of the ward, let alone the building."

She looked up. Dr. Stone stood above her. She hadn't even noticed the woman approach. Either she was still foggy from the opiates she'd been given or she was losing her focus. Neither was acceptable. "I don't know what you're talking about."

"No, of course not." It might have been her imagination, but Claire thought the other woman rolled her eyes. "I need to check your wounds."

"Aren't you afraid I'll try to overpower you?"

Wooden legs scraped the floor as Dr. Stone pulled a

chair to her bedside. "Are you afraid I'll give you enough laudanum to ensure you never wake up?"

"No," she scoffed. "That wouldn't be in your best interest." She was useful to the Wardens. She just had to make certain she remained so until she'd recovered enough to make an attempt at freedom.

"And trying to escape wouldn't be in yours." The doctor hitched her dark brown trousers and sat down. "I'm going to lift your gown. Let me know if anything hurts."

She already hurt—all over. The carriage might have broken her fall, but she felt as though it had broken a few bones at the same time. Claire gritted her teeth in anticipation of the pain to come. "Go ahead."

Dr. Stone lifted the gown and peeled back the blood-stained muslin over Claire's side. Claire sucked in a breath as the fabric pulled at her skin, her dried blood acting as a kind of glue.

"Care to dump some salt on it while you're at it?" she demanded. "Maybe poke it with a stick?"

"You're very lucky," the doctor said. "The shot missed anything vital; elsewise you'd really have something to whine about."

Whining? The woman accused her of whining when she'd just been shot and fallen off a roof. Claire gave her a grim look. "So lucky I ended up in Warden custody and your charming care."

The darker woman shot her a surprised glance. Then her lips twitched. "Better than dead."

"That depends on your view of the world."

Dr. Stone's dark gaze went back to her work as she

applied salve to Claire's side. "Dead is dead, Miss Brooks. Anything else means there's still hope."

"And what exactly do you think I should have hope for?"

Clean bandages were smoothed over her ravaged flesh by gentle hands. "That the Earl of Huntley is inclined to plead your case."

Claire shrugged. The movement pulled at her stitches and made her wince. "Either he will or he won't." Inside, she wasn't nearly so disinterested. If Luke couldn't do anything for her, she would have to try to escape on her own. The longer she was held in Warden custody, the farther ahead of her Howard would get, and she wasn't going to give him much of a chase in her current condition. "What do you care?"

The doctor stood. "I believe in the sanctity of life. Occupational hazard, I suppose. Get some rest. They'll be moving you to a cell as soon as you're ready. You'll be more comfortable there."

Her brows rose. "I doubt that."

"Suit yourself. I'll check on you later. Rest now."

Claire closed her eyes, but sleep eluded her. Her mind insisted on worrying, working over every detail of her pursuit of Howard. How could she have been so stupid as to let him get away? It was the mistake of a green agent, which she was not. She'd been with the Company since she was fifteen. Thirteen years of experience should have at least kept her out of Warden hands. Instead, she'd allowed her emotions to rule her and got herself not only shot, but captured.

Robert would be rolling in his grave right now—if

he had one. She had his pocket watch and that was it. Even his signet ring, the one that had belonged to their father and grandfather, had been lost to the explosion that claimed her brother's life.

She was completely alone in the world, and it was all Stanton Howard's fault.

Tears threatened to slip from beneath her lashes, but she refused to let them go. She would cry for Robert once she had avenged him, and not a moment before. It was senseless, she knew, but if she cried now, she feared she might lose her memories of him, along with the rage that drove her. Grief was all she had, and she would not give it up. Not yet.

So she forced herself to think of happy times, of years long ago when her mother and father were still alive, and the four of them had been a family. Occasionally they'd been a happy one when she was a child, before her father began to drink more and more often, lost his job and became a mean, self-loathing creature. She thought of Christmases spent together, of birthdays, town picnics and dances when she got to wear her finest dress and hope that John Taylor would *finally* notice that she was no longer a little girl.

Sleep must have come for her after all, for when she heard the male voices above her, she opened her eyes to find her vision blurry and her head foggy. Her hand immediately went for her aether pistol, only to find nothing. Right. She was a prisoner. John Taylor had married Althea Bowers, and Robert was dead.

"Claire."

Her heart rate slowed. She knew that voice. She'd

heard it in her ear many a night. Her gaze lifted and locked with one of purest blue ice. "Five."

He winced at the name, and Claire cursed herself for using it. But that was how she knew him. She hadn't known he was an earl when she shared her bed with him. She hadn't known he was a married man with a wife waiting for him at home.

It would have made a difference, knowing that he was married. Sometimes being a spy meant seducing men one didn't particularly like, or men who didn't hold themselves to the same vows of constancy as their wives. Spend enough time with such men, and finding one you did fancy—who didn't belong to another woman—was a rare find, and one to be taken advantage of.

She hadn't known he was a damn Warden. Then again, neither had he.

He looked better. Fitter. Happier. His black hair was a little longer, the angles of his face a little less sharp. He had another man with him. This one wasn't quite as tall as Fi . . . Lord Huntley, but he was more muscular. He was definitely English, with reddish hair and gray eyes.

And the way he stared down his nose at her. It was a strangely nice nose, for an Englishman. He had brackets etched on either side of his mouth that suggested he knew how to smile and did so often, though they might have just as easily been cracks from attempting to smile just once. He didn't look like a man who laughed all that often—or ate, for that matter. He could stand to gain a few pounds.

"Who are you?" she demanded.

Broad shoulders straightened beneath an olive green coat, and a gingery brow rose mockingly. "Alastair Payne, Lord Wolfred." Ah, the fine lines around his eyes and mouth weren't made from humor, but from mockery. She wasn't impressed, despite his pretty face. Christian names meant little in their line of work. "What do the Wardens call you?"

His expression didn't change, though his eyes went as cold and flat as a rain-soaked street. "Wouldn't be very deserving of such a surreptitious title if I told you, would I?"

No, of course not, but that didn't change that she'd like to know who she was up against. "That's hardly what you English call 'sporting' when you know who I am."

To her surprise, the rugged man turned that stormy gaze of his to Huntley, who shot him the barest of glances. "The Company called her the Dove."

Payne's eyebrows pulled into a deep scowl. "Jesus Christ," he muttered, his gravelly voice a harsh rasp.

Claire might have smiled in pride if not for the hatred dripping from his words. Hard gray eyes locked with hers. For one disconcerting second they flashed like twin mirrors. "You're lucky no one's sneaked in here to kill you."

She hadn't thought of that. Her mind had been too clouded by the laudanum to think clearly. When word got out that she'd been captured, there were Wardens who would try to kill her. The Company would as well. They wouldn't want to risk her spilling their secrets.

Hell's bells.

Huntley cleared his throat. "I don't know what you think I can do for you, Claire, but I'm not technically with the W.O.R. anymore."

She looked into the eyes of the man who had saved her life on more than one occasion and saw that he was telling the truth. She nodded, resigned. She was on her own, then. "I want you to know that I had no idea what the Company did to you." It was just another reason to hate the bastards. It was one thing to capture an enemy; it was another to meddle so deeply with his mind that he didn't know who he was. They'd sent him home to kill his own wife as the ultimate revenge—not only against the wife, but against Huntley as well.

"I never thought you did," he replied in that low, dark voice of his. He frowned as he sat down in the chair Dr. Stone had occupied earlier. "How did they even catch you?"

It was meant as a compliment, but it didn't feel like one under the weight of Payne's steely gaze. "I got myself shot and fell off a roof." She managed a smile. "Rough night."

"What can I do for you, pet?"

Claire's heart warmed at the nickname. "You know me. I need you to vouch that the information I give the Wardens is true."

"Why would we take anything you give us as fact?" Payne demanded. Color had risen to the jut of his cheekbones, and she noticed he had a smattering of freckles there.

Claire turned her focus back to Five. Damn it, *Huntley*. "Robert is dead."

Sincere sympathy softened his austere features, eliciting a hot wash of tears behind her eyes. She blinked them back. She'd rather be shot in the face than cry in front of Payne.

"Claire, I'm so sorry."

"Who's Robert?"

Huntley glanced up at his scowling friend. "Her brother. He was a friend of mine."

She expected Payne to twist the knife and rub a little salt in the raw meat of the wound. He did not. Instead, he inclined his head, the waves of his thick hair flashing copper under the lights. "My condolences."

"I don't need sympathy from you," she snarled. It was rude of her, but anger was the only thing that could keep the tears at bay. "You would have killed him yourself had you been given the chance."

His eyes brightened with emotion—a spark of lightning in the middle of a thunderstorm. "Yes, I very well might have, but if you're as eager to hand over Company secrets as you seem to be, I wager it wasn't the Wardens who ended him at all, was it?"

There was no cruelty in the words, just cold, hard assumption. Claire swallowed against the hatred clogging her throat. She didn't know this man, but she'd love to rip that lovely face right off his damn English skull.

"No," she replied from between clenched teeth,

holding his gaze. "It wasn't. My brother was killed because of the Company." She turned to Huntley. She couldn't give too much away. "He was betrayed by another agent and died in an explosion of that same agent's design. There wasn't even a body left for me to bury."

"I'm sorry, Claire. Very much."

He meant it, she knew. "They didn't do a thing to avenge him. The agent responsible is still free."

"Who is it?"

"I don't know." It was the first time, she realized, that she'd ever lied to him.

Huntley stared at her with those piercing eyes of his, weighing the truth of what she'd told him. "What can you offer the Wardens to justify leniency?"

That was simple. Her chin lifted. "I'll tell you every Company secret I know—including how to find Stanton Howard and the man who tried to destroy your mind."

"Surely you don't mean to take that seasoned liar at her word?" Alastair shook his head. "Christ, Luke. I shouldn't even have to ask."

They were in the study at Luke's house in Mayfair, not far from Alastair's own. He paced because he was too agitated to stand still. Luke, however, seemed terribly calm as he poured a dram of whiskey for each of them.

"I've never known Claire to be a liar," Luke replied, offering him a glass. Alastair took it and downed more than half its contents.

"That was when she thought you were on the same side." Heat from the liquor blossomed in his chest. "For the love of God, she's turned her back on her own agency."

"Careful." Luke gestured to his glass. Alastair glanced down. He was holding the crystal so tight, a fine crack ran down it. "I gave the W.O.R. everything I had on the Company as well."

Alastair flexed his fingers, forcing the metal beneath his skin to ease its grip. "It's hardly the same. You were a Warden for years. The Company abducted you, erased your memories and sent you back here to kill your own wife, all as a kind of vengeance against you, Arden and the W.O.R. Of course you turned over all you know about their operations."

"The Company has allowed her brother's death to go unpunished."

"Maybe for good reason." He downed the rest of his whiskey.

Luke's face took on a dangerous tightness. "He was my friend."

Alastair made a face. "And you were shagging her. Neither of those things says much for your clarity of judgment."

"I would think, given the circumstances, you would be the last man to question anyone's judgment."

Alastair straightened. This conversation was becoming far too heated. "That's why I question you. I know how attachment can cloud a man's sense."

Luke scowled at him. "Claire and I worked together,

and occasionally we slept together. It was not an attachment."

"What exactly was it, then?" came a crisp voice from the door. "And why does it matter now?"

Alastair closed his eyes. He did not want to be part of this. Arden, Luke's wife, was his friend as well, but this was none of his business.

He set his glass on a small table beside the sofa. "I'll give the two of you some privacy."

"Stay." Arden had come into the study and now stood on the richly patterned carpet. Her pale cheeks sported high splotches of red, and her whiskey brown eyes glittered in the lamplight. In her hand she held what appeared to be a compass, but Alastair knew it was nothing so mundane. It was her sentimentometer, and she was going to use it to ascertain her husband's— and likely his—emotions. All she had to do was point the bloody thing at either of them. "What's going on, Luke?"

Luke, to his credit, didn't look the least bit guilty. He faced his auburn-haired wife with a regretful but sincere expression. "The W.O.R. captured a Company spy—Claire Brooks, also known as the Dove. We often worked together when I was under the Company's control."

His wife obviously wasn't familiar with the name, or she didn't care that one of the Company's most dangerous and successful operatives was now in custody. "You slept with her."

Luke nodded. "I didn't know about you then, Arden.

I didn't know I had a wife; otherwise it never would have happened."

"I know." Arden didn't even consult the gadget in her palm, a fact that did not escape Alastair's notice. He would have looked. He would have *had* to look. She had that much faith in her husband that she had no doubt of his sincerity.

Alastair frowned. What must it be like to trust so completely? He hadn't really loved Sascha. He'd never loved anyone *that* much. The realization was like a kick to the chest. Had he been Arden, he wouldn't have taken Luke at his word any more than he would the word of that damn American. There was nothing wrong with being cautious. Better safe than sorry.

He'd already had enough sorry to last a lifetime.

His friends stared at each other. Both radiated regret, but there was tension as well—tension that would remain as long as he stood there, a reluctant bystander.

"I really must go," he announced, already walking toward the door. "The two of you need to discuss this, and I do not wish to bear witness."

"Alastair." It was Arden who stopped him.

He turned slightly. He really just wanted to be gone. "Yes?"

Her face was pale, but there was nothing waifish in her expression. If there was one woman who could handle this sort of situation with grace, it was Arden. She rarely listened to her heart without consulting her brain first. Though at times that was just as frustrating as an emotional response.

"This woman. Is she pretty?"

She was the most incredible-looking woman he'd ever seen—even pale and bruised. A man would go a long way for such seductive green eyes and a thoroughly kissable pout. "Passably," he lied.

Arden's shrewd gaze narrowed. "And is she a skilled agent?"

She was the bloody Dove—and like the bird Noah sent out from the ark, she did not return until her job was done, and she always returned victorious. Despite being dangerously feminine, she was hard as iron, and she fought her way out of trouble as often as she used her charms. She'd outmaneuvered several W.O.R. agents over the years and had made them look as capable as children. "Not skilled enough to avoid capture." They never would have caught her had she not been wounded and unconscious. She'd escaped capture several times in the past.

"Damn and blast." Arden's hands went to her hips. "The next time you speak to her, I will be present. I'm obviously the only one who will see past her reputation and looks." Her gaze moved to her husband. "Do you trust her?"

Luke nodded, his expression both resolute and wary. "I do. If she says she's no longer with the Company, I believe it."

"And you want the man who took control of your mind," Alastair reminded him. He regretted the words as soon as Luke looked at him. If it were possible to stare daggers at someone, he'd have been on the floor bleeding from several lethal wounds.

Astonishment lit Arden's features. "The Doctor? She knows where to find him?"

The man called the Doctor, who invented the procedure and mechanisms with which the Company was able to overtake Luke's mind, had escaped after Luke started to get his memories back. The Wardens hadn't been able to find him, despite extensive searching. All they had was a bag of his implements that Luke had managed to steal during their last encounter. The man was as twisted as they came.

"She says she knows where he is," Luke informed his wife. "She's even offered to lead us to a high-ranking Company operative here in Britain."

"What does she want in exchange?"

"To avenge her brother. Her freedom."

"Of course she wants her freedom," Arden said with an unladylike snort. "They all want that. You know Dhanya won't give it to her."

Dhanya Withering was the director of the W.O.R. She wasn't exactly known for acquiescing to enemy demands. In fact, when Luke had returned, she had made it clear to Arden that if he was determined to be a liability, she would have her husband executed. Ashford was acting in her stead while Dhanya was on personal leave, but she would be back in charge of things in a few days.

Luke's brow pinched. "I know."

Alastair had to admire the bastard. He shook his head as Arden's expression softened into sympathy. With those two words, declaring his loyalty to her and the W.O.R., Luke had diffused a situation that very easily could have become worthy of a Shakespearean tragedy.

"She wants me to be her liaison with the Wardens."

And then he ruined it. Alastair swallowed a curse and reached for the doorknob. He most assuredly did not want to be present for this.

"No." Arden's voice was quiet, but it was as effective as a slamming door.

Luke sighed. "I know this is difficult, but it will only be for a little while, until she feels she can trust them."

"She can't trust them," Alastair reminded him. Why was he still there? More important, why was he jumping in on the side of a woman he'd like to see rot in a cell for all she'd done? There was Warden blood on her long, slender hands. He had known two agents who died in pursuit of her, and she had ruined at least two operations, one of which resulted in the freedom of Victor Erlich. Lucas was taken and sent home by Erlich's brother to kill Arden, his wife, to avenge Victor's death at Arden's hands.

Both Arden and Luke ignored him. "We promised each other no more intrigue." Arden folded her arms over her chest. "We promised we would only do jobs for the W.O.R. that we could do together or from home. If the Company finds out we have her, they'll send someone to kill her, and you will be right in the middle of it."

"I have to do this," her husband insisted. "It's the only way they can find out what she knows. Arden, this is my chance to alleviate any misgivings the W.O.R. has about me."

"I said no." Her cheeks were flushed, her eyes bright.

"You're being irrational."

Luke said something else, but Alastair was trying very hard not to listen. He turned the knob and slowly nudged the heavy oak open. He could just sneak out. . . .

"I'm pregnant."

He froze on the threshold, heart jacked up beneath his ribs. Arden was pregnant?

There had been a time when he'd once entertained the thought of being the man with whom she had a family. He'd loved her for years, but she'd clung to the belief that Luke was alive. She'd been right, and his heart had broken for it. He loved her still, but no longer in that manner. She was better with Luke, and vice versa. They belonged together. Christ, Luke had even gotten a tattoo similar to Arden's when he was so far under the Company's spell that he didn't know who he was, let alone that he had a wife. The two of them were made for each other.

They were the only things in Alastair's life that made it worth living, which was why he turned to them. He could not ignore the myriad emotions playing over both their faces: shock, joy, regret, worry, love. He tried to look between them rather than directly at them.

"I'll do it," he promised. "I'll be the liaison. And if the American spy doesn't like it, she can rot." Awkwardly he added, "Congratulations."

And then he finally crossed the damn threshold and went the hell home—alone.

Chapter 3

They moved her to a cell.

They called it a cell, but it had a four-poster bed, thick rugs on the floor and steam circulating in the iron heating pipes. She was comfortable and cozy. It was nicer than some of the places she'd holed up while working for the Company. They even gave her a lovely beef dish and a glass of red wine for dinner.

Claire didn't fool herself that the Wardens were somehow better than the agency she now betrayed. The W.O.R. was treating her this well because she was of use to them. The oh-so-very-polite British believed in encouraging cooperation through kindness rather than violence.

Of course, if she hadn't proved useful, they would have shot her in the head and left her in just the right place to send the right message to the right people.

There were no windows, so she had no idea what time of day it was. She knew that they had brought her underground after wheeling her from the hospital ward in an invalid chair. They'd strapped her in with shackles and used a large key to wind a mechanism in the back of the chair that caused a wire and metal dome to close up over the front of the chair. It had been disconcerting, but Dr. Stone explained that it was not only to protect them from her, but to protect her in case anyone tried to kill her.

Apparently word had gotten out that the Wardens had "the Dove" in custody.

It was such a hideous name, but every agent had to have a code name. She'd been given hers because Robert had made some stupid joke about how many doves were at the funeral for a Napoleon-type character she'd sent to his maker. She wasn't supposed to kill him, but he'd shot a child in front of her, just because he wanted to make a point. She'd done the world a favor by disposing of him in kind. He'd gotten off easy; she had planned to let the child's father have him.

And then there was that silly rumor that she'd earned the moniker because she was like the dove sent out by Noah, but that was just a fanciful story.

She picked up the tin cup the guard had brought her tea in. It was still warm. She wasn't a big fan of tea, but it gave her something to do. She could read one of the books on the shelf, but that would require moving, and her entire body felt as though . . . well, as though it had been shot and had then fallen off a roof.

The clock was ticking. She had to get back on Howard's trail. He'd be at that country party a few days at best before moving on to the next phase of his plan. Even if they let her go tomorrow—in Five's custody—she was in no condition to travel hell-bent for leather. It was going to take longer than she wanted to catch up to the bastard.

She'd seen the look on Payne's face when she offered up information on Company operatives. He wanted what she knew, but he was disgusted with her for turning on her former comrades so easily, even though she'd explained what happened to Robert. All her strength had gone into showing as little emotion as possible as she talked about her brother, and that ginger-headed bastard looked at her as if she were dog excrement on the bottom of his shiny boot.

Claire would have looked upon herself with the same expression once upon a time. Now she didn't care what anyone thought of her or how anyone looked at her. She didn't even care that what she was about to do was tantamount to putting nails in her own coffin. She was going to make certain Stanton Howard paid for her brother's life. If that satisfaction cost her own life as well, then so be it.

She took another sip of tea. She was going to have to make her way to the toilet soon. It was hand-painted porcelain that swept waste away with the pull of a chain. Back home in New York, they'd had chamber pots. Apparently England believed even her enemies needed posh pots to piss in.

There was no fighting it any longer. Claire pushed herself to her feet with a throat-ripping growl of pain and clung to the bedside table for support while stars danced before her eyes. Her breath came in shallow gasps. She gripped the top of the chair that sat in front of a little writing desk—where she was expected to commit all she knew to paper—and used it as a make-shift crutch as she shuffled across the carpet.

By the time she finished her business and began her return to the bed, her legs were trembling and cold sweat clung to her hairline. It was of course at that moment that a rap sounded at her door, followed by a key in the lock. She heard the grinding of gears as the locking mechanism disengaged, then a solid "thunk" before the door eased open. Claire looked up, expecting to see Dr. Stone.

It was Payne.

Had he come to kill her? She'd heard of such things happening to Company agents in W.O.R. custody. They were taken and never heard of again. Or had Huntley changed his mind about helping her? That would be unlike the man she used to know, but then he wasn't that man anymore.

"What do you want?" she demanded. Why did he have to show up when she was in need of a bath and trembling like a leaf in the wind? She had to look a fright, and her looks had always been something she used to her advantage. Men—and some women—generally found her very attractive.

Payne was obviously not one of those men. "I came to talk," he replied in that voice that reminded her of velvet rubbed the wrong way—rich and rough. "What the hell is wrong with you?"

There was no advantage to lying. "The loo," she informed him, using a word she'd heard other Brits use. "Seems I wasn't quite up to the task."

His cinnamon brows pulled low into a scowl as he stomped toward her. Was he swearing under his breath? Claire might have laughed had he not seized her by the arm and slung it over his shoulders as he bent low and put his own arm around her waist. "Lean on me."

She'd rather stick her face in a wasp's nest, but she did as she was told and was grateful for his support. He practically carried her to the bed, then set her upon the mattress with surprising tenderness. It still hurt like the devil, but not as much as it would have if she'd done it on her own.

"Thank you."

The earl seemed to understand how difficult those words were for her to say. He gave a curt nod and pulled the chair she'd abandoned closer to the bed so that he might sit. He could have remained standing to intimidate her, but he didn't. She would not assume it was out of chivalry. The Earl of Wolfred didn't need to stand to be intimidating. The man was built like a prizefighter, albeit a rangy one, and he had a gaze as cold and hard as steel.

He braced his forearms on his thighs and leaned toward her. His black greatcoat pulled across his back, the fine wool stretching to accommodate the movement. Normally she would love that he put himself so close, as it would make it all the easier for her to strike him in the throat or crotch, but right now she was painfully aware of just how little of a threat to his safety she was in her current condition. He was no doubt aware of it as well.

"Are you going to tell me why you are here, or are you going to stare at me all night?"

He didn't so much as blink at her words. "It must be difficult for you to be locked up."

"Yes, because these are such spartan conditions," she replied drily. As if she would ever confide just how confined she truly felt. How vulnerable. Were the room any smaller or the ceiling any lower, she'd be sitting in a corner, foaming at the mouth, mindless.

He arched a brow. "Indeed. Still, it must wound your pride as the Dove to have been so easily delivered into Warden custody. That's an absolutely rubbish code name, by the way."

Claire drew back. It hurt, and she winced. That would teach her to react. "I didn't choose it," she informed him—why, she had no idea. It wasn't any of his business. "Will you tell me what they call you?"

"Reynard."

She frowned. "As in the trickster fox?"

He looked impressed. What, did he think because she was female she was ignorant? Or perhaps it was because she was American. "That's somewhat insipid, isn't it?" She might have put more sarcasm behind it, but she had heard stories of Reynard, and being in the same room as him—within striking distance—bothered her. The man was augmented with metal "bones" and supposedly incredibly sharp eyes that . . . *glowed* when they caught the light.

Good God. It was *true*. He had the eyesight of a cat.

"No more than calling a dangerous woman 'Dove.' "

Whatever her reputation, this man's was just as formidable—or worse. The last woman to cross him—a sympathizer sleeping with a Company agent—had left him for dead beneath an overturned carriage. He not only survived; he was part of the team that tracked down the woman and her lover.

No one knew what happened to the pair after he captured them.

"You came here for a reason," she said, all bravado. "Either tell me what it is, or leave."

Something flickered in his eyes—something would have made her squirm were it not that it would hurt too much. "You're hardly in the position to order me about."

"Where's Five? Huntley?" She'd never get used to calling him by that name.

"At home with his beautiful wife."

Ah. Claire smirked. "She must be quite the woman if her jealousy was enough to send you here in his stead."

"The countess is not the least bit jealous of you." He couldn't have sounded any more disdainful if he'd stepped in dog dung as he said it. "Lord Huntley no longer works for the W.O.R, and therefore is in no position to hear or answer any demands or requests you might have."

"Then I have nothing to say. You may as well kill me now."

"We don't kill people, Miss Brooks."

"Of course you do."

That eerily glowing gaze of his met hers. "Sometimes we leave them to rot until the entire world forgets they ever existed."

That struck real fear in her heart. She wasn't afraid to die. Hell, she had embraced the notion the day she set off after Howard. No, dying held no sway over her, but living out the rest of her days in this box with no windows or sunshine . . .

"And here I thought you English gentlemen were supposed to be so very charming."

He let out a short breath. "Either you work with me or you don't work at all. That's the only choice you have at the moment."

She didn't know this man. She certainly didn't trust him, but when she looked at him, she knew he might be the one person who wanted Howard as much as she did. Not because he had a personal stake, but because it was his duty. She might not be able to trust him with her life, but she could trust him to hunt the blackguard to the ends of the earth once she put him on the right trail.

And she was running out of time.

"Fine." The word left a bad taste in her mouth. She wanted Howard's blood more than anything, but agreeing to work with the Wardens went against everything she and Robert believed in.

She'd joined the Company with her brother shortly after their parents' death. They fought against enemies of the United States before journeying to Europe for missions on that continent. The Company didn't pledge allegiance to any one country, though it had cells all around the globe. No, the Company was everywhere, fighting against dictatorships, monarchies—any system that kept the common man in the dirt while the wealthy made yet more gold off his back.

The man sitting across from her embodied everything the Company stood against, such as monarchy, class systems and oppression of the people. And she— for lack of a better term—was about to sell her soul to him. The real kick in the arse was that she found him terribly attractive. In other circumstances she might have seduced him, or allowed him to think he was seducing her.

Instead, she was left with an odd respect for him.

"Do we have an understanding?" he asked. "You work with me, and I speak to the director on your behalf once we have Howard and the Doctor in custody."

Claire shrugged. "Why not?" The lie rolled off her tongue with practiced ease. It didn't matter if she liked him, or wondered for a brief second what it would be like to rub her naked skin all over his. It didn't matter because she had no illusions about surviving this. If Howard didn't kill her, the Company or the WOR would once they knew she'd betrayed them. Howard wasn't going to be anyone's prisoner or bargaining chip.

Stanton Howard was going to die—by her hand. And if Payne got in her way, she'd have to kill him, too.

On street level, number 13 Downing Street did not exist. It was merely a door absorbed into other buildings near the "official" residence of the prime minister. Of course, the PM lived in a much grander residence than the rather nondescript brick town house tucked behind a wrought-iron gate. Alastair wasn't there to see Salisbury, however. He was there at the request of the director.

Last evening he'd unlocked the same door, crossed to the same gated lift and entered the correct punch card that would operate the lift and, after dropping it a couple of floors like a discarded toy, pushed it backward, deep below the street. There was a slight variation in this series of events, as he was here to see an entirely different sort of woman than he had the night before when he'd been there to see Claire Brooks.

He had gone to his club after that meeting, where he'd hoped to meet up with Luke, but his friend hadn't made an appearance. Probably he was with Arden—and that was a drama Alastair wanted no more part of. It was bad enough he was being forced to work with that *woman* Claire Brooks. Better him than Luke, though. Luke was too easily convinced of her honor, whereas Alastair was certain she had none.

And yet he'd felt some compassion for her when he saw how much pain she was in. And he'd felt a little grudging respect when she stared defiantly down that pert nose of hers. Women—agents—like her normally turned on the seduction in an attempt to gain affection or trust. She hadn't used her wiles against him at all. In fact, she seemed all too willing to do what he wanted. Why?

After the club, he returned home, and after a glass or several of whiskey, retired for the evening. Sleep had not come easy. He'd lain awake for hours, playing bits of the conversation with Brooks over in his mind, and one question remained.

How did such a woman become such a spy? She was beautiful and unusual enough to adorn the arm of any important man. Then again, beautiful women—women with presence—often made the best spies. And one might ask why he chose such a profession when he certainly wasn't in need of it. Perhaps Claire Brooks thought she'd been doing the right thing when she joined the Company.

But being misguided was not something that was going to earn his sympathy. Everyone had decisions to make in the course of his or her life, and each of those decisions carried consequences.

He was about to face the consequences of his decision to keep Luke away from Claire Brooks.

The lift jerked to a stop, and the door slid open. Alastair opened the gate and walked out into the grand foyer of Warden headquarters. He'd heard others describe it as looking like the great hall of a country house with its columns and marble, but to him it was more like a gallery—ostentatious, pretentious and far too quiet. And that bizarre blue glow given off by the lamps on the wall always made him feel as if he'd just stepped into a fantasy world.

Armed guards dressed in black and gold—the colors of the Wardens—flanked the large oak double door that led into the inner sanctum. Alastair approached them with an easy stride, his hands loose at his side. He wanted to hold them behind his back, but that might present the misconception that he had a weapon he was prepared to use, and that would not be good.

"Alastair Payne, Lord Wolfred, to see the director," he informed them. It was such a foolish procedure. These guards knew who he was, for pity's sake.

Without the slightest change in expression, one of the guards continued to stare at a point over his shoulder, and with practiced movements, extended his arm and turned the handle. The door opened.

Alastair crossed the threshold, into an interior that had always reminded him of a high-class brothel, though he would never voice that opinion aloud.

A pale carpet with a demure pattern covered the floor. The walls were papered in a delicate cream peppered with brightly colored exotic birds. The furniture was dark wood, upholstered in bloodred velvet. Clocks on the wall gave the time in several foreign cities, and behind an ornate desk sat a gentleman in his forties with a kind, round face and a receding hairline. He looked like a jovial sort, but Alastair knew for a fact the bloke would kill a man as soon as look at him.

"Good morning, Finchley," Alastair said in greeting.

"Wolfred." Even his voice sounded cheerful—cheerfully mad. "Bit late, aren't you, old boy? Go on in. She's expecting you." Then he pressed a button on the ornophone box—a polished teak affair about the size of a cigar box with a small polished horn, like those on a Victrola, on top—and announced Alastair's arrival.

He'd had less trouble getting an audience with Queen Victoria, even though this meeting was not his idea. Yes, it made sense after Dhanya's last secretary turned out to be a Company agent, but it was still a pain in the arse.

Walking into the director's office was like walking into a Bengal market with its silk-swathed walls and bright, richly colored decor. At the back of the room was a large desk formed of a huge slab of ebony on the back of four temple elephants. Behind it was Dhanya Withering, rumored to be the illegitimate granddaughter of Her Majesty, and director of the W.O.R. She was tall and shapely with long black hair coiled on the back of her head, dark eyes and a complexion that was a perfect blend of exotic and English. She wore her usual work uniform of snug trousers tucked into boots, white shirt and waistcoat—this one a rich violet.

"Alastair," she said, using his Christian name as easily as his own mother. "Thank you for coming."

As though he'd had a choice in the matter. He smiled. Part of Dhanya's charm was that she was impossible to stay annoyed with. She was supposed to be on leave, but she had returned to work when she heard of Claire Brooks's apprehension—and when Evie threatened to quit if Ashford wasn't made to step down. "Finchley said I was late."

Her lips tilted up on one side. "Mr. Finchley needs to have his pocket watch adjusted. Come sit. Tea? I have chai. It will put some color back in your cheeks."

"Sleep could have done that," he replied drily as he approached the desk.

She shot him a sideways glance from the sideboard where a teapot of hot water sat on an ornate warmer. "It is not my fault you cannot get to bed at a decent hour."

Alastair flipped out the tails of his coat and sat down in one of the plush chairs in front of the desk. "The devil it's not."

"You were at your club into the wee hours. Is that my fault?"

How the hell did she know these things? "No, but the fact that I'm here before noon is."

Dhanya returned with a tray carrying two cups of fragrant, milky chai and a plate of sweets that no doubt came from her mother's bakery. The woman made a variety of edibles, but her traditional desserts simply had no equal. He immediately plucked a small, orange-colored square from the plate and popped it in his mouth. It was all he could do not to moan in delight.

"Poor thing," she teased. "Having to actually get out of bed in the morning. How awful."

This was not a debate he had any chance of winning. "Thank you for the chai."

She smiled in that closed-lipped manner so many women seemed to employ when they knew something the man did not. "You are welcome. Now, shall we discuss why you are here?"

"Of course." He crossed his legs. "I assume it has to do with the Dove."

All trace of humor disappeared as Dhanya met his gaze with the fathomless gravity of her own. "She is quite the acquisition."

"She's a spy, not a pair of shoes." Acquisitions couldn't stab one in the throat. Or tremble because they were in so much pain.

Dhanya tilted her head, continuing to watch him as

if she were an owl and he a damn mouse. "Quite. I'm told you wish to take responsibility for her rather than Lucas Grey."

"Arden's pregnant." There was no point in saying anything other than the truth. Dhanya probably already knew.

The director nodded, the light reflecting off the dark of her hair. "Yes. And you still see yourself as her knight errant."

Alastair smiled slightly. She did not know everything, Miss Withering. "No. I'm no knight. I simply think it would be wrong to separate Luke and his bride again. Last time it took him seven years to find his way back. Claire Brooks works for the people responsible for that."

"She did work for them."

"You believe she's turned traitor, then?"

Dhanya nodded and took a sip of tea. "Huntley believes it, and I'm inclined to trust his judgment. He knows how to handle this woman, Alastair. You do not."

He snorted. "I'm no stranger to women like her."

"Precisely. The last one almost killed you. I'd hate for you to take any unresolved feelings you might have regarding that misfortune out on our prisoner."

"You think I'd abuse her?" He couldn't keep the indignation from his voice. He'd kill her if necessary, but he would never make sport of her—or any other woman. "I may be an idiot, but I am not cruel, Dhanya."

"I would never suggest that you were. Only that . . .

you're not exactly an excellent judge of character when it comes to women."

Carefully, Alastair set his cup and saucer on the desk. He leaned back and linked his hands over his stomach. He put every ounce of will into presenting a calm façade rather than tell his superior exactly what she could do with her opinion of his ability to judge character.

"Perhaps not, but I am an excellent friend. Lucas Grey no longer works in a professional capacity for this organization. He is entirely unsuitable for the task of guarding Brooks. I've volunteered my services. You do not have to accept them, but regardless, you will not *use* Luke."

Brows as black as raven wings lowered over her eyes. "You do not make those decisions, Lord Wolfred."

He leaned forward. "He's a civilian. You have no dominion over him. Leave him alone, Dhanya."

"Or what?"

"Or you'll prove my judgment of women faulty indeed."

They stared at each other a moment, and then she laughed. There wasn't much humor in it, but there was enough to make him relax. "Well played, my lord. You let me walk right into that."

He shrugged. "It would have been ungentlemanly of me to stand in your way. Are we agreed? Luke stays home, and I deal with Brooks?"

"We are. If you wish to have the assignment, it's yours. But have a care, my lord. If this goes badly, I will hold you responsible. I want the Doctor, Stanton Howard and Claire Brooks delivered to me alive and ready to divulge all their secrets. Am I understood?"

"Perfectly."

"Good." She took another sip of tea. "Now have something else to eat. You are far too thin."

Chapter 4

"Sweet hell! Are you trying to kill me?" Claire's eyes watered as she glared at the woman hovering over her.

Dr. Stone shot her a dry glance. "Luvie, if I wanted you dead, you would be already. I'm trying to help you, so be a good girl and stay still—and quiet."

Claire might have smiled or had a smart-ass remark in reply if the wound in her side didn't hurt so damn much. "What is this for?" Two guards had "escorted" her to the hospital ward but hadn't told her why she was going. She had assumed it was so Stone could check her wound, but now she wasn't so certain that it wasn't torture the good doctor had in mind.

"It's to help your body heal faster." The other woman removed from Claire's torn flesh the tip of what had to be the largest syringe ever made. It had to been buried at least two inches inside her.

"I thought you gave me some of that already."

"This recipe is better."

"You mean it's the stuff you give to your agents rather than your prisoners."

The doctor didn't even bother trying to look contrite as she covered the raw tissue with a fresh bandage. "Exactly. My employer wants you well quickly, so it's my job to ensure you are ready for duty."

"Aren't you afraid I'll escape and take this miracle serum of yours back to the Company?"

Large dark eyes turned to meet hers. "No."

"You don't think that's a little naive?" No matter how much she tried, she couldn't seem to irk the woman. It made her mood even darker.

Dr. Stone straightened and pointed at a long sideboard against the far wall. "Do you see those three bottles there?"

Claire pushed herself upright, swore at just how difficult movement still was, adjusted her shirt and looked. There were three glass bottles, each filled with a slightly pinkish liquid. "Yes. Is that what you used on me just now?"

"One of them is. And one of them is a synthetic toxin that could kill you instantly."

"I could take a sample of all three with me."

"The third is a compound so noxious, a whiff of it would burn the tissues of your nose and throat so badly, you would die a slow and agonizing death."

No wonder the woman was so confident. "I could hold my breath."

"Shall I tell you what it would do to your eyeballs?"

Claire stared at her. "You're bluffing."

Stone put her hands on her hips. "Go check for your-self."

"I'm skeptical but not stupid, Doctor. Your formula is safe from me."

Full lips lifted slightly. "No, 'stupid' is not a word I would use to describe you."

"Though I was stupid enough to get caught."

The other woman's expression was guarded, but there was a shrewd glint in her eyes. "You don't seem to have suffered so badly for it."

"Except now I'm going to prove myself a traitor and work with a man who would kill me as easily as a dog."

"Lord Payne would never hurt an animal."

Claire stared at the doctor, fighting back a bark of unexpected laughter. The woman's dark eyes sparkled with mirth. "Why don't you hate me?"

Dr. Stone instantly sobered. "I've always thought hate a useless emotion."

"Really?" Her tone was so dry, sand poured off her tongue.

The other woman began gathering up her medical supplies. "My mother was from Sierra Leone. Are you familiar with it?"

Claire shook her head. "I am not."

"Many former slaves went there when the government abolished slavery. She was born free. My father was a doctor who went there as a young man. He met my mother, married her and eventually—when I was eleven—brought her back to England. Do you know that there are people here who despise me because of the color of my skin?"

Claire met her direct gaze. "There are many people in my country who would despise you for the same reason." Slavery in America had been abolished before her birth, but there were people who still clung to the beliefs behind it.

"And it's such a foolish reason. Did you believe you were doing the right thing when you joined the Company?"

"Of course."

"Then I'm not going to hate you for it. You've done nothing to earn my dislike." The doctor glanced up at the sound of the door opening. "I cannot speak for her, however."

Claire glanced over her shoulder. Entering the surgical theater was a pretty woman of good height with rich auburn hair and skin the color of cream. She could hate this woman for her perfect complexion. What would the good doctor think of that?

"Who is she?" she asked, turning her attention back to the darker woman.

"Arden Grey," came the low reply. "Lady Huntley. I believe you know her husband." There was a wealth of implication behind that judgeless gaze.

"Hell." And there she was with a hole in her side and no gun. "Is there going to be trouble?"

"Not in my house," Dr. Stone replied. She went to greet the redhead, putting herself between Claire and the other woman. Something pinched in Claire's chest—hard. She wasn't afraid of Arden Grey. There wasn't much in the world that scared her. No, what she felt was surprise. No one had ever put himself between her and a potential threat before. Not Five—Huntley—not her brother, not even her mother had ever stood at her defense.

If Evelyn Stone asked Claire to kill for her, she would do it without a blink. Did the woman have any idea of the loyalty she'd just earned with a simple confounding act?

Claire remained on the examination table but maneuvered her body so that she sat facing the women, watching. A lot could be learned from simply paying attention to how a person stood. Dr. Stone's posture was relaxed, but she held her arms across her chest in an almost defensive manner. Arden Grey held a carpetbag in front of her like a shield, but her face was open and free of tension. Neither woman wanted trouble, but they were prepared for it.

And all because of little old her.

She didn't blame the countess for coming. Were the situation reversed, she would also want to see the woman who had screwed her husband—just to see how she measured up. It was a little perverse, perhaps, but human nature.

The two women stopped talking and turned to walk toward her. Claire kept her expression neutral.

"Claire Brooks, this is Arden Grey, Countess Huntley. She's here to discuss your upcoming assignment with Lord Wolfred."

Of all the things she might have said, that was not

one Claire had even entertained. "What of it?" she asked, directing her attention to the redhead.

Arden Grey wasn't afraid of her, either. Good. It would be horribly disappointing to think of Fi... Huntley with a weak woman.

"Many of the weapons and equipment employed by W.O.R. agents are of my design," the woman began in a voice that seemed better suited for a schoolmistress than a countess. "I've studied the items found on your person when you were brought into custody, and I would like to discuss them with you." She drew her shoulders back, as though she expected Claire to refuse.

"What would you like to know?" She didn't care if she gave away Company secrets. They'd lost her loyalty the moment they let her brother's murderer escape. Nothing mattered except justice for Robert.

The countess set the carpetbag on a waist-high table beside her. She opened it and withdrew not only Claire's gun, but several other familiar items. For a split second Claire imagined herself grabbing that gun and making a run for it. Foolish thinking, of course. The ravaged flesh around the bullet wound tingled—it was already healing—but not enough that she could move that quickly.

"I studied this pistol and its operation. I am correct in that it channels aether as ammunition?"

Claire nodded. The inlaid pearl handle had been molded for her grip. The wide barrel needed a bit of a polish, but it gleamed in the light, a few scratches on its surface. That gun had saved her ass more than once.

"It has a small aether absorption tube inside, and concentrates a tiny amount into a powerful blast. It refills almost instantly because the force of each use helps draw more aether into the tube. There's a vacuum extension for the barrel that effectively silences the discharge. I shot a man in a lending library once, and no one heard anything until his head hit the table."

"Effective." She sounded genuinely impressed—by the weapon, not her. "And this?"

It looked like an ornate, heavy cuff bracelet made of gold. "Plated gregorite." She didn't need to tell this woman that gregorite was the strongest metal known to man. "If you press the large stone in the center once, it releases a length of spun gregorite wire suitable for a garrote. Twice releases a much longer length, and the cuff itself converts into a grappling hook."

Arden pressed the stone. A length of wire not even as thick as a boot lace spilled out of the bracelet. "Genius. How does it retract?"

"Press the pearl." The wire was sucked back in when she did.

They went through the rest of the gadgets—a locket with a secret compartment for cyanide, a ring that concealed a small device that, when swallowed, emitted an aetheric signature that could be tracked using a matching compass hidden within what appeared to be a pocket watch, and a fan that appeared demure but was actually made of wickedly sharp blades.

"These are good work," Arden remarked when they were done. "Is there any chance the Company could also track the device in the ring?"

"I'm not certain, but probably."

The redhead nodded. "I will have to alter the transmission frequency, then. These items will be returned to you when you depart on your mission with Alastair."

Alastair, was it? Just how close was this woman with her husband's best friend? "Even my gun?"

"Yes, though it will probably be trusted to Lord Wolfred's care."

"Of course," Claire replied flatly.

"I will also have a few new devices for you, such as a pair of garters made with gregorite threads."

She frowned. That sounded ridiculous. "So my stockings will be certain to stay up?"

Whiskey eyes met hers. This woman had to have been a schoolmarm in a former life, because Claire suddenly felt as though she should be cleaning a chalkboard in penance. "They can be used to slide across wire or beams without injuring your hands, and may also be used to bind an enemy's wrists and ankles. I know one female agent who survived a particularly nasty gunshot wound simply by using a garter as a tourniquet."

"A variety of uses, then. Excellent."

The woman gathered up Claire's weapons and placed them back in the carpetbag. Claire wanted to fight Arden for her gun, just so she could have its familiar metal—the comfort of it—in her hand.

"You'll be traveling as husband and wife. The agency has seen to it that suitable clothing will be provided for you. Dr. Stone provided your measurements."

Husband and wife? She and Reynard? "No one will believe we're married."

"Why not?"

"Because we can't stand each other."

"Oh no. That's fairly commonplace amongst the English."

Claire snorted, eliciting a small smile from her companion. She hadn't noticed before, but now she could tell Dr. Stone was only pretending to work at her table. She was obviously listening and watching them and making sure no one got all riled up. Honestly, Huntley was one of the best men she'd had the privilege of knowing, but he wasn't worth shedding blood—not to Claire.

Arden fastened the bag. "I understand you weren't wearing one of the earpieces we've seen on several of your associates."

"Those are used only on the ones they need to keep tabs on." She watched the woman's expression. Huntley had been outfitted with one of the devices.

"Ah. That makes sense." She lifted the bag and turned to leave.

"Why did you come here?" Claire inquired. "Surely they could have sent someone else to discuss gadgetry and what's expected of me. Why you?"

"I asked to come."

"Of course you did." She would have done the same. "Surely there's more? Questions you want to ask? Don't you want to hurt me a little?"

Arden lifted her slightly pointed chin. "I have no wish to hurt you. I simply wanted to see you with my own eyes."

"And now that you have?"

The other woman stared at her, unflinching and a little detached. This wasn't what Claire expected. She'd slept with more than one married man in the course of her life, mostly in the line of duty, or out of her own need to connect with a human who wouldn't try to court her afterward. She'd never met any of the wives, until now. It wasn't pleasant knowing she might have hurt this woman, or anyone else.

"I'm not jealous of you," she was told. "Not in the way you might think. I waited for him. For seven years I waited, and he was shagging you. Living his life as though I didn't exist. Can you comprehend how that makes me feel?"

"No. For what it's worth, he tried to remember you. One night he said your name in his sleep. The next day he saw the Doctor and went back to being their good little machine." That didn't seem to make the other woman feel better. "I never loved him, and he never loved me. His mind might not have remembered you, but I think his heart did."

The woman was positively white in the face—not difficult given how fair she already was. "Why would you say something like that?"

"Because it's what I think, and I have a tendency to say what's on my mind. It's not as if it hurt me to say it."

They stared at each other, unblinking. It didn't matter what the other woman might see in her eyes, either. Claire didn't care. In another life they might have actually been friends, which was an odd concept for her to

begin with, let alone trying to fathom it with the wife
of her former lover.

"Most women would have tried to take my eyes out
by now, or would have dissolved into tears."

The redhead made a face—as if tasting sour milk. "I
find I don't make tears as easily as some women. And
you will need your eyes to assist Alastair. That is more
important than any desire to make you less beautiful.
Never mind that it wouldn't change that you know my
husband in a most intimate manner. I will simply have
to accept that and carry on."

Claire stared at her, an unwanted feeling of appreciation coming over her. She admired Lady Huntley.
No wonder the Company hadn't been able to remove
her completely from her husband's mind.

"I told Wolfred you must be quite the woman for
Huntley to be so loyal. I said it with malice, but I was
right. You are."

Arden Grey smiled—it seemed a mix of amusement,
irony and regret. "Funny. I said the same about you."

"What the devil were you thinking?" Alastair raked a
hand through his hair as he regarded Arden. They were
in the parlor of Huntley House, having tea. Only he
was on his feet now, unable to sit still any longer. He
whirled around to confront Luke. "How could you let
this happen?"

His friend's brow lifted. "I didn't 'let' anything happen. My wife is quite capable of making her own decisions."

They were mad—the pair of them. Mad as a bag of

cats. "She met with a dangerous enemy agent. By herself."

"She did what either you or I would have done when wanting to assess a situation. Dr. Stone was present, and it's not as though Claire would harm Arden."

"Because she's so very trustworthy?" Sarcasm dripped from his words. Honestly, he understood Arden's jealousy, but this was beyond sense. And now she actually *felt* for the woman.

Luke scowled. "Because it wouldn't be in her best interest to hurt my wife, not when I'm the only friend she's got."

"I don't understand how you can call yourself her friend. She's a Company agent, for Christ's sake. Forgive me, Arden."

She made a face at him. "The fact that you seem to find me incredibly stupid offends me more than your language, Alastair."

He opened his mouth to respond, but Luke cut him off. "You cannot be so naive as to see the world in such drastic black and white, my friend. The Company is really not that different from the Wardens. Both sides think their way is the right way and would die—or kill—to protect that way of thinking."

"The Company is made up of anarchists determined to reshape the world into their ideal. They talk of freedom from oppression, but they want to enslave us all under a large dictatorship. Their manifesto goes against everything I believe in—everything you once believed in."

"I still believe in those things." He could punch

Luke for sounding so bloody calm. "I simply acknowledge that the entire world doesn't necessarily agree."

"I was not without weapons," Arden spoke up, "and Dhanya asked me to consult with Miss Brooks in regard to Company scientific advancements."

"Dhanya had no right asking you to see that woman." He'd been glad that his friend was back from her leave, but obviously her judgment was impaired.

"On the contrary, she had every right. I'm still employed by the Wardens as a gadgeteer." She looked at him and sighed. "If I'd been in any danger whatsoever, Luke would have never allowed me to go alone. You know that."

Alastair grunted and looked away. Honestly, he agreed with her, but the whole thing made him inexplicably angry.

"Actually, I somewhat liked her."

He scowled. "You have got to be joking! Are you mad?"

"Have a care, Wolfred. That's my wife you're speaking to." Luke wore an expression that promised an altercation if Alastair's familiarity continued. He'd been so accustomed to speaking however he wanted to Arden when Luke was gone that he'd forgotten she wasn't just another one of his cronies.

When had he stopped thinking of her as the woman he wanted to live out the rest of his days with, and started thinking of her as simply an old and dear friend?

"My apologies to you both," he said, sincere though still annoyed. Brooks was a master at subterfuge, and he had no doubt that she could charm the wings off a fly if she set her mind to it. She was the sort of woman entirely too accustomed to having everything her way and everyone tripping over themselves to please her—especially men.

She was duplicitous, a trait he personally abhorred, despite being something of an expert in it himself.

"Your concern does you credit," Arden told him with a gentle smile, "but I am fine. She did not hurt me in any way. In fact, she made me feel rather better about the situation."

"Rather better?" Incredulity had his voice an octave higher at the end of the remark. "How so?"

Arden cast a glance at her husband, who gazed back at her. Why did they insist on sharing these intimate moments in his presence? It was bloody uncomfortable and time-consuming. "She said some things that make me understand what Luke went through while under Company control."

Ah. She was trying to come to terms with her husband's unfaithfulness. Yes, it had to be deuced uncomfortable to come face-to-face with "the other woman," especially when that woman looked like Claire Brooks. Even with her hair mussed and dirty, and pain clouding her mossy green eyes, she was an incredible-looking woman, the sort that could make a man's heart stop. But there was a hardness to her, a certain strength that would make her intimidating to other women—hell, to many men!

Alastair did not find her intimidating, but he would think twice before turning his back on her.

Despite her being the embodiment of almost everything he disdained, she had something intriguing about her—something challenging. He was almost looking forward to working with her.

What the hell was wrong with him? The woman was poison, no way around it, and already he was curious about her. Had he not learned any lesson from almost dying? Had his life not had enough two-faced people mucking about in it?

"You don't think this is a trap?" Alastair turned to Luke, who could barely look away from his wife. "Could Brooks turn on me once we find the Doctor or Howard?"

"Not unless she's a completely different woman than the one I used to know. She's turned on *them*, my friend. There's no way she'd do this otherwise. I've seen her withstand torture that would have broken many men."

Arden frowned. "Were you tortured as well?"

Luke shifted in his chair. "Yes."

"By whom?"

Oh hell, Alastair thought. "Wardens." He had a fairly decent idea of what that torture entailed, having doled it out on a few Company agents himself. If she hadn't cracked under that, then either she had indeed turned her back on the agency as she had claimed, or she was playing them all.

His friend nodded. "I believe so." A humorless smile curved his lips. "So you see why I don't think the Company and the W.O.R. are all that dissimilar. Both want power and will stop at nothing to defend their ideals."

"Yes," Alastair replied. "I can see it." He also saw the pain in Arden's expression as she regarded her husband. This was quickly about to become one of those intimate moments he no longer wished to be a part of.

"I should be on my way." He rose to his feet. "I must prepare for the journey ahead."

His friends also rose. "You'll keep me informed?" Luke asked.

"As much as I'm able." Luke was his best friend and a former agent, but the mission he was about to undertake was a sensitive one, and Alastair couldn't jeopardize it by discussing it with unauthorized persons.

Luke extended his hand. "Good luck. Punch that Doctor in the bollocks for me."

Alastair accepted the handshake and clapped him on the shoulder with his other hand. "I'll bring him back so you can do it yourself."

He hugged Arden and took his leave, grateful to be away from the oppressive force of their affection. He did not begrudge them their love. In fact, he often envied it, but hell and blast, it took up so much of their lives! It was all well and good to adore one's spouse, but Luke and Arden rarely spent any time apart. Occasionally Luke would come to the club, or they'd take their Velocycles for a ride out of the city, but Luke inevitably would end up in a rush to get home to his wife. And he'd seen Arden cease work on a device for the Wardens simply because she felt as though she hadn't spent enough time with Luke that day. She resumed work only when her husband joined her in her workroom.

If that was the sort of behavior one could expect once married, then Alastair reckoned he'd do well to remain a bachelor.

He left Huntley House and climbed into his touring carriage parked in the drive. It was a damp night, and he was thankful for the oilskin canopy that kept the vehicle dry. The steam engine added more moisture to the air, but it also provided a little warmth, so that by the time he reached his own Mayfair address a few minutes later, he was only slightly chilled. He'd barely opened the door when one of his men from the stables ran up to take the carriage away, driving it behind the house to the building where it was kept.

Being a Warden made him cautious; hence the two security locks on his front door. One was a regular lock-and-key affair, while the other required the right combination of numbers to be selected on its dial. Only once those numbers had been entered would the locking mechanism disengage with a sharp clink, allowing the door to be opened. He alone knew the code for this particular door. The servants' entrance had its own code, which only the housekeeper and butler were privy to. Any employee out after dark—or who had left the house for whatever reason—would have to ring for admittance or remain out.

Alastair stepped into the foyer of his family home, absently rubbing his right hand as he often did whenever a problem perplexed him. He would run his fingers over his own palm, over the back of his knuckles, squeezing each joint. It was the joints that reminded him that he was no longer an ordinary human. The metal "bones" in his hand behaved as they ought, but they were stronger than he could have ever imagined. The knuckles felt hard beneath his fingers; yet they were almost delicate by design. Because of them he could drive his fist through a brick wall and feel only surface pain.

Tonight's problem was Claire Brooks. He couldn't seem to quite shake the thought of her. She was there, in the back of his mind, even when he was engaged elsewhere.

He told himself that his reaction to her was normal, that she had been trained in the arts of subterfuge and seduction to the point of being an expert. She could probably seduce an archangel if she put her mind to it. No, being attracted to her—or rather, intrigued by her—was not a problem. It would become a problem only if he lost his damn mind as he had with Sascha.

He was not going to be that foolish ever again. He'd rather sleep with a viper than share his sheets with Claire Brooks.

Well, perhaps not a viper, but something nasty regardless.

When he reached his bedroom, he entered it to find the bed turned down and a glass of whiskey sitting on the bedside table. A little nip before retiring always helped him sleep. He took the glass with him to what looked like an ordinary armoire, and opened the doors. Inside was an aether engine—a large device with a typewriting machine keyboard for typing in commands and requests, and a specially crafted glass screen that allowed him to see images. This model was connected to the W.O.R. engine via a transmitter antenna on the roof of the house designed to intercept and interpret as well as send aetheric transmissions.

Alastair took a sip of the whiskey before sitting down in front of the contraption; then he turned the key on the front of the cherrywood housing. The guts of the machine came to life with a click of gears and a gentle chug. He waited until the engine fully engaged and the inquiry box appeared on the screen to type "Claire Brooks." He struck the SEARCH key. Within moments, the Warden databank returned several images and articles for him to read.

Claire Brooks stared at him, a study in gray on the screen. He moved the handle on the machine so that it brought up the next page of evidence, only it brought up another photo—this one of Brooks dressed as a can-can dancer. "Sweet Jesus," Alastair whispered, taking another drink. "That should not be allowed."

Once he got beyond the photographs, he was able to begin reading all the information the Wardens had ever acquired about the attractive spy. She was skilled in combat, was known for her ruthlessness and determination, and had once killed a man with a pair of sugar tongs. Her main alias was Claire Clarke, and apparently she was well known under it as an American actress. It was a good cover, and judging from the photograph of her in the scanty dancer costume, a thoroughly distracting one.

It made for fascinating reading. And he was going to read it all, regardless of how long it took. Luke might trust Claire Brooks, but he did not. There was a glimmer of desperation in her eyes that unsettled him.

Luke said there wasn't much difference between the Company and the W.O.R. Brooks had supposedly been a loyal agent—as loyal as Alastair himself was to the Wardens. So what would make someone such as himself turn against his agency? Nothing but the deepest of betrayals would sway him to forsake his vows of duty and obligation. Perhaps the Company had been responsible for her brother's death after all.

Still, she was a little too eager and agreeable for his liking. She was planning something; he could feel it in his bones, so he would prepare as best he could. He would learn all he could about Claire Brooks, because she was as much his enemy as the Doctor and Stanton Howard.

He flexed his augmented hand and ran his thumb along the faint scars softened by a pinpoint ray of aetherically particalized light. He could easily crush a man's throat with that hand—even a skull. He did not need Arden's fancy weapons to get himself out of a bad situation. *He* was a weapon.

So when Claire Brooks eventually turned on him— and he knew she would—Alastair would be ready.

Chapter 5

It was nothing short of a miracle.

Claire rotated her torso, stretched and bent. There was little to no discomfort, despite her having been torn open by an aether blast just days ago.

"You should sell that concoction," she told Dr. Stone as she soaked in the bath the good woman had prepared for her. "You could make a fortune."

The doctor smiled. "That's not why I invented it. You've soaked long enough. The salts in the water are designed to reinvigorate. Too much and you'll feel as though you have ants under your skin. To your feet now."

Dutifully, Claire stood, not the least bit embarrassed about her own nudity. "Isn't this a little beneath you? Helping a prisoner bathe?"

"It's part of your recovery, which is my responsibility. One I take very seriously, thank you." There was surprisingly little censure behind the words. She still couldn't figure out why the doctor didn't dislike her, no matter what was said. "Here, dry yourself."

Claire accepted the towel and began rubbing at her wet skin. There was a fire in the grate, and hot steam circulating through the pipes warmed the room, but a chill caressed her naked shoulders regardless, reminding her of winters back home when the water would freeze in the washbasin.

She dried off quickly and stepped into the clean clothing Dr. Stone handed her item by item. Her eyelids fluttered as she pulled on the trousers. Having been heated over the pipes, they instantly infused her chilled flesh with warmth. She shivered in delight. "Thank you."

"You seem so surprised whenever I show you kindness," the doctor observed. "Not all of us here are like Ashford, the man who was the acting director when you were brought in."

"Yes, where is that dear man? I haven't seen him since I first woke up."

The other woman's full lips tilted. "One too many complaints against him. The actual director decided to return from leave early."

"Would you know anything about those complaints?" Claire asked as she pulled a fine linen shirt over her head and tucked it into her trousers.

"Of course not." But there was just enough false protest that she knew the doctor lied. "The man's a tosser. He never should have been in charge."

Claire had no idea what a tosser was, but it certainly wasn't a compliment. "Why was he?"

"Because Alastair wasn't available."

"Payne? He fills in for your director?" Hell's bells, and this was the man they paired her with? Why not just hand her over to the damn queen? Or at least to the Prince of Wales.

It was obvious from the other woman's face that she believed she'd said too much. "Yes. On occasion."

"But not this one."

"No."

"Why not?"

"He was still on leave himself. He'd been injured in the line of duty."

"I remember hearing about that. A couple of Company agents left him for dead in Spain. I suppose he has you to thank for such a good and speedy recovery?"

"Me and his own determination. When I went to Spain to care for him, he was already recovering. It helped that he was in excellent physical shape to begin with."

"Yes, there's nothing wrong with his shape," Claire agreed. She drew on a boned waistcoat that also served as a corset and began tightening the laces in the front. "Have you and he ever . . . ?"

Dr. Stone laughed. "God help me, no! Lord Wolfred is fine, to be sure, but I learned a long time ago not to shag where I eat, if you catch my meaning."

"I understand you perfectly. I wish someone had given me such sound advice; then I might have faced Lady Huntley with a less guilty conscience."

"You wouldn't have bedded him if you'd known? Even though he didn't?"

She tied the laces into a bow and began rolling up her sleeves. "No, I wouldn't have. There are some things that just aren't right, and sleeping with a married man simply because he doesn't know he has a wife is one of them. How do I look?"

Dr. Stone cast a critical eye from her head to her toe. "Like a pirate. Would you like me to pin your hair?"

No one had pinned her hair since her mother died. "Yes . . . thank you."

There wasn't a mirror in the room—too easy to break and use as a weapon, she supposed. Or perhaps they thought she might use a shard to take her own life. "I'm going to trust you not to make me look atrocious."

"On my honor," the doctor replied. "Sit."

Claire did as she was told. As the other woman brushed her hair—she'd forgotten how delightful that could feel—she let her mind wander a bit. Perhaps she had spent too much time in the bath, because she did feel jumpy, although that was probably anticipation. Soon she would be back on Howard's trail. If luck was on her side, she'd be standing over his corpse in a day or two.

Hopefully Wolfred would give her a moment to savor her victory before killing her. If she was very fortunate, he'd bring her back to London to face execution. She might really be able to savor Howard's death then.

"He won't hurt you."

Claire's head jerked up. "What?"

Nimble hands coiled a plait on the back of her head. "Wolfred. You have no reason to fear being alone with him. He's very honorable." The way she said it made it sound as though Dr. Stone had known her share of dishonorable men. Hadn't they both.

"Yes, he seems very honorable." And proper. And righteous. And brave. Those traits only agitated her.

"Anyway, you won't have to worry about him harming you or taking advantage."

Claire laughed. "That man wouldn't touch me with a yardstick unless it was the only weapon at his disposal."

"You underestimate your appeal."

"No, you underestimate *him*." Wolfred was rich, noble and gorgeous. The idea of forcing a woman was more alien to him than it was even to her. No doubt he had ladies pitching themselves at his feet every time he stepped out of his house. "He should be here soon, should he not?" She'd been told they would be leaving on a northbound train that evening, in the hopes of catching up to Howard the next day.

"Yes. Soon." Another pin pushed against her scalp. "There. You look lovely."

Claire flushed. "Thank you." Such compliments often came to her from men, but rarely from another woman, and never in such a sincere tone. Of course, Dr. Stone was as exotic as Cleopatra herself, and she was hardly likely to be intimidated by another pretty face. Claire didn't claim to be a great beauty, but she knew the extent of her charms. It would be a weakness not to.

"Lord Wolfred will have your new clothing, and whatever devices Lady Huntley has provided."

Claire turned in her chair. "Will he give me my gun?"

"I don't know. They don't tell me these things. I'm not usually this . . . involved with prisoners."

"You're the closest thing I've had to a friend in a long time," Claire confided, despite how pathetic she knew it must sound. "Thank you for being so kind."

"I find in the world of intrigue a little kindness is much more effective than many weapons." She patted Claire's shoulder. "I have to get back to work. I'll have the guards take away the bath."

Claire stood. "Will I see you again before I leave?"

Dr. Stone shook her head. "Probably not, no. But I'll be here when you return."

A lump formed in Claire's throat. If she came back to this place, the doctor wasn't likely to be this nice to her. "Until then." She offered her hand.

The other woman looked at it, chuckled and then put her arms around Claire instead. Claire stood there, frozen, uncertain what to do with her own arms. Finally she closed them around the doctor and patted her awkwardly on the back as her eyes began to burn.

She was not a sentimental woman. It was only because she could practically see the end of her life that she was being so . . . vulnerable. Before the tears could come, she was released. The darker woman gave her a smile. "Until then."

Claire watched her leave and felt the clank of the lock in her bones as the door closed behind her. She had not missed the company of another female since she had been a young girl.

But then she'd never felt her own mortality so deeply as she did at that moment. Being adventurous and reck-

less had always left a sensation of being so alive, but this
mission—this last mission—would be the death of her,
one way or another. Knowing one's clock was slowly
winding down was sobering, to say the least.

Fortunately she was not left to melancholy for long.
Approximately thirty-three insanely long minutes later,
there came a knock upon her door, immediately followed by the clanging, hissing and thumping of the
locking mechanism. When the heavy slab swung open,
two guards stood at the threshold.

"Time to go, miss," the smaller of the two informed
her.

How formal and polite these Englishmen were.
Were she a man, would they call her "sir"? Or was it
some unshakeable sense of chivalry that made them
defer to her, even though she was a prisoner?

It hardly mattered. Claire rose to her feet, gathered
up what few items she had and stood quietly while one
of them locked shackles over her boots. Not so polite
now, she thought. Then the other guard took the bag
with her belongings in it from her hands. "I'll carry
that, miss."

Remembering her own manners, Claire thanked
him. Each guard took hold of one of her arms—her
wrists shackled in front—and led her from the cell.

The corridor looked like something out of an up-
scale hotel fallen on hard times. The carpet was of good
quality but a little shabby. The wood could have used a
good buff and polish. She'd lived in worse.

They took her to an ascension room—or lift, as she'd
heard them called over here. Inside, one of them in-

serted a punch card into a slot located in a box near the gate. Once they were shut in, the enclosure jerked into motion and carried them upward.

Three floors later, the lift finally lurched to a stop. The guard opened the gate, and the two of them escorted her into a vestibule that reminded her of the waiting area of a doctor's office. There were a couple of chairs and a sofa, a scuffed coffee table—did they call them tea tables here?—and a small sideboard with a pot of water sitting on a heating coil, and all the necessary items to make a cup of tea.

But Claire didn't care about tea, or the decor. Her attention was riveted on the man who rose from the sofa as she was led toward him. Alastair Payne. Her heart stuttered at the sight of him—one of the few men who didn't look at her as though they'd been hit in the face with a brick, or as though they thought they might smugly charm their way into her bed. His handsome, rugged face was void of any sort of reaction as she approached—a fact that only made him that much more interesting in her eyes.

His thick, wavy hair shone with copper highlights, and his storm-cloud eyes looked all the more intense when paired with a dark teal tailcoat—a hue only redheads could wear and look good. The coat appeared to be new, and it fit his broad shoulders perfectly. His waist and hips were narrow—perhaps a little too narrow—but his trousers were snug enough to make any warm-blooded woman regard his backside with appreciation. There was nothing as disappointing as a handsome man with an unfortunate arse.

He was as pretty as a peacock, and she felt as drab as a hen.

"Take the shackles off," he commanded with a scowl at the restraints.

"But she's the Dove, my lord!" one of the guards replied.

Claire smiled at the man. "Flatterer."

The guard flushed and turned back to Wolfred, who looked at him even more fiercely. "I said *take them off*."

Good lord, he was stern. "Or you could just give me the key and I'll do it myself."

Gray eyes locked with hers, and the smile faltered on her lips. Not since her father had any man made her feel so completely put in her place with little more than a look.

"Give me the key." He held out his palm. Claire noted that he had faint calluses on his fingers. No idle nobleman was he.

The guard removed the heavy iron key from one on his belt and placed it in Wolfred's hand.

The earl knelt before her, one booted foot still on the floor. The supple leather was polished so well that it shone. His gleaming hair—almost cinnamon in the light—blocked her from watching, but she felt a tug on the iron around her ankles, and she heard the clang and clunk as they slid to the floor.

"Are you certain that's a good idea?" she asked him. He was in the perfect position to get the heel of her boot in the chin.

Wolfred lifted his face to look up at her. The sight of him, kneeling at her feet, so close, seemingly supplicant but so obviously in control . . . Damnation, but it made her tremble inside. She wanted to grab him by that gorgeous hair, pull his head back . . .

"Are you an animal, Miss Brooks?"

Claire blinked. She didn't flush because she was not embarrassed—even if he did appear to be a mind reader. "What's that?"

"I asked if you were an animal. Are you so ignorant and lacking in rational thought that you need to be restrained? Or are you intelligent enough to know that striking out at me would be a mistake?"

Damn, but he was arrogant. He regarded her so casually and without concern that she wanted to kick him just to prove that she was a little bit of an animal, yes.

But that wouldn't get her to Howard, and she was so close now, she couldn't betray Robert by letting her own arrogance get the better of her. "I am not an animal, sir."

He unlocked the shackles on her wrists and rose to his feet, holding her gaze, so that she was forced to inevitably look up at him. "I didn't think so."

Was that a compliment? Who the hell could tell? They stood there, inches apart, staring at each other like two children, each determined to make the other blink first.

"We won't be traveling as husband and wife," he informed her. "Too many people at the house party you told us about will know me. They know I'm not married. You'll have to be my mistress. That will provide a much more believable cover for you if you're recognized—either as your true self or as Claire Clarke."

"Mistress," she sneered. "I'm sure you'll enjoy that, won't you?" Perhaps the earl wasn't as honorable as she had first thought. Everyone knew a mistress wasn't treated with the same respect as a wife. Well, he'd be sorry if he or any other man tried to abuse her. "Will we be forced to share a room as well?"

One of the guards coughed, but neither she nor Wolfred paid the man any mind. A muscle in the earl's jaw flexed. He leaned in closer so they were almost nose to nose. She refused to draw back. Her mother always said she was like a rat—when cornered, she decided to put up a fight.

"Trust me, woman. I'd rather put my cock in the rudder of a dirigible than let you anywhere near it. Do I make myself clear?"

Claire glared at him. "Perfectly." Had the remark not stung so much, she might have accused him of liking boys just to bait him, but common sense told her to drop it and fast.

"Good." Wolfred drew back and swept his hand in front of him. "Then after you."

She kicked the shackles aside and strode past him with her head held high. For some reason she had the insane urge to smile.

Perhaps Lord Wolfred was an honorable man after all.

There had to be something wrong with him—seriously wrong.

As they boarded his private railcar for the journey north, Alastair had to force himself not to notice how

Claire Brooks's backside looked in her snug trousers. There ought to be a law against women wearing such form-fitting garb. How did they expect a man to concentrate?

Especially a man who always seemed to be attracted to the worst possible women.

There was no denying she was a beautiful woman, so he wouldn't bother. And he truly would rather trust his privates to a rudder blade than to her person, but that didn't stop him from thinking about it. She wasn't overly soft, but she was firm and strong, and there was nothing demure about her. She was brash and direct, and he knew without a doubt she would be the same in bed. Of course he thought about it—how could he not? That didn't mean he was going to allow himself to make that mistake again.

Because it would be the biggest mistake of his life. Sex was just another weapon to her, one she wielded with great skill. Women like her were always well aware of their power over men, and he refused to be made a fool of by his own rigging—again.

Nonetheless, she'd seemed sincerely offended when he told her she'd be assuming the role of his mistress for the journey. He didn't doubt that she'd been taken advantage of in her life. It happened more often to female spies than he wanted to consider. And he certainly didn't want to think about some man doing that to Claire Brooks. He didn't want to have any compassion for the woman.

And yet . . . It made him angry that she thought he might be like those men. "Your baggage is in the bedroom," he informed her, nodding toward the open door at the end of the car. "Before we arrive, you will need to change into something a bit more suitable for a house party."

She turned to face him. "You mean something more feminine."

"I mean something more suitable. You know, this getting defensive every time I speak is getting tedious."

Arched brows lowered. "I'm not defensive."

"Indeed," he drawled, and moved toward the cold box—a specially designed metal-lined container kept cold by means of the substance Cardice—which was certain to be stocked with all manner of refreshment. He was famished.

He'd just reached the cold box when the train gave a loud hiss and lurched into motion. He braced one hand against the wall to keep from stumbling. Claire, he noted, did the same, only he doubted she almost put her fingers right through the wall.

"Hungry?" Alastair asked, once the locomotive found its pace and he felt secure in his footing.

"Sure," she replied, glancing around. "It looks like a brothel in here."

He followed her gaze. Yes, the paneling was dark and the furnishings a tad too crimson, but that was how it looked when he purchased the bloody thing. "Been in many brothels, have you?"

She glanced at him over her shoulder. "A few, yes."

He carried a platter of bread, cheese and cold ham to the table. "Come sit."

She regarded him warily as she moved closer. "You

don't want to know what I was doing in the brothel, or who I was doing it to?"

"To whom you were doing it. And no. I don't."

She ignored his correction of her grammar. "What if I told you I was with another woman?"

Alastair paused. He was a man, after all, and the idea had a certain lasciviousness he appreciated as a lover of the feminine form. "Not even," he responded, returning to the cold box for cider.

"Does the thought offend you?"

Christ on a Velocycle, the woman was the most provoking creature he'd ever met. "No. Should it?"

"Most men would be aroused by it."

He set the cider on the table and sat down on one of the benches bolted to the floor. "Would you like to arouse me, Miss Brooks?" He was not a fool; he had played these games before. He'd wager he'd used his own looks and charm to worm his way into almost as many confidences as she had, though perhaps not with the same success. But this was not his first assignment, and she was going to have to do better than that to trick him.

She leaned across the table, flashing him a coy look. "It would be so much easier for that rudder to do its job if I could."

He laughed. For the first time in too long to remember, he laughed well and hard.

Then the damnedest thing happened. Claire Brooks smiled—really smiled. And it was as though someone hit him upside the head with a cricket bat. He could only stare at her like a stupid boy.

He was playing right into her hands. If there was one thing of which he was certain, it was that this woman would chew him up and spit him out if given the chance.

Alastair cleared his throat. "Right. Here, eat something. We won't be north till well into the night. We'll stay at a hotel and then venture on to the house party later that day."

She shifted, as though ill at ease. Well, what did she expect? That she'd make one joke and he'd be hers? "I thought we'd be there tonight."

He didn't blame her for being eager to get it all over with, but a few extra hours in the free world must surely hold some temptation? "No. We need to make sure we give the same information if asked. I assume you want to use your alias of Claire Clarke?"

She nodded, a hint of that beguiling smile returning. "Yes. I meant to ask you how you found out about that."

"I have my means." He tore off a bit of bread and popped it in his mouth. "You never thought that perhaps actress was a bit high-profile for a spy?"

"It's perfect. I started doing a little acting before I joined the Company. No one suspects me of anything. They either think I'm traveling or doing a performance somewhere, and it usually saves me from having to hunt people down by bringing them to me. Men always think I'm trolling for a new lover."

Alastair shook his head as he tore another chunk of bread from the soft loaf. "All right, that works." He wasn't known for being a lothario, but he'd had a few relationships in his lifetime—enough that the idea of his seeing an actress wouldn't be a surprise to anyone. No one would question why he was with her, though some might wonder what the devil she was doing with him when she could easily have a duke or a prince as her lover.

"Where did we meet?" she asked, also helping herself to the simple but delicious fare.

"London. We can say you were in the city because you've been asked to appear in a production of *Hamlet*."

"Argh." She made a face. "Not Shakespeare. I despise trying to do Shakespeare. No, I'm thinking of playing Mrs. Cheveley in Wilde's *An Ideal Husband*."

"You're hardly old enough to play Mrs. Cheveley."

"That doesn't matter. It's a good role, and one that will immediately make all the women at this event think of me in the proper manner."

"You want the women to dislike you."

"Yes. It will make the men like me all the more—and endear you to the women because they'll all think you deserve better."

"What does it matter? We won't be there for any length of time. We find the Doctor and Howard, and we're done."

She rolled her eyes at him. "The Doctor may not be at the party with Howard but somewhere close by. And Howard, as you must surely know, is a master of disguise."

Yes, of course he knew this. "I assumed you would recognize him even with a disguise."

She snorted. "He's a master for a reason, my lord."

Provoking indeed. "And you reckon he's traveling with the Doctor because he needs some sort of surgery done?"

"I think the Doctor is going to surgically change Howard's facial features so that he can avoid capture permanently."

"Damnation. Is that even possible?"

She looked at him as though he were a dolt. "This coming from a man whose eyes have been altered so he can see in the dark."

Alastair froze. "How do you know that?"

"Please. Everyone in the Company knows about you." She waved a piece of cheese at him. "You're like the bogeyman."

Yes, there was a certain pride inherent in being feared by some of the most devious agents in the world, but at the same time he didn't like them knowing all his secrets. And he truly did not like Claire Brooks knowing them. Though, thanks to his research, he now knew plenty of hers.

It was time to draw the conversation away from himself. "You don't seem the least bit bothered that we're going after your former cohorts."

"I'm not." She took a bite of ham, chewed and swallowed. "You're not surprised, are you? You know how the game is played; you're only as loyal to your agency as it is to you."

That wasn't always the case, he thought, fighting off the cold that threatened to wrap around his heart. He knew of one traitor who had been treated very well by his agency. "And yours is responsible for the death of your brother."

Real pain flickered in her eyes. "Yes. They betrayed me, and now here I am helping you catch two of their most prized assets to save my own arse and spank theirs."

There was something in her voice that made him think she was lying, but he couldn't put his finger on it. Perhaps he just wanted to distrust her because it made her that much less appealing. Perhaps it was easier to simply see her as the enemy.

Regardless, it made him wonder what secrets Claire Brooks was hiding. Would one of them get him killed?

Chapter 6

Wolfred wasn't stupid. He knew she wasn't being entirely truthful. These were but just two thoughts that passed through Claire's mind as she and the earl made the journey from the train station to their hotel very late that evening.

He became quiet earlier as they ate. She wasn't stupid, either, and she knew it was because he had suspicions about her. Hell, she had her own about him. It shouldn't matter that he didn't trust her. He was right not to trust her. Normally she wouldn't care what he thought of her, but she no longer looked at Wardens as her enemy. How could she when the Company so brutally betrayed Robert? They'd betrayed her, too.

If nothing else, all these years as a spy had taught her something important—regimes changed. Ideals changed. There was no such thing as an agency or government or political party that had only the good of the people in mind. You gave your loyalty to the right people at the right time to achieve your goal, and the rest was up for negotiation.

Wolfred seemed to be a good man. She'd always thought of herself as a good woman. A good agent, risking her life for a better world, because she believed that one person should not have all the power over the people, that people shouldn't suffer and starve so that another might indulge himself in luxury. She might still subscribe to such naive beliefs if the people she believed in hadn't allowed her brother's murder to go unpunished—and if she hadn't experienced such kindness at the hands of a Warden. Evelyn Stone had had a more profound effect on her than she would ever know. Her world was no longer black and white, good and bad.

Alastair Payne did not see her as good. She was still his enemy in his eyes. That was for the best, because he was too handsome, too witty and too dangerous for her to play with.

Some time after they finished eating, she reclined on the chaise near the window and watched darkness fall over the countryside as they raced across it. She nodded off and didn't wake up until the car was shrouded in darkness.

From the stillness around her she deducted that the earl was asleep as well. She could probably sneak out if she wanted. She'd jumped from trains before. She could make her own way to the house party and slit Howard's throat in his sleep.

But the Doctor might get away, and she wanted that weasel to pay for what he had done to Huntley. She wanted to make certain Wolfred took him back to London so Luke could have a go at him. So, even though her head was screaming at her to escape, she found herself listening to her heart.

And then she found a pair of glowing eyes watching her in the dark.

"Hell's bells!" She pressed a hand to her chest.

"Apologies," came Wolfred's voice. There was a scratching sound, and then a match flared. The burning tip was put to an oil lamp on the wall, and soft golden light illuminated that corner of the car. He turned to face her, a slightly abashed expression on his face.

"I sometimes forget about them." He gestured to his eyes. "I didn't mean to frighten you."

Claire felt like an idiot for having been frightened. "Obviously I forgot as well."

He actually smiled. "Yes, I assumed as much from your reaction. 'Hell's bells,' was it?"

"It was my grandmother's favorite saying." Now, why had she just confided that?

"She must have been an interesting woman."

"That's one way to put it. And she was." That was all the thought she was going to allow herself. If she started thinking about family, she'd remember how alone she was in the world, and then she'd either start crying or fly into a fit of rage over the injustice of it. Neither was something she wanted to do in front of this man.

"My maternal grandmother used to like to say 'balls' whenever she was agitated. I don't know where she learned it. Mortified my mother, but gave me and my cousins something to snicker at."

Claire smiled—more at her mental image of Wolfred as a child than at the story itself. She imagined him with a huge head of thick, curly red hair and a face full of freckles—and a missing front tooth. "Is she still alive?"

"Yes. She'll be two and eighty in December."

"Just a few months then. Impressive that she's lived to such an age. You're lucky to still have her."

"Stubbornness and sherry make a great preserver. I am lucky, except for when she harps on me about grandchildren." He moved away from the wall, graceful despite the train moving beneath his feet. "As though the eleven she has weren't enough."

"I can't imagine having children, let alone grandchildren." Too late she regretted the words. She'd never had a problem with being too candid before. What was it about first Dr. Stone and now this man that made her so careless with her words?

Wolfred seated himself in a wingback chair not far from her—the spot where she assumed he had slept while she napped. "No. Our line of work makes that difficult."

"But you don't need to do this," she reminded him—once again being careless. "You are rich enough on your own. People like me, this is all we have. And how could I be so cruel as to bring a child into this life? I'd have to leave it with someone, and that's no way to be a mother."

"Do you want children?"

She turned her head. "Doesn't every woman?"

"No. Nor does every man, I'd wager. Though it is bred into most of my social sphere that it's one's duty to produce heirs, propagate the line and all that."

Her gaze returned to him, against her better judgment. He was watching her with an expression that looked a bit too much like pity. Had he been closer, she might have pinched him. "Of course, it's different for you as a man. You could father a dozen children and still run off whenever you wanted."

He nodded, infuriatingly unprovoked. "I could, but I wouldn't. I remember what that was like. I saw little enough of my own father." He tilted his head. "What is it about me that puts you on the defensive? I realize we have been conditioned to be enemies, but I've never met anyone who seems to want to fight me as badly as you."

It was a simple question, asked without an ounce of emotion, save for curiosity; yet it was like a hard slap to the forehead. "I don't know," she replied honestly. "I suppose I feel as though you judge me."

"I suppose I do. We're predisposed to it, are we not? You're Company and I'm Warden. Puts us at opposite ends."

"But I'm not Company, not anymore." It was important that he know that.

"Forgive me if I don't quite believe that just yet."

She shrugged. "That's fair, I suppose. I don't completely trust you, either."

"We're going to need to trust each other a bit, aren't we, though?" A crease appeared by his mouth as his lips lifted to that side—a self-deprecating little smile if she'd ever seen one. "Can you do that?"

"If you can." She felt as if she were ten years old again, and she and Robert were daring each other to see who could climb higher in the tree in their back-yard. The thought of her brother was enough to strengthen her resolve. If nothing else, she could trust this man to get her to Howard, and that was all she needed. And he could trust her to help him find the Doctor.

The earl watched her closely, scrutiny in those strange eyes of his that sometimes lit up when the light caught them a certain way. "I believe I can." He offered his hand. "Shall we shake on it?"

For a second, Claire actually hesitated. It wasn't a complete lie—he could truly trust her to a point. It didn't make her an awful person. She slid her hand into his. His fingers were firm, warm. When they closed around hers, they felt . . . odd. Human, but something more. She took his hand in both of hers, then turned it over so she could peer closely at his palm.

The scars were no bigger than a thread, and so well healed that they barely stood out against his skin. She traced one of them with the tip of her finger, curiosity getting the better of her. There wasn't even a ridge.

Wolfred flinched. Or was it a shiver? She couldn't tell; it happened so quickly and was over just as fast. He pulled his hand away. "Forgive me. The scarring is sometimes . . . sensitive."

Had he been any other man, she wouldn't have believed him. She wasn't an innocent; she knew when men wanted her, but this man—well, she didn't know what to make of him. "I should apologize for being overly familiar. I've never met anyone who was augmented before—other than Five. I mean, Huntley."

His brow puckered as he leaned back in his chair and crossed one ankle over his opposite thigh. "I thought the Company had been doing such procedures for years."

"They have. I was never selected for the program. There was concern that the procedure might interfere with my agility and flexibility."

"Yes, I've heard that you are rather . . . flexible."

Was that innuendo in his tone? "What do you mean by that?"

"Exactly what I said. I've heard tales of your daring escapades. Did you not once escape through an opening barely large enough to fit a child? In St. Petersburg, I believe."

Claire hesitated. Should she be concerned or flattered that he knew such details? "The window wasn't that small. I was simply fortunate that the Russian guards chasing me were on the sturdy side. But what of you? I heard you once disappeared practically into thin air while being pursued by French gendarmes."

Wolfred chuckled. "I ducked behind a drapery and hopped up on the windowsill so they wouldn't see my feet beneath the fabric. Then I opened the window and escaped through the back garden. Hardly the stuff of legend."

"As uninspiring as portly Russians," she replied

with a faint smile. "How very disappointing that neither of us can live up to our reputations."

"Speak for yourself." His expression was all mock indignation. "I earned every accolade."

"I won't argue. I've heard what happens to people who cross you."

He went very still. Hell. So much for a moment of easiness between them. "Yes. I can just imagine what you've heard about that shite. Tell me, did the Company paint me as a fool or a villain?"

She blinked. "Neither. You were not the only one played for a fool by those two. The details of how you survived, tracked them down and apprehended both of them were recounted with respect and fear. You *are* something of a legend, my lord."

He scowled. "Foolishness."

Claire wasn't certain what to say. She wasn't accustomed to men who didn't like to hear themselves praised. She was saved from having to say anything by the slowing of the train.

Wolfred consulted his pocket watch. "We'll be arriving soon."

When they disembarked at the station, Wolfred put a coin into an automaton torso that sat on a weathered podium. It looked like a metal man with no legs, and it had a large dial in its chest with a tarnished knob. Its right arm was raised, the hand holding the rim of a dented brass bowler hat.

Gears and clockwork parts wheezed into service, clicking and clacking. The aetheric engine kicked in as well. The metal man's jaw dropped open with a screech. Claire cringed—it needed a good oiling. "Please dial the number of the service required," it crackled in a heavy brogue. "Dial one for a porter, two for a cab, three for a porter and a cab. . . ." Alastair—she had to get used to thinking of him as such—turned the dial to three. The automaton responded by lifting its bowler hat to reveal a steam whistle coming out of the top of its head. It rent the air with three sharp blows. Then it ground back into its original position.

"That was painful," Alastair remarked with a wry grin.

"Modern innovation at its finest," Claire retorted.

His only response was a dry chuckle before a porter hurried to greet them with a luggage cart in tow.

Now they were in a richly appointed steam carriage driven by a man with an accent so thick, Claire hadn't understood a word he said. Wolfred didn't have the same trouble, it seemed. He even laughed at something the old man said before climbing into the cab. Porters had taken care of their luggage, carefully stacking and securing it high on the back of the vehicle.

They were alone, and entirely too close in the confined space.

Claire opened the shade to let moonlight inside. She didn't like tiny little quarters like this. Large rooms like the train car or even the cell the Wardens put her in were fine because they were spacious enough for her to move about comfortably. This wasn't much bigger than a closet.

"Are you all right?" Wolfred asked.

"I'm fine," she lied. "I just wanted to see some of the countryside. I've never been to Scotland before."

He glanced at the window. "Can you see much of anything?"

"No, but the moon is very pretty."

She could feel him watching her, damn him. "What am I to call you when we arrive at our destination? If we are to be lovers, we should have a degree of intimacy, shouldn't we? I can hardly call you Lord Wolfred all the time."

"Many people refer to me by my title," he said, the gravel of his voice filling the carriage. It was soothing. "You could call me Wolfred, or better still, call me Alastair. There will be no doubt as to the nature of our relationship, and it will lend a slightly scandalous cast to the whole thing."

Claire raised a brow. "Using a man's Christian name is scandalous?"

"You're in Britain, Miss Brooks; table legs are scandalous here."

She chuckled. "Call me Claire. Might as well if we are to be lovers."

He leaned back against the faded velvet seat. A glimmer of moonlight reflected in his left eye, and for a moment it shone like a mirror. She envied his enhanced vision. He could see her so much better than she could see him.

"Yes, I reckon I ought. I should have a pet name for you," he mused. "Something obnoxious that will make me sound terribly infatuated with you."

"Such as?"

"I've no idea. Bunny, perhaps. Or maybe sweetling."

Claire winced. "Surely you can do better than those, Mr. Love Cannon."

He laughed. "I will have to put my mind to it, if for no other reason than your superior ability to come up with obnoxious and humiliating monikers."

"Mmm-hmm." She hid a smile and went back to looking out the window. His gaze was unsettling—it made her feel as though he could see into her soul.

They arrived at the Hart and Hound Inn shortly after two o'clock in the morning, waking the innkeeper—an ill-tempered, round little man with florid cheeks and thick white hair that stood out around his head like a cloud. His mood changed drastically when he realized his late guest was an earl who appreciated his kindness and paid generously for it.

"You gave him far too much money," she commented over her shoulder as they climbed the stairs to their room. The staircase was so narrow, she was forced to walk in front of him.

"If it gets us a decent room with a comfortable bed and a hot meal in the morning, I don't give a damn."

She shrugged. "Your purse." What was it like to have so much money you didn't have to be careful with it? She made a decent living as a spy—a better one as an actress—but her total per annum earnings were probably on par with what he spent on shirts during the year.

"Here we are, my lord," the innkeeper announced with a wide smile. "Best room in the house." He opened the door and gestured for them to enter.

As she stepped over the threshold, Claire had to admit that there might be something to this overpaying business. The room was large and smelled of beeswax and lemon. Their luggage, brought up while they talked to the innkeeper, was piled neatly in the corner. The wallpaper was cream with exotic birds painted on it. The carpet was thick and soft, and the bed . . . The bed was huge.

But there was only one.

A maid had just lit the fire, and she bobbed a curtsy to Claire as she scurried from the room at the innkeeper's insistent gesturing.

"Will you be needing anything else, my lord?" he asked.

Alastair shook his head and handed him several coins. "That will be all, thank you."

The man thanked him profusely and backed out of the room. "Good evening to you both."

When they were alone, Claire turned to him. "Thank you."

Wolfred tossed his greatcoat over the back of a chair. "For what?"

"This." She waved a hand. "It's lovely."

He stared at her a moment. "You're welcome." He removed his jacket and began loosening his cravat. "There's a private bath. You may make use of it first."

He didn't have to tell her twice. Claire looked for toiletries and a nightgown in one of the bags provided for her, and she found everything a traveling woman might need and more. She grabbed a brush, tooth powder, face cream and a soft nightgown and wrapper that was new and smelled of jasmine.

At that moment she didn't care if she was going to be in a state of undress in front of Wolfred. She didn't care if they were going to share the same bed. She just wanted to feel that nightgown against her skin and settle her tired bones on that thick mattress. Her days on this earth were numbered—if the Wardens didn't end her, the Company would—so she intended to enjoy whatever luxuries came her way.

She didn't even care when she saw him outfit the door with a portable alarm system. It was little more than a bell with a combination lock that had to be entered correctly or the bell would begin to clang. She wasn't offended. On the contrary, she'd be more offended if he didn't take precautions—it proved that he thought her his equal. She made quick use of the facilities but vowed to indulge in the claw-foot tub the next morning if there was time. When she returned to the main room, Wolfred stood in the middle of it in nothing but a pair of loose linen sleeping trousers that hung low on his hips.

Sweet God in heaven.

He wasn't pale like most redheads. Instead, his skin had a natural golden hue. His shoulders were broad and well defined, with a smattering of freckles across them. Auburn hair covered his sculpted chest, narrowing as the trail disappeared beneath the waist of his trousers. Beneath that warm skin, his ribs were faint ridges, his stomach so flat it was almost concave. He was muscled there as well, like the statues she'd seen once in a museum in New York. And his arms . . . He had biceps a woman couldn't even begin to get her hands around.

It had been a long time since she'd been with a man, and even longer since she'd been with one she was truly attracted to. Alastair Payne was the worst possible man for her to want. He was also probably the last man she would ever see in a state of undress. Given that realization, there could be no harm in looking.

And he was staring at her as though he liked what he saw. He would never act on it; she knew that. But if some time in the night her hand "accidentally" slipped between his legs, he just might be persuaded to do what came naturally.

That, or he'd go looking for that dirigible rudder.

"It's all yours," she rasped, gesturing to the toilet with her bundle of dirty clothes. She was as jittery as a virgin, for pity's sake. This was how it felt to have met one's match. She would have to be very careful not to reveal her intentions to him.

"Thank you." He brushed past her, and she caught a whiff of his scent. He smelled like man—warm skin and exotic spice.

"Cardamom," she whispered.

"Did you say something?" He was already several feet away.

"Nothing," she replied, and hurried to her bags to put her things away.

Once she was alone, her thoughts turned briefly to escape, but she had to admit that it would be a foolish risk. She also had to admit that she didn't want to escape. Tomorrow she would find Howard, or he would find her, and then she would face whatever fate had in store. This was the last time she would ever sleep in such a decadent bed, especially with a man. Never mind that he might just as easily gut her in her sleep. He would certainly have to deal with her once she killed Howard. She could forget about him laughing at her wit then.

She went to the bed and climbed in, sinking into the soft mattress. The sheets were cool, but they were made of velvety flannel that soon warmed around her. By the time Wolfred—Alastair—returned from the toilet, she was already half asleep.

He extinguished the lights until there was nothing but the glow from the fire, then pulled back the blankets and slid into bed beside her. It didn't feel the least bit strange to have him there. In fact, she had to resist the urge to inch closer to his delicious warmth.

"Claire?"

"Mmm?" To her embarrassment, she yawned as she opened her eyes.

He was propped up on his elbow, all russet and gold in the firelight. "Can I trust you not to escape? I don't want to have to shackle you to the bed."

That might not prove entirely unpleasant, she thought. Nonetheless, she appreciated that he hadn't trussed her up at all, though that was probably because he'd armed the door, and most likely the windows as well. "I'm not going anywhere, Alastair."

It was probably the fire, but she thought she heard him hiss—like a sharply indrawn breath. "You're not going to kill me in my sleep, are you?"

Did he actually believe her? She yawned again and

closed her eyes. The damn things refused to stay open any longer. "No. I'd want you awake for that."

Silence descended, and for a moment she thought he was going to watch her all night just to make certain she didn't break her word. "I've decided what I shall call you."

"Oh?" She snuggled deeper into the downy embrace of her pillow. He had the sort of voice that could lull a woman into oh-so-pleasant dreams. "What?"

"Belle."

"As in beauty?" It was sweet, but not terribly original. Robert had called her something similar when she was a child. Good enough for a mistress, she supposed.

"No, as in hell's."

Then he rolled over, and she was glad that his back was to her so those damn sharp eyes of his couldn't see her smile.

Alastair woke with Claire, her nightgown riding up her thighs, curled up against him, and an erection so hard, he could have broken ice with it.

This was deuced inconvenient. Thank God she was still asleep; otherwise he'd be mortified. She was warm and firm, with feminine softness in all the right places, and she smelled good, like cake. Worse, she felt so terribly right pressed against him, as though she belonged there.

He shouldn't be surprised. Number one, she had been Luke's lover, and he seemed to have an annoying habit of sharing his friend's taste in women. Second, she was the last woman he should want; therefore it made a perverted sort of sense that he wanted her as much as he did.

He was surprised, however, to have slept through until morning. He truly thought she'd try to get away from him in the night, despite giving him her word. That he'd expected her to break her promise left him feeling slightly lowered. That she hadn't only confounded him.

Quickly and carefully he eased himself out of the bed. The room was not nearly as chilly as he expected, having heating pipes that were obviously turned on in the wee hours to make up for banked fires. Damn, he'd hoped the chill might ease the raging cockstand tenting the front of his trousers.

No wonder Luke had climbed into Claire's bed. She had to be one of the earthiest, most sexual creatures he'd ever met. There was no coyness to her, no artifice as there was with many women of his acquaintance. It wouldn't occur to her to tease or flirt unless she intended to follow through, because she was doing it for either business or pleasure. She must have reminded Luke of Arden a little that way—all brash and blunt.

He could speak plainly with her, be brutally honest if necessary, and she would give it back. She'd taken his remark about the dirigible rudder—a desperate lie, but oddly true at the time—and turned it into a joke between them. There shouldn't be any warmth between them at all, no camaraderie; yet they didn't seem able to avoid it. He'd set out on this journey determined to dislike her, and after some sixteen-plus hours in her company, he was already losing the battle.

He wanted to ask her more about betraying her agency. About how she came to the decision. Oh, he knew it was because of her brother, but there must be more to it. If she explained it, perhaps he would understand his father a little better—a man rumored to have betrayed the Wardens, though it was never actually proved.

But he wasn't going to think about his father while sporting an erection that seemed to have been forged from gregorite.

Claire was entirely too likable when she wasn't trying to provoke him. Though he had to admit to being guilty of provoking her as well. He should have known better. Nothing could happen between them. In a few hours he would meet with another W.O.R. agent already in attendance at the house party of Lord and Lady Dunrich. He'd be foolish to walk into such a situation without backup he could trust—he'd learned that lesson the hard way, thanks to Sascha.

Once he'd made contact, all that would be left would be to take the Doctor and Stanton Howard into custody. Claire would draw them out, he and the other agent would apprehend them; then they'd return to England, and he would very likely never see Claire again. She would be taken back to her cell, and left to whatever future the Wardens offered her, and he would be back to trying to atone for a life of mistakes that weren't his own. He hoped his father paid for his sins or found absolution—whether in heaven, hell or somewhere in between.

Such thoughts should have been as effective as a bucket of ice water on his libido. They were not.

Alastair took clean clothing from his valise and went to the bath, where he filled the sink with hot water and slathered his face with shaving soap. As he swiped the sharp blade of his razor over his jaw, he thought about how he'd reacted last night when Claire said his name. The woman had a way of making ordinary words sound sensual as hell.

And the way she'd looked at him when she came out of the bath . . . He'd known quite a few women over the course of his life, and none of them had ever looked at him like that. Not even Sascha, who'd gone out of her way to seduce him. Sascha had looked at him in a manner that suggested she thought of all the things he might do to her. Claire looked at him as though she was thinking of all the things *she* might do to *him*— arousing as hell, and very tempting.

Thinking about those very things did nothing to ease the insistent tightening in his groin.

He rinsed soap residue from his face, blotted the water with a towel, and then massaged a small amount of lightly scented oil into his skin to ease the redness shaving sometimes left on his face.

He was still hard.

Sighing, Alastair knew there was no point in denying the damn thing. It was determined to poke against the sink, chafe against the front of his trousers, and make an all-around nuisance of itself until he literally took it firmly in hand.

It was all Claire's fault that he was reduced to servicing himself in the bath like a horny boy. He braced one palm flat against the wall as he loosened the drawstring of his trousers and let them fall to the floor; then he wrapped his fingers around the rigid length of his erection and set himself to the task of ridding himself of the damn thing.

But as his hand moved, he began to think of all the things Claire might do to him if given the chance, and all the things he might do to her. For a few moments, until bringing himself to climax, he forgot about the fact that she was the wrong woman, that he couldn't completely trust her, that there could never be anything between them, and he indulged in what might have been under different circumstances.

The result left him trembling, weak in the knees, feeling guilty as hell, and surprisingly sad.

Chapter 7

What the hell was that?

Claire sat up right in bed. For a moment, she didn't know where she was; then memory came flooding back. She was alone, but the pillow beside hers held the indent of having been slept on, and there was a familiar cinnamon hair on it.

"Alastair?"

She heard the sound of taps and then running water. He must be in the standing-bath. The thought of him standing naked beneath a spray of hot water was a fleeting but effective one. Now was not the time for distractions.

In a few hours Stanton Howard's throat would be at the mercy of her blade, if she could get her hands on one. Or perhaps she'd stab him in the ear with a hat pin. Or shoot off bits of him with her gun—provided Alastair gave it to her.

Alastair. He was going to end up one of her biggest

regrets; she could feel it. It was bewildering, as she had known him only a short time. How sad that the first man she felt a real . . . *connection* with was the one she could never have. Fate had a perverted sense of humor.

Her stomach growled. She was ravenous. Surely he wouldn't object to breakfast? She climbed out of bed and slipped into the wrapper draped across the footboard. Then she went to the call box on the wall. There was no dial or crank on it, so it was useless for outside calls unless the inn had a switchboard—which she doubted. She brought the handset to her ear and waited.

"Good morning! What might we do for you?"

Claire smiled. Thick as mud was the woman's accent, but at least she understood it. "I'd like to have some breakfast sent up to my room if that's possible."

It was, and she rattled off what she would like. The woman assured her it would arrive "in a tic" and hung up. Claire began choosing her clothing for the day while she waited. The Wardens had supplied several gowns for her to wear, each of good quality. Not the best, of course, but they were well-made items suitable for a successful American actress who didn't like her clothing to overshadow her looks. Simple but elegant. There was a small assortment of cosmetics packed in a vanity case as well. They truly had thought of everything.

She selected a lovely day gown that wouldn't be too injured by travel. It was a rich violet that would complement her eyes and complexion. The gown was in need of an iron, however. She shook the garment out and draped it over the back of a chair. Perhaps the rest of the wrinkles would fall out. A knock sounded upon the door just as the water shut off in the bath. Perfect timing. Two maids bearing trays loaded with food and a coffee service entered without triggering Alastair's lock. The food smelled so good, Claire's mouth watered. One of the maids spotted her wrinkled gown and immediately offered to take it away to have it pressed. Claire thanked her and let her take it. It wasn't as though she could do it herself.

The maids closed the door behind them, and Claire pounced on the food trays, left on a small table near the window.

The door to the bath opened, and Alastair stuck his head out. "Who was that?"

Claire glanced over her shoulder and wished she hadn't. Wet, his hair was darker, and it curled about his nape. And the towel he held about his waist rode even lower than the trousers he'd worn to bed—it was shorter, too, so now she was treated to a glimpse of well-shaped and muscular calves.

"For God's sake, man, put some clothes on. I ordered us breakfast."

He came into the room. "Oh good. I'm starving." Claire was thankful that he stopped and grabbed a dressing gown from the same chair where he'd draped his outerwear last night. She watched, her breath held as he lifted his arms and slid them into the arms. The muscles in his stomach shifted. Any second that towel was going to let go. . . . The heavy velvet brocade settled across his back, hugged his shoulders, and tied snugly about the waist.

Relief and disappointment drifted through Claire's mind. "Did you drop something in the bath earlier?"

Alastair removed the silver cover from a plate and sat down at the table. "No."

"Oh, I thought I heard you cry out."

He hesitated, just for a second, as he reached for the salt. "Not that I recall."

"My mistake then." Was that a flush in his cheeks? What the hell . . . ? *Oh.* To her astonishment, heat flooded her own face as well. She sat down opposite him and busied herself with her own breakfast. Men. Couldn't keep their hands off themselves.

She was so tempted to tell him she would have gladly taken care of that for him, just to see his reaction. He didn't seem the type to blush often, but given what she'd seen, he was magnificent when he did.

Instead, she poured a cup of coffee for them both from the silver pot. It was hot, and she had to pull the sleeve of her wrapper over her palm to keep from getting burned.

"There's something I don't understand," she said.

He barely glanced up from slathering strawberry jam on his toast. "What's that?"

"The woman you were involved with. Why did she try to kill you? If she got the information she wanted, why not just leave?"

He looked as though he'd rather chew nails than discuss it. "I didn't give her any information during our affair. I'm better than that. And she wasn't the one responsible for the carriage falling on me. He was."

Claire nodded. "That makes more sense to me."

"Oh? Pray, then explain it to me."

She plucked up a piece of crispy bacon with her fingers and took a bite. Heavenly. "Obviously he was jealous. She probably started to fall in love with you, if she hadn't already. She had to go along with him to save face and her relationship."

"She didn't care about me. It was her idea to leave me with the carriage."

Clearly he didn't like this turn of topic, but he hadn't told her to shut up, so she pressed on. "I reckon he wanted to put a bullet in your skull?"

"Yes. She said leaving me as I was would make it a slower death. A more painful one."

Claire snorted. "Or give you plenty of time to be discovered."

He frowned at her. "You women will look for a shred of romance in anything, won't you? Leaving me for the buzzards was not an act of feeling."

She pointed the bacon at him. "When you made love, did she let you kiss her?"

"That's none of your business."

Claire smiled, not the least bit offended. Oh, but she loved poking him. And maybe she wanted to show him that not all women in her profession were untrustworthy, as easily bought as a three-cent whore. "She did. Women do not kiss men they don't like—not much. Did she look at you when you made love?"

It was temper, not embarrassment, that flushed his

cheeks now. "Have you no shame whatsoever? Not even a shred of decorum?"

She rolled her eyes. "Don't be a prude. I'm an actress, remember? And a spy. I know all the lies and truths women use. If she looked into your eyes while you were inside her, she cared about you, my lord. You were not the one who made the mistake. It was her." She bit into the crisp bacon.

"I'm not a prude," he grumbled. "I don't want to discuss it because I'm mortified of having made the mistake of believing her affection for me was true."

She made a face. "Because that was her *job*, and she was good at it. Then she began to believe it as well. That was when she should have gotten out. You would not have been hurt, and she and her lover would not have been hunted by the fox like baby rabbits."

Alastair set aside his toast as she devoured another piece of bacon. "Does the Company train its women agents to be skilled in seduction?"

"Yes. Some of the men as well. It's not all about sex, you know. It's about making the target feel good when you're around. It's about making them want to connect with you, think about you, even when you're not there. You become what they need you to be."

"Like a well-trained whore."

Ah, who was poking at whom now? "Doesn't pay as well, though."

"Have you been trying to seduce me?" His lips tilted mockingly. "Because you're doing an excellent job of it."

Both of her brows rose, but she refused to be baited.

"You told me you'd rather stick your cock in a rudder than in me, remember? No, I'm smart enough to know better than to try to seduce a man like you."

"But you pity me for being stupid enough to be seduced by her?"

"No, because you're the kind of man who makes it easy for a woman to lose her wits. You try to be so hard and tough, but beneath that you are a good man, and no woman can resist that. I don't care how well-trained or determined she is. You will make her want to please you, to win your trust and the ultimate prize of your heart, and then she's lost." It was an honest answer to his question, but he looked as though she had slapped him. "That's not an insult. Merely an observation from a woman who has met enough bad men to know a good one when he takes her shackles off."

"I . . ." He ran a hand through his damp hair. "I know it's not, but the Warden in me can't help but see it as a fault."

"Then the Warden in you is an ass," she retorted, strangely angry at him. "If you can't bring yourself to use it as a weapon, then you need to avoid missions that put you up against women."

His gaze was the color and intensity of a thunderstorm. "Such as this one?"

"Well, yes." She spread jam over her toast. "I asked for Huntley, remember?"

"Huntley has retired and has a pregnant wife."

"She's pregnant?" The news surprised her, but that was the extent of it. "Well, he's come out of all this all right then, hasn't he?"

"You're not jealous?" He sounded surprised.

"Of course not." Claire picked up another piece of bacon and placed it on the toast; then she took a bite of both, savoring the sweet and salty delight on her tongue. "I'm happy for him."

Alastair didn't look convinced. Claire regarded him as she chewed. "Why don't you just ask me what it is you want to know?"

His eyes narrowed as he lifted his toast. "And just what is it I want to know, oh omnipotent one?"

She moved forward, leaning over the table. "If I loved him."

He leaned closer as well. "Did you?"

Where was all this anger coming from? How did they inspire each other to such intensity? "No. I never loved him, and he never loved me. We were both too good at the game. Does that make you feel better? Or do you feel even guiltier about wanting his wife?"

For a second she swore she saw lightning in his eyes, but it was more likely a flash of sunlight coming in the window. "Woman, you need to learn when to shut that fucking mouth of yours."

A thrill—perverse and hot—raced through her once she knew she had inspired such coarse language. For a moment, she'd made him forget honor and duty and propriety. She pushed harder, knowing full well she might push him way too far. "You'd like to teach me, wouldn't you, Lord Wolfred?"

"Yes, I would." Before she knew what he was doing, he reached out and grabbed her by the back of the neck, hauling her onto the table. Claire's heart hammered against her ribs, not in fear, but in anticipation. The tines of a fork dug into her knee and she didn't care. She reached out with both hands and seized the front of his dressing gown. The bare flesh of his chest scorched her thumbs. Their gazes locked.

"Do it," she whispered. Commanded. Begged.

He growled low in his throat, and his mouth claimed hers.

Claire's mouth felt exactly as Alastair had known it would, though he had imagined her tasting of berries or spice rather than of bacon and sugary jam. It really didn't matter, because her full lips yielded beneath his, letting him inside without hesitation. Her mouth was hot and wet, inviting. Her fists held him just as tight and close as he held her, and the table be damned.

He was already hard for her, despite having relieved himself of the same affliction not long ago. Christ in a dirigible, he felt as if he were eighteen again. If he slipped his hand beneath her nightgown, would he find her equally enthusiastic for him?

If he took her to bed, would she look into his eyes? He would keep his open just to see.

The thought was exactly the shock of reality he needed. He released her, then pulled away. He sat back in his chair and made a show of brushing toast crumbs from the rumpled front of his dressing gown.

Claire slowly moved off the table and sank into her own seat. She had a smear of jam over her left breast. It looked almost like blood against the ivory silk of her wrapper. She lifted a hand to her mouth, the pads of her long, slender fingers pressing as though to check for bruising or injury. Had he hurt her?

"That . . ." She cleared her throat. "That was . . ."

"A mistake," Alastair blurted before she could. "My apologies, Miss Brooks. I forgot myself. It won't happen again."

It was undoubtedly his male pride and wishful thinking, but he thought he saw disappointment flicker in her eyes.

"Of course," she replied softly, her sultry voice a little strained. "Obviously we were overtaken by the moment."

Alastair frowned. That sounded more like something he'd expect out of an Englishwoman rather than this bold American. What had he expected? That she'd declare her lust for him after he had said his for her was an error in judgment? It was, but no woman wanted to hear that.

"I want you to know I would never take advantage of you," he said, though he wanted to. He really, really wanted nothing more than to take advantage of her right there, on the table.

Her lips twisted—a little bitterly, he thought. "No, of course you wouldn't. You are an honorable man, after all, and despite my being a Company whore, I am your prisoner. Wouldn't want to abuse your power. Would you excuse me? I should really get cleaned up and dressed if we're going to venture on to the house party as planned."

He barely had time to stand before she leaped up from the table, grabbed her things from the bed, and bolted to the bath. The door closed firmly behind her.

Alastair slumped into the chair. He'd certainly mucked this up well and good. Perhaps it was time for him to give up being a Warden. He certainly didn't seem to be very good at it anymore, at least not where Company females were concerned.

Sighing, he stood and went to a case sitting on top of his baggage. From it, he withdrew a small brass and leather box that had seen better days, and returned to the table with it. He might be an idiot, but he was still hungry, and not about to let all this food go to waste. He ate two slices of bacon and a piece of toast as he opened the box and set the machine to working order.

It had to be used near a window or outside for the best aetheric reception, and it always behaved better on clear days such as this one. He pressed several keys on the small typewriting keys, struck the carriage return and then waited. From the bath he heard the sound of water filling the tub.

The small, circular screen flickered and crackled with static; then a grainy image appeared—a face Alastair had heard several ladies describe as terribly handsome, though he didn't see it. "I've been waiting on you, Wolfred."

"Don't get your knickers in a knot, Blackstone. This is the first chance I've had to make contact. You're an aristocrat; you shouldn't be up yet regardless."

"There was a hunting party this morning. I had to plead a hangover." Declan Frost, Lord Blackstone, was not the type of man who drank to excess, and Alastair doubted the man would know a hangover if one chose to cosh him over the head.

"Is Howard with the party?"

"How the devil should I know? I haven't been downstairs. If he's the bloke I think he is, then he talked as though he wouldn't miss the chance to shed a little blood on the hunt. That odd friend of his is going to join the party for the midday meal. Are you certain he's the Doctor?"

"That's what our intelligence tells us. They'll be out for a little while longer at least. We should be there before luncheon."

"We?"

"I have a traveling companion with me." It was ridiculous, but he didn't want to tell this man about Claire; he didn't want him to know the truth about her.

Blackstone's eyes twinkled—or it might have been more static. The aether was being temperamental today. "Good to hear. For a while there was speculation that you might never bother with a woman again."

"Indeed," he remarked drily. He shouldn't be surprised. He'd taken part in similar speculation regarding other agents over the years—it wasn't that different from the betting books at the clubs—but he'd rarely been the object of such wagering before. "I hope you didn't bet against me."

"Never. All right, get your arse dressed and up here. I'll meet you when you arrive."

"Excellent. Make certain you're armed. See you soon." He flicked the switch to disconnect communication and packed up the machine once more. He'd just set it in his bag when there was a knock on the door.

His fingers closed around the handle of a scatter pistol, but he left his hand inside the luggage, out of sight. "Come in."

It was a maid, carrying a freshly pressed purple lady's day gown. She curtsied to him and carefully avoided his gaze. "Begging your pardon, my lord. I'm just returning the lady's clothing."

"Thank you." He let go of the pistol, and dug a couple of coins out of his change purse. He gave the silver to the girl. "Excellent work."

She flushed. "Excuse me, sir, but will the lady need any assistance? I can come back."

Alastair glanced at the closed bath door. Who the hell knew what Claire needed? "We'll ring if we need you."

The girl bobbed another curtsy and exited. Alastair had to let her out because of the lock bieng used to keep Claire in. He hung the gown on a nearby hook on the wall. It was a lovely color. Whoever did the shopping for the W.O.R. had excellent taste. It was probably the work of Madame Cherie, popular seamstress and W.O.R. agent. The dress was quality without being pretentious. Fashionable but not fussy, it was exactly the sort of thing one would expect of a woman who knew she needed little adornment.

He finished his breakfast while he dressed, putting on dark gray trousers, a white shirt, a dark gray brocade waistcoat, a dark green cravat and a dark gray jacket. The drab color of his own ensemble would make

Claire stand out even more, and they needed her to at-
tract attention. It was the only way to draw Howard
out into the open.

She would draw Howard to her, and when the bastard made his move, Alastair and Blackstone would be
there to capture him. Then he'd return to London with
Howard, the Doctor and Claire in custody. As far as the
Wardens would be concerned, he would have proved
that he had his balls back, and he would be out of his
father's shadow once and for all. Life would go back to
how it had been before.

And Claire Brooks would rot in a W.O.R. prison cell.
If she gave them enough information, they might let
her go eventually, but not until she was too old to be of
use to either agency.

That one kiss would haunt him until the end of his
days, as would the woman herself.

He stood in front of the mirror, tying his cravat.
Claire was fortunate Howard hadn't killed her that
night. He'd made the mistake of thinking the fall would
do her in.

Or had he? He must have seen the carriage below. If
he truly wanted to protect himself, he should have put
a bullet in her brain just to make sure she didn't get up
from the fall.

Her situation wasn't like his own, was it? Had Howard let her live because he had feelings for her, just as
Claire claimed Sascha had for him? She could be after
him for a little lover's revenge.

No. It didn't make sense—not just because he
thought she'd have better taste in men, but because he

couldn't believe any man would walk away from Claire.

Alastair glanced at the bath door. He could hear water draining out of the tub. She'd be in there, naked and wet, her body slick. . . . He swallowed. He'd known her only a few days, and she already had him by the wedding tackle. Jesus, he needed a wife or a mistress—someone to occupy his body and encourage his affections. Then he wouldn't sniff around every unsuitable woman like a randy hound.

Though he couldn't imagine any Englishwoman, mistress or wife, demanding that he "do it" as Claire had.

He was packing his toiletries when she emerged from the bath. "Did the maid bring my gown?"

"It's on the wall," he replied, not looking up. "She said she'd return to assist you in dressing if you needed her help."

"I'm fine, thank you."

He looked up just in time to see her standing there in a chemise, drawers, stockings and corset. The drawers were short and lacy, giving him a view of thigh above her garter and stocking. She had long legs—shapely and strong. It was too easy to imagine them wrapped around him. The corset nipped in her waist and pushed up her breasts so that they swelled over the low neckline of the chemise, which was so thin he could make out the faint blush of a nipple.

She didn't notice him staring—thank God—or the obvious interest his crotch had in the proceedings. She simply pulled the purple gown over her head and began buttoning the multitude of fabric-covered buttons that ran up the front.

"Did Lady Huntley send my fan?" she asked as she worked.

Alastair's gaze jerked up to meet hers. "Yes."

She arched a brow. "May I have it?"

He turned to retrieve it. He was such an idiot—acting as if he'd never seen breasts before, while she was cool and collected, as though she almost devoured a man every day.

Perhaps she did. Perhaps she flirted and reacted the way she did with him to keep him off balance and keep him from asking the wrong questions.

Well, he'd damn well ask them anyway. "Was Howard your lover?"

She went perfectly still—like a doe at the end of a hunter's sights. She looked up from shoving the fan in her reticule and met his gaze with one that burned and snapped like wildfire. Her fingers tightened on the item, and for a moment he wondered if she'd whip it open and use it on him.

"I would never let that man touch me. And if you ever again insinuate that I would, I'll make it impossible for you to ever jerk yourself off again."

Her words should have shamed him, but they didn't. They made him angry, but they also ignited his lust for her. Even the most skilled of actresses could not put that much truth into a performance. She was not in league with Howard; she never had been.

He wanted to go to her, turn her to the wall, throw up those skirts and shag her until she screamed. He wouldn't care if she lined her cunny with razor blades and lye; he'd still want to be inside her.

But he was a "good" man, and he'd never force himself on a woman, though he reckoned there would be little force involved. She was more than a match for him. He was also trying to be a smart man, and that was what kept him from acting on his desires.

"It will be difficult to do that from inside a prison cell," he informed her coolly. "But duly noted. My apologies for offending you."

She nodded stiffly and went back to her reticule, leveling an uncomfortable and thick silence between them.

A short time later, they'd packed up their things, had the baggage taken to their carriage and began the short journey to the Dunrich estate, just outside of Ayr.

"How did you procure an invitation to this party?" Claire asked as the carriage rumbled along, putting them closer and closer to their target.

She deigned to speak to him again? In his experience it generally took much longer than this for a woman to forgive a lesser slight. "I'm an earl. I get invited to many of these sorts of things. Once the season is over, it's assumed that gentlemen and ladies of the aristocracy are bored and have nothing better to do than go live in someone else's house for weeks at a time."

"Not everyone shares your dedication to the Crown, I take it?"

"No, though it would make the Company's job easier if some idiots did." He avoided her gaze, not wanting to decipher what he saw there when she looked at him.

"Howard must be masquerading as nobility then," she surmised. "Or at least as someone important."

"Most likely he'd pretend to be foreign. Debrett's Peerage is required reading amongst my set."

She said something about wagering that the Wardens required their agents to know just as much about the ruling classes of every European country and went back to staring out the window.

Alastair stared at the countryside as well. Things wouldn't be nearly so tense between them if he hadn't kissed her. If he hadn't finally wondered why Howard hadn't killed her and asked a stupid question. But he had, and it was just as well. He'd rather have coldness between them than lust. Lust led to mistakes and regrets. Coldness was much better in regard to self-preservation.

They arrived at the Dunrich estate forty minutes later. It was a large, stately structure built at least two centuries earlier, but outfitted with modern conveniences. The gate at the end of the drive worked on punch cards, which each guest was sent along with an invitation. For the duration of the party, the code carried by the cards would allow access to various parts of the estate. After the party, the code would be changed. Guests were also given similar cards to access their rooms.

Their driver pulled the carriage right up to the front door, which had a long flight of shallow stone steps leading up to it. As his door opened, Alastair saw Blackstone practically running down the steps toward him. What the hell . . . ? The man was usually a much more discreet operative.

"Blackstone, what's going on?" he demanded, stepping to the ground.

The man regarded him with an agitated expression. "Howard and the Doctor. They're gone. They're sailing from Ayr in half an hour."

"To where?" Alastair demanded, ignoring Claire's sharp intake of breath.

Blackstone shook his head, his expression turning to resignation. "I have no bloody idea."

Chapter 8

"No." Disbelief seized Claire with icy fingers. "He can't get away. He can't." She didn't care that Alastair watched her with curious eyes, or that his friend looked at her as though she were a lunatic. He was obviously a W.O.R. agent, there to provide support if they needed it.

Why the hell hadn't he stopped Howard? If he'd known they were leaving, he should have stopped him. What sort of Warden allowed not one but two Company agents to simply wander away?

As though reading her mind—something that seemed to be another Warden talent—the man looked from Alastair to her and back again. "I didn't find out until after they'd already left. I would have tried to delay them if I could."

For all the good it did them.

Claire grabbed Alastair by the coat, shoving him toward their vehicle. "Get back in the carriage. We have to go after him."

"Claire . . ."

"Get in the damn carriage!" She knew her eyes had to be as wild as a cornered animal's and didn't care. Robert's killer was not going to slip through her fingers, not after she got herself captured. Spending the rest of her days in a cage would be worth it only if she could relish the specter of Howard's blood on her hands.

Something in her insanity must have gotten through to him. He turned to the other man. "Send word to the director. Let her know we're in pursuit."

The man nodded. "I will. Be careful, Wolfred." He cast a wary glance at Claire. "Miss."

Claire didn't wait for him to turn his back on them before jumping into the carriage. She grabbed Alastair by the arm and pulled. "Come on, we have to go!" She hit her fist on the roof of the carriage, signaling the driver to move on.

Alastair climbed in and grabbed her wrists with his fingers. She could feel the difference in strength between his hands. One was much stronger than the other. His eyes weren't the only part of him that was augmented then. "Claire, calm down."

"How can I calm down when Howard is getting away?" she demanded, and pounded on the roof again. "Move the damn carriage!"

Alastair pushed a button on the wall. There was a tiny ornophone horn next to it. "West toward Ayr, Tavish. We need to get to the city docks as quickly as possible."

"Yes, my lord," came the reply, and the carriage jerked into motion, the steam engine wheezing.

Claire released a breath. "Now he decides to move." She closed her eyes and pinched the bridge of her nose between her thumb and index finger. This wouldn't have happened if she and Alastair hadn't wasted time sparring with each other—kissing each other. She had lost sight of her purpose—vengeance for Robert—and this was the price.

The steam engine chugged faster, carrying the carriage along at a faster pace. By the time they reached the end of the drive, they were tearing along at full speed. Claire watched the ground whip past, convinced she might run faster than the carriage if she jumped out. It was idiotic, of course, but anxiety sat heavy in her chest, making her restless.

She could feel Alastair's gaze upon her, curious and suspicious. It had been a mistake, letting him see her agitation, but it couldn't be taken back now.

As if on cue, his voice cut through the sound of the engine and wheels. "Why didn't Howard kill you?"

Of all the things he might have asked—such as whether or not she was insane—*this* was what he chose?

She turned from the window. This was a distraction both welcome and frightening. If she said the wrong thing, the satisfaction of killing Howard would never be hers. "He shot me and pulled me off a building."

"But you lived. He must have known you weren't dead."

"I would expect there might have been too many witnesses. The people in the carriage got out." She looked him dead in the eye. "Why do you think he left me alive?"

"I have no bloody idea, but something about it's not right." He glanced at her and saw the glint in her eye. "Don't look at me as though you'd like to kill me if you don't have the guts to just do it."

"You don't know what I have the guts to do. Stanton Howard knows what happened to my brother—why he was killed. I've chased him all over Europe for the answer, and I'm not going to stop until I find him. If that means slitting your pretty throat, I'll do it."

Alastair had no doubt she would do just that if provoked. Oddly enough, it only served to make him like her more. There seemed to be no guile about her at all; yet he couldn't escape the feeling that she wasn't being completely honest with him. He really oughtn't be so surprised that she trusted him so little. It wasn't as though he trusted her.

"How did he look at you before he pulled you off the roof?"

"What do you mean?"

"What was his expression?"

"I couldn't tell. He was wearing a disguise that made it difficult to discern his true features."

"How do you know it was really him?"

"I know."

He watched her for a moment, and she could tell he was trying to figure out whether or not to believe her. "Alastair, I may not be the brightest of candles, but I know Stanton Howard. Maybe not immediately, but I will find him. He has eyes as cold as a Siberian winter, and he is as heartless as anyone ever could be. He is a monster, and I would know him by smell."

"By smell?"

"He often smells of stage makeup. And spirit gum. I think anyone with theatrical knowledge would know him. My brother once said he thought Howard must have been a professional actor at one time, because he is so talented with disguise."

"And the two of you, having theater backgrounds, recognized this."

"Yes. It's not a common smell, though I doubt many outside of the theater would be able to identify it."

"You do realize there's a slight chance we won't catch up with him."

"We have to." Her vehemence was almost as unsettling as the wildness of her expression. He'd seen it before when an agent got too involved in an assignment and began to make something personal out of it.

"Listen, I know you want justice for your brother, but you have to accept . . ."

"I don't have to accept anything. We are going to catch this bastard, and we're going to bring him to justice. He will pay for what he did to Robert, and we're going to catch the Doctor and make him pay for everything he has ever done. Are you listening to me? I did not come all this way to lose him now."

For what *he* did to Robert? Damn. She gave herself away.

"What are you planning to do to him, Claire?" Alastair asked in a low, careful tone.

"Give him to Warden custody, of course." She met his gaze evenly, praying he couldn't see the lie in her soul. If she told him she planned to kill Howard, he'd have her on the next train to England, with an armed guard. "I want justice, Alastair. I don't want my brother's murder to go unnoticed. The Wardens will make certain it doesn't." She didn't believe that for a moment, but he did.

"The Company won't look fondly on your betrayal."

"I don't look too fondly on the Company right now, either, so that should make us even."

"There's a good chance they'll send assassins after you."

"I realize that as well. I should be relatively safe in Warden custody, should I not?" For a moment, she wondered if he knew that she had already resigned herself to her fate of life imprisonment or death. If she was going to die, she was going to make certain Howard went first.

"Yes, the Wardens will do whatever they can to ensure your safety."

"Perhaps the Doctor will teach Dr. Stone how to change a person's features through surgery. Think of all the spies and witnesses you could protect then. The Company would never be able to find them."

"We'll never find Howard if he goes through such a procedure."

"No. That's why we have to find him now, Alastair. We have to catch him before he gets on that ship, or he'll be lost. And my brother will have died for nothing." The admission, that almost complete baring of her soul, left a heavy feeling in her chest.

"Why did Howard kill him?"

She could lie, but now was the time for truth. She

knew enough about Alastair Payne to suss out that he had a weakness for damsels in distress—or women who he believed needed him. She did need him. She wouldn't catch Howard without him. Not now.

"I'm not sure. I believe it was because Robert figured out that Howard planned to double-cross the Company. He apparently stole some documents of a sensitive nature—documents he planned to sell to the highest bidder at a private auction. Robert followed the bastard to a warehouse where he planned to meet a potential buyer. Next thing you knew, the building went up in a jet of fire and smoke. There wasn't enough left of my brother for me to identify his body. I buried an empty coffin."

"I am sorry."

"It was hardly your fault, unless you are Stanton Howard."

He didn't laugh, and for one split second, she wondered if she had been mistakenly, horribly right. She'd seen stranger things in her career.

His lips twitched, and she almost sighed aloud in relief. "I'm not Howard, no. I'm sorry for your loss, is what I meant to say."

"Thank you. I appreciate it. You know what it's like to lose people you care about to this line of work. You expect it to happen, but when it does finally occur, you can't seem to believe that it actually happened."

"You expect it to be part of a ruse, or maybe an assignment. Any moment they'll walk through the door and explain it was all for show, and apologize for not being able to tell you all about it in the beginning."

"Exactly. I keep hoping he'll send a note, or show up somewhere in a crowd and tell me it was all a mistake."

"And then he'll break you out of Warden custody, I suppose?" There was a little amusement in his tone, but not the mocking kind.

"Yes. He'll be masquerading as a guard and take me away from all of this."

"And then what? In your imagination, what do you and your brother do when you've managed to escape it all? Do you go back to the Company?"

She gave him a disgusted look. "Never. We buy a little house in the country and retire there. It's in up-state New York, where there's nothing but lakes and trees. It's peaceful, and there's no one trying to kill you every time you turn around. You have to drive a couple miles into town, and every once in a while you go to a dance or some community event, and no one cares what you used to do; they just offer you a drink and food and friendship."

"It sounds lovely."

"It is." She laughed. "We'd be bored out of our minds within a week, and we'd probably start a fight at a church supper."

He laughed as well, and she was glad of it. It made sense that he understood. He probably felt the same way. "I reckon that's why people like us get into this line of work. We're bored by life."

"Not bored. Dissatisfied. I was never comfortable watching bad things happen to people, or sitting back and putting all my trust into a government that seemed to have money in mind more than the interests of its people. I joined the Company because my brother joined, and because I thought it was the right thing to do."

"My father and grandfather were both Wardens. It's in my blood. I suppose I inherited a position in it. It was certainly expected of me—just like actually sitting in my chair in the House of Lords."

"Yes, I'd heard that your parliament was made up of many nobles. Doesn't that defeat the purpose?"

"Not if you're a noble. Tell me about your brother. This talk of governments and duty—true as it might be—bores me. I want to hear about something worthy."

His words brought a strange burning sensation to her eyes. With that simple request he had honored Robert more than any of the Company agents she spoke to after his death. "You don't have to ask me about it. It's all right."

"I mean it. I want to know, and it will help pass the anxious moments until we reach the dock. Tell me. What did you love most about your brother?"

"His bravery. His quick thinking. I've seen him get into situations that I think are utterly inescapable. The next thing I know, he's escaped. He was always the smartest and fastest, winning accolades and honors. Before our parents died, he wanted to be a lawyer. He would have been brilliant at it. If not for the accident that killed them, he could have realized that dream instead of getting caught up with the Company and Stanton Howard."

"Perhaps he believed he could achieve more through the Company. Howard may have played on your brother's desire to make the world a better place. He more than likely pretended to be a friend."

"Maybe, but Robert was really good at judging people. He seemed to have a knack for knowing the heart of a person."

"The two of you had that in common. You obviously admired him very much."

"I did. I wanted to be more like him. He was so smart. Funny, too. He could do so many things. I'm sure the Company must have been disappointed with me. I'm sure they expected me to be more like Robert. He had an excellent service record."

"Your reputation does well by you. You are two different people. There is no comparison."

"Maybe not, but I can't help but think one was made. The only distinction I have is that I am better with weapons than he was."

"Only distinction?" He shook his head. "So the name the Dove, as in the bird often associated with death and funerals, was a mistake? It was meant for someone else?"

"No. I earned it, but at first it was a joke—started by my brother. It only became real because I was hell-bent on proving it to be true."

"I know the feeling. I struggled to distinguish myself as well."

"Were you constantly compared to your father and grandfather?"

Something changed in his expression—a slight shuttering behind his eyes that told her he didn't want to discuss it. "Oh yes, in both flattering and unflattering ways. It was the old man who reminded me that we can be measured only by our own accomplishments, not anyone else's. You leave yourself open for disappointment if you judge yourself by another person's yardstick."

"But comparing yourself to someone else can sometimes push you to do better than you would without that hanging over your head."

"When was the last time that comparing yourself to your brother made you feel better rather than worse?"

He had a point. "I don't remember."

"Indeed."

Claire glanced out the window. She really didn't want to get into what she thought of herself with him. There was a sign for Ayr up ahead, but she couldn't read what it said. "Are we close?"

"We should be. Tavish is making good time. Hopefully he won't flip the damn thing and kill us all."

She looked at him. He seemed so calm. Her insides were dancing and jerking like a line of Irish dancers. "Thank you," she said.

"For what?"

"For distracting me with this conversation. For not bringing up the kiss from this morning, and most of all, for not expecting more, or reminding me of what a bitch I can be."

"I do have that whole honorable reputation to live up to. But now that you've mentioned it, I am sorry for this morning."

"Are you? Truly?"

Their gazes locked. "No," he replied easily. "I'm not

really sorry at all. It wasn't the best idea I've ever had, but I don't regret it. I'm probably going to regret confiding that to you, though."

Laughter escaped her, despite the anxiety of the journey. "Thank you. No woman wants to hear a man say kissing her was a mistake, if even she agrees with him."

"So you regret it then?"

"No. I should, but I don't. I regret the circumstances surrounding us. Were things different . . ."

"Were things different, we'd still be at the inn and we'd still be in bed. I think both of us can admit that."

"Yes. Impulsive as it would be. So, maybe it's better that things are as they are."

"Maybe," he agreed, and when he looked at her, she saw the desire in his eyes. It wasn't a burning desire—he didn't want to take her right there in the carriage, but he wanted her. It made her a little sad—thinking of "might have beens" and "if onlys." "You can be a topnotch bitch, though."

She laughed at that, and he grinned, softening the lines of his face. Those brackets around his mouth weren't a lie after all; they just didn't get used as often as they once did.

It wasn't until he turned his face toward the window that she noticed the lines around his eyes and mouth had deepened. There was tension in his jaw and shoulders. He was as concerned about losing Howard as she was.

They sat in silence for what felt like forever, but it was probably only a handful of minutes. Claire watched the countryside give way to more urban surroundings, until they were driving through the streets of a bustling town.

"We're here, aren't we?"

"We're in the town of Ayr, yes. We'll be at the docks in a few moments."

She didn't ask if he thought they'd catch them. It didn't matter what either of them thought or feared or hoped. They would either catch them or they wouldn't.

The carriage got held up in traffic, much to Claire's chagrin. She was literally chewing her nails by the time they started moving again. The fingers of her other hand—already chewed—gripped the strap just above her head, knuckles white.

Finally she saw it—water. There was water ahead. She pressed her face against the glass. "I can see the docks."

Alastair leaned forward as well. "Yes. I think I see the ship."

Claire didn't ask how he could possibly know which one they were after. A port this size had to have any number of ships in and out of it during the course of a day. Still, she hoped he was right, and that they were about to catch their prey.

The carriage stopped, and the two of them practically dove out of it. They ran toward the ship, Claire managing to keep up with Alastair's slightly longer stride despite wearing a skirt. She'd wrap the damn thing around her neck if she had to.

"There!" she cried, pointing. "The Doctor!"

The thin, unassuming man also heard her as he

stood on the docks, looking as though he'd been used as a punching bag. There was blood on his coat, and his face was battered. He didn't look like the monster he was. Unfortunately, he had heard her exclamation, and he took off running at the sight of them. Or rather, he took off at a hobble. Someone had beaten him soundly. Had she had her pistol, she could have already shot him.

Alastair caught up with him quickly and tackled him to the wooden slates. People skirted around them, staring and pointing, but no one tried to interfere or help. The difference in their sizes made it easy for the earl to overpower him. But as Claire neared them, she saw something in the small man's hand. It was a syringe.

"Alastair!" she cried, running closer. She wouldn't get there in time.

He glanced down, saw the syringe just inches away from his arm and gave the Doctor's wrist a wrench. Claire's stomach dropped as she heard bones snap. The smaller man screamed in pain.

Alastair stood, hauling the Doctor to his feet by the throat. "Where is he?" he demanded. "Where is Howard?"

The Doctor snarled at him, clawing at Alastair's fingers with his good hand. It didn't matter how much he struggled; he'd never loosen that augmented grip of his. "I'm not telling you anything."

Lifting him so his feet left the dock, Alastair shook him like a dog would a rabbit. "Tell me where he is and I'll let you live, you worthless piece of shite."

The threat seemed to work, or perhaps it was the sight of Claire that loosened his tongue. His pale, scary blue eyes actually brightened. The malicious glee there froze her on the spot. She'd never seen such evil in anyone's eyes before. Never. "The bastard double-crossed me. Beat me, stole my case, and boarded the ship."

"Which ship?" Alastair's expression was a mask of fury. If she had been the Doctor, she'd have been afraid for her life at that moment.

"The one that just left," the smaller man told him with a grin, revealing bloody teeth.

Claire turned her head at the same time Alastair did. Her heart plummeted as she saw the large vessel plowing through the waves at least two hundred feet from the docks. It was already leaving, and there'd be no calling it back.

Stanton Howard had escaped.

Chapter 9

Alastair thought Claire was going to have a hysterical breakdown right there on the docks. He'd never seen such rage and anguish on a woman's face before—on a man's face, either, for that matter. She literally crumpled to her knees as the ship put more and more distance between them and it.

At that moment, he would have jumped into the water, swum after the damn boat and hauled it back to shore himself if he could have. Instead, he turned to the Doctor, whose jaw was resting between his thumb and forefinger.

"Where's it going?" he asked, giving the vermin a little shake.

The man had stopped clawing at his fingers, and he now held on to his wrist in an effort to support his own weight. He smiled. It was an unsettling expression, given that his face was already distorted by Alastair's grip. "America. New York City. You'll never catch him."

Alastair tightened his hold ever so slightly. "You seem pretty happy for a man who was just double-crossed."

"Anything that makes life difficult for the Wardens makes me happy."

"You know I'm going to send you to the W.O.R."

"They won't break me."

"Lucas Grey might." He had the satisfaction of seeing real fear flicker in the worm's eyes.

Tavish arrived then, with the shackles Alastair had brought along for the Doctor's capture. There was a set for Howard as well.

Damnation.

Once the Doctor was locked up and immobile, Alastair tossed him over his shoulder like a sack of apples and carried him back to the carriage, locking him securely in the boot. For a moment, he leaned against the side of the vehicle and silently swore. If only they'd been a little earlier. If only he and Claire had spent less time needling and challenging each other—flirting—they might have arrived in time.

Sighing, he straightened and looked out at the water. The ship sliced through the waves like a hot knife through butter. He could almost imagine Howard on deck, waving a gleeful good-bye.

As his gaze turned toward the woman still kneeling on the docks—the woman he felt he had disappointed beyond repair—he spied a submersible peeking out above the surface of the water.

"Will we be leaving then, my lord?" Tavish asked.

Alastair shook his head. "We're not defeated just yet,

my good man. Keep an eye on the lady for a moment, will you?" He didn't think Claire would run off on him, but losing both Howard and her would be more than his pride or reputation could take. People would wonder if he hadn't taken after his old man after all. Plus, he wasn't certain that she wasn't contemplating jumping in after the bastard as well.

It took nearly a quarter of an hour for him to locate the dockmaster, and then another ten minutes to find the owner of the submersible, but another five minutes after that, he returned to where he'd left Claire.

She was gone.

Alastair's heart skipped a beat. Where the hell was she? He actually peered over the side of the dock to make certain she hadn't jumped in. He looked down one side of the dock, then the other, panic rising. Then, he glanced toward his carriage and saw her standing outside the boot, which was open.

She was talking to the Doctor.

A nasty suspicion crawled up his spine. He was attracted to Claire, but that didn't mean he trusted her—not completely. She'd done nothing to make him doubt her, but then, neither had Sascha right up until that fateful moment. Claire was a desperate woman, one who knew the life she'd had before was over. All she wanted was to catch the man who killed her brother and have him tell her why.

Desperate people tended to do desperate things, and their victims ended up with augmentations that weren't just for the job, but for life. If Evie hadn't been able to put metal in his legs, he wouldn't be walking right now—at least not with any grace.

Alistair approached quietly, turning his head ever so slightly so that his left ear was toward them. The W.O.R. had augmented his hearing as well—nothing so startling that he could hear conversations in other rooms, but enough so that it was sharper than ordinary. If he concentrated, he could sort through the noise of the bustling shipyard and eavesdrop on their conversation. Not very honorable of him, he knew, but there were times when a man would rather be dishonorable than a fool.

"Why did he do it?" he heard Claire demand. "Why did Howard kill my brother?"

"You traitorous bitch, if you think I'm going to tell you anything, you're insane. If my hands were free, I'd kill you."

"Well, that's where I have the advantage, Doctor. As you can see, my hands *are* free. And I didn't just have one of my wrists broken by Reynard. It's going to be difficult for you with only one good hand to do procedures on people. I wonder how difficult it would be with only one eye?"

Claire raised her hand, and something glittered in the weak sunlight. Alastair didn't know what it was. He didn't care what it was. He knew only that Claire was in danger of seriously damaging his prisoner, and if anyone was going to have that pleasure, it was Luke.

He ran toward them, grabbing Claire's wrist just as she was about to strike. She whirled toward him, and he found himself staring down the barrel of a very fancy, very deadly-looking pistol. She'd gone through the bags and found her gun.

What other items had she reclaimed?

"Alastair!" she admonished. "This doesn't involve you."

"Put the gun down, Claire," he commanded in the most gentle tone he could manage. He wasn't keen on dying on the Ayr docks.

"I can't do that," she replied. "Not until the Doctor answers my questions."

The Doctor was still shackled, but a strange apparatus had been attached to his head. Little wire arms extended down from his temple and up from his cheeks, holding his eyes wide open, so much so that Alastair could see the curves of his eyeballs, and the ruddy inner flesh of his lids.

His stomach rolled. He hated anything to do with eyes. He couldn't think about what had been done to his own without gagging a little.

Then he spied what Claire wore on her right hand—claws. They were sharp brass talons that looked perfect for the job of scooping an eyeball right out of someone's head. He'd forgotten he had them, and now they'd fallen into the worst possible hands—literally.

"Jesus Christ," he whispered. "Claire, don't do this."

Her face was a study in stone. "I want to know why Howard killed Robert."

She was on the verge of madness; he could see it. It was that cold detachment of emotion that enabled people in their line of work to do whatever was necessary to achieve their goal. Though often a good thing, in times like these, it could go very, very wrong. He knew because he'd felt it himself once or twice.

"The only person who can tell you that is Howard, Belle." The foolish nickname came easily to his tongue. "We need the Doctor intact."

She reached out and swiped the smaller man's face with the claws, leaving deep cuts in his cheeks. The Doctor tried not to scream, but his pain would not be denied and came out as a guttural cry.

Alastair didn't think. He swatted the hand holding the gun away with his augmented arm. He didn't want to hurt Claire, but he would if he had to. She cried out as the pistol tumbled from her fingers. It discharged when it hit the ground, blasting a hole in a nearby shack.

"Holy hell," he swore, and turned back to Claire. She held her injured arm to her chest, and her "talons" were just about to tear into the Doctor's eye socket. The man didn't say a word; he just stared at her, daring her to do it. He would rather die than be taken to London as a prisoner. Alastair could not let that happen. He drew back his fist. He hadn't struck a woman in a very long time, but he would do it now to stop Claire from making an awful mistake.

Suddenly there was a sharp buzzing sound, and Claire fell. Alastair just barely managed to catch her before she hit the ground.

"Sorry, my lord."

Alastair glanced up from her unconscious face to the apologetic countenance of Tavish, who stood just a few feet away holding one of Arden's "discombobula-tors." It had a fancier name, but he could never re-member it. Basically it was a little device that shot prongs into a body and then jolted it with an electrical shock. It was very handy for rendering attackers inca-pacitated.

"Well done, Tavish," he said on a sigh, pulling the small sharp prongs from Claire's hip. "Get that con-traption off our prisoner, will you? And shut the boot so I don't have to look at his ugly face. You're going to return to London with him tonight."

Tavish stood there, holding the contraption as though it were nothing more dangerous than a daisy. "What about you, my lord?"

Alastair swung Claire up into his arms. "I'm the new owner of a submersible, and I'm going after Stanton Howard."

The world around her was moving. And it smelled like the inside of an old boot. What was that noise? It sounded something like a dirigible, but muted, as if the inside of her head were full of cotton wool.

Slowly Claire opened her eyes and sat up. She was on a small bed, and her muscles were rubbery, weak, twitchy. The last thing she remembered was getting ready to take the Doctor's eye out, and Alastair telling her to stop. . . .

Damn him. He'd done something to her. It had felt like the kind of shock she sometimes got from a car-riage door in the winter, only multiplied by a thousand.

She ran a hand over her forehead and glanced

around at her surroundings. Was she in a cell? It was small—smaller than the one at the W.O.R. She didn't like it. It was too small. The walls curved at the ceiling—she could imagine them closing in on her. . . .

She leaped to her feet, knees rubbery as she hurried to the door. It opened, and she stepped out into a narrow corridor. The invisible band around her chest tightened. Where the hell was she? It was not much bigger than the room she'd just escaped, the walls lined with equipment and various gadgets and gear.

Staggering down the corridor, she moved toward the only sound she could hear above the muffled "whomping." She spied Alastair, sitting at a console where he was listening to a cylinder recording of Beethoven's "Für Elise."

"Where are we?" she demanded. And why was it so damn tiny? They weren't on a train, and this was nothing like any carriage she'd ever seen.

Alastair's entire chair turned as he faced her. His brow furrowed, and the lines around his mouth seemed sharper. "How do you feel?"

"Like hell," she replied, her heart pounding in her throat. "What did you do to me?"

"Tavish used one of Arden's devices to incapacitate you before you could harm the Doctor any further."

That he hadn't been the one to injure her didn't make her feel better. "You should have let me have him. You had no right to do that to me before I got an answer from him."

"He had no answers to give you, and if he's going to be tortured, Luke's going to be the one to do it. You promised him the Doctor, remember? If you had killed him, all of his secrets would have died with him."

She did remember. She also knew he was right, but that didn't mean she had to like it. She wrapped her arms around herself and glanced around. "I can't stay here. It's too close. Where's . . . Where the hell is the door?"

He pointed up. Claire followed the line of his finger and saw an airtight hatch above her head.

"Oh my God." Her knees buckled beneath her. Her head swam as she gasped for breath. "Where are we?" She didn't really need to ask; part of her—the paralyzed part—already knew.

"Claire?" Alastair was suddenly there beside her, catching her in his wonderfully strong and warm arms. She felt like such a . . . *girl*. "Claire, are you all right?"

"No, I'm not fucking all right!" she yelled. "You've put me in a box! A tiny little box that's going to crush the air right out of me!" As if on cue, her breathing became shallow and labored as she gasped for breath. Her lungs couldn't seem to get enough.

"It's a submersible," he told her. "Claire, we're going after Howard. Claire!"

She heard him, but she couldn't respond. It was such a tiny little box inside the ocean. Even if she got out, the water would claim her. Surround and suffocate her. Oh God, it was worse than the closet. Worse than any cell could ever be. Blackness swamped her mind, tugging her down. Blackness was good. If she passed out, she couldn't panic anymore.

"Claire." He shook her. "Speak to me. You're all right. I have you. Close your eyes."

That she could manage. When she did, he pulled her against his chest and soothed her with a gentle rocking motion. "Just keep them shut and listen to me. Can you do that?"

She nodded against his waistcoat. Her starving lungs continued to gasp for air, but it wasn't quite as bad as it had been. Large, warm hands stroked her back, easing the chilling pinpricks that assaulted her skin. The darkness behind her eyes, inside her own mind, was the one that didn't terrify her.

"You're safe." The low, rough timbre of his voice washed over her. "The walls are sturdy and strong. They will not collapse on you. We have plenty of air. Slowly breathe in through your nose and out through your mouth, pet. That's it. I won't let anything happen to you. You are all right."

Claire focused on his voice and tried not to think about those horrible times as a child when she misbehaved and her father would lock her in the closet as punishment. The more he did it, the worse it became, until she would start to shake at the very thought of the closet. The sight of one was enough to make her throat go dry. Being "good" had become a full-time occupation for her.

In through the nose. Out through the mouth. In through the nose, and out through the mouth.

But she wasn't in a closet right now, and Alastair wasn't her father. She wouldn't have ever gotten on this thing if she'd been conscious, and now they were on their way after Howard once again. All was not lost.

She had to pull herself together. She would not allow fears from years ago, caused by a man long dead, to stand in the way of what she wanted. And she wanted to catch up with Stanton Howard.

She remained curled against Alistair until most of the panic passed, leaving her feeling drained and even more shaky than she'd been when she woke up. Oddly enough, she didn't feel the least bit ashamed. He had seen her at her worst and her weakest, and he hadn't exploited it. He hadn't made her feel inferior or broken.

"How much longer?" she asked.

"I'm not sure," he replied. "Not long. An hour or so. They got a head start, and then we lost a little more time getting on board. The ship he's on is one of the fastest passenger ships in the Bright Star line, and this is an old sub, but we're gaining on her. I'm going to get you justice for your brother, I promise."

Justice for her brother. Not that he was going to get Howard for the Wardens or for his own advancement. Of course, those things had to be a consideration, but he had thought of her as well. He made it sound as though they really were partners in this rather than prisoner and Warden.

"Thank you." She sniffed. Damn it, she'd been crying and hadn't known it. She pulled away from him and wiped at her eyes with her fingers. "I'm sorry. You must think I'm an idiot."

"No, I don't. We all have things that scare us. I'm afraid of heights."

She peered at him from beneath damp lashes. "But you helped take down Erlich on a dirigible." She'd heard about it because Erlich was a Company agent who had infiltrated the Wardens and began working on his own agenda without Company consent. It had been a shocking scandal when it broke, and Five—Huntley, blast it—had been right in the middle of it, along with Alastair.

In fact, if it weren't for Robert's death, if she didn't want Howard and to stick a spike in the Company's eyes, she would have knocked him out the night before and taken him as her own prisoner. That would have earned her some respect from her fellow agents.

He nodded and continued. "And I thought I was going to piss my trousers the entire time. I refuse to let my fears get the better of me."

"You're not even like a real person," she told him, half joking. "You don't let fears or insecurities stop you. You do the right thing at all times. Don't you ever make mistakes?"

A chuckle escaped him. "Plenty. Remember the woman who tried to kill me? And you were right. I did allow myself to develop feelings for Arden. Even though I knew there was no chance of ever truly claiming her affections."

"So, your mistakes have been with women?" No wonder he tried to deny their attraction. She was a reminder of every bad choice he'd ever made with a female.

"Most of them, yes."

"When you look back on this, will you think of me

as a mistake?" She forced herself to meet his gaze, because she knew that he would regret ever laying eyes on her by the time she was through.

He smiled at her—a little lopsided affair that made her heart hitch. "Maybe. Though it was a thoroughly enjoyable kiss."

Heat filled her cheeks, much to Claire's horror. "Yes, it was."

Alastair's smile faded. "I'm sorry about what I said earlier—about wondering if you'd been involved with Howard. It was cruel of me, given what he did to you. Not to mention petty."

She shrugged, though she felt as if a huge weight had been lifted from her. "I would have thought the same." In fact, she was thinking about what he'd said in the carriage, wondering why Howard hadn't killed her. At first she'd thought Howard had made a mistake—but he rarely did that. Then maybe she thought he'd wanted to humiliate her, let her live and be taken into custody. She still wasn't completely convinced of that, but she wasn't paranoid quite enough to come up with a different reason.

In all truthfulness, she'd already mentioned the best explanation—he'd been wounded and there were witnesses to summon the police. He'd chosen escape over her death. She would have done the same thing.

Alastair gestured toward the console with his thumb. "I need to steer this thing. Want to help? It may prove to be a good distraction."

"I don't know the first thing about marine vessels."

"I'll teach you." He rose to his feet and offered her

his hand. She took it. His skin was warm and slightly rough.

"Do you ever crush things?" she asked. "By accident?"

"In the beginning. Now, not so much. I don't even notice it most of the time now. It's just me."

Yes, that made sense to her. He didn't see just how exceptional he was. Claire stood, waiting until she was certain her legs would support her before she moved. The submersible moved beneath her feet. She could feel the motion of machine and ocean. If she thought about it, though, she'd get hysterical again, so she simply wasn't going to think about how deep they were and how they'd die a horrible death if anything went wrong. And she certainly wasn't going to think about her father.

Instead, she did as Alastair had instructed, breathing in through her nose and out through her mouth until she felt calmer.

Alastair continued to hold her hand as he led her the few feet to the chairs bolted to the floor in front of the console. He took the one on the right; she sat to his left. Each of them had a steering column and a series of buttons and levers in front of them. A rounded window formed the front-most part of the ship, and a light above the glass, outside on the vehicle, illuminated the water around them. It should have made her feel even more trapped, but it didn't, because she could see the surface and the daylight above. They weren't that deep, and knowing that made it easier.

"Here's how you guide the vehicle," he explained,

wrapping his fingers around the handles as she watched. "You move it like this to turn, like this to rise or surface. . . ."

Claire listened as he explained, paying attention as best she could. It was a little difficult when she was still a bit distracted by her fears, and very distracted by the fact that he was so . . . kind.

And gorgeous. She mustn't forget that. She'd never fancied a ginger before. He wasn't quite ginger, though—not in the way she imagined ginger to be. His hair was red, yes, but it was a rich dark red—not quite auburn, but a far cry from orange. He wasn't pale or abundantly freckled, though he did have some freckles.

He was more handsome now than he had been the first time she saw him. She wasn't foolish enough to believe he'd actually improved in looks. And she was honest enough to admit that the attraction no doubt had something to do with the fact that he would be the last man—who wasn't a guard—she would be this close to in a long time, perhaps the rest of her life.

He explained things to her for about a quarter hour, demonstrating each thing before giving her a chance to try. He was right; it was good for keeping her mind occupied, and by the time the lesson was done, she was steering the submersible with a fair degree of confidence, monitoring their progress on the panel instruments. They were inching closer and closer to Howard's ship.

She didn't begin to understand how it all worked, but there was a grainy screen on the panel that flashed their location and that of the ship they pursued. It probably had something to do with the aether and me-chanics. Arden Grey could probably explain it.

Then again, Arden Grey seemed the capable sort of woman who could poop gold if she set her mind to it. The universe wouldn't dare deny her, and if it did, she'd find a way around it. No wonder the Company hadn't been able to take her away from Huntley. No wonder he came back to her despite all their work and deceit.

"How do we get on board once we catch up?" she asked, turning her attention back to what was impor-tant.

"I've telegraphed the ship's captain, letting him know the Wardens have confidential business on board. We'll surface and be lifted up into the ship. The sub will be held by the boat until we dock in New York."

"It will be the first time I've been to New York in a long time," she confided.

"I'm sorry we won't be there long enough for you to enjoy it." The honest sincerity in his voice made the back of her eyes burn. She did not let it show, however. She still had some of her pride.

"So am I," was all she could let herself say. When this was over she would have a long list of regrets, but they would all be worth it when Howard died at her hand. If she was lucky, Alastair or some other Warden would kill her immediately so she didn't have long to dwell on those regrets.

Regret had a way of growing—like a cancer—and it wouldn't take long for her to doubt that she'd done the right thing and wish that she'd taken a different road. She didn't want to live that long.

"I think you succeeded in scaring the Doctor," Alastair commented a few minutes later. She had wondered when he was going to bring that up.

"I wasn't going to kill him," she confided. "Hurt him, yes. I just wanted to know why Howard did what he did." She wouldn't have taken the little bastard's eye out.

Well, she might have taken his eye, but she would have cauterized the wound with her aether pistol. He wouldn't have died from it.

"You may never know why." There was an edge to his voice that hinted at questions of his own. "Sometimes people do things, even people we love, and we never understand why they did them."

"Are you talking about Sascha again?" Claire had known the woman only by reputation, but she was on her way to despising the cow. If she wanted Alastair dead, she should have just killed him, and if she wanted to protect him, she should have done all she could for him, rather than being a coward and letting him suffer because of her lover's jealousy.

And yes, she was well aware that she'd practically defended the woman at the inn with all the "she loved you" nonsense. Probably Sascha had developed feelings for him. That was all the more reason she should have done all she could to protect him.

If she'd loved him, she should have just walked away.

"No." He looked so sad, she wanted to console him,

but she had no idea how to do it in a manner he'd accept. "Not her. I wish I were." And that was obviously all he was going to say.

"I didn't mean to pry," she told him. "God knows I'd be the last person to criticize someone for having secrets."

A humorless chuckle met her words. "You're not prying. It's just something I swore I'd never talk about. I've already said more about it to you than I have to anyone else in the last two years."

"It's easier to tell a stranger private things. I don't know why, but they say it is." Regardless, warmth filled her chest at his confession. Lord knew she'd told him things she shouldn't have. And she couldn't remember the last time she told anyone about Robert.

"Yes, they do say that, don't they?" His stormy eyes twinkled. "*They* say a lot of shite. And you're not quite a stranger. Not anymore."

Maybe not, but she wasn't exactly a friend, either, was she? And after she killed Howard, he'd think even less of her. She would have to live with that, because nothing would deter her from her goal. Not even that she and Robert hadn't been close in a long time—much longer than she cared to admit.

At least she wouldn't have to live with it for long.

Chapter 10

They finally caught up to the *Mary Katherine* at around five o'clock that afternoon. They'd made better time than Alastair had expected, and that was a welcome thing indeed. Claire managed to hold herself together for the rest of the trip, but he could tell it took a lot out of her just trying to remain calm.

He hadn't asked about the cause of her terror, but when she likened the submersible to a closet, he'd gotten the impression that was where the fear began. Someone had locked her in a very small, dark space, and now anything remotely similar brought back those childhood feelings of being powerless and terrified.

He'd like to meet the person responsible for that—meet him and have five minutes alone with him and a cricket bat.

Before rendezvousing with the steamship, Alastair took sole control of the steering and began the task of slowly raising the sub at the right speed and angle. Too fast would cause problems for both himself and Claire. Too slow and they'd miss the boat.

It had been a long time since he'd docked a submersible to a ship, and he didn't have time to second-guess himself. He watched through the viewing window of the submersible, and used the periscope during the process. They broke the surface right beside the *Mary Katherine*. As soon as he got the signal from the crew member on the deck, he engaged the magnetic docking mechanism that would "lock" their vehicle to the ship's retrieval apparatus.

There was a long, whirring sound and the screech of metal on metal as the sub was grabbed and pulled into place. Once he heard, and felt, the "arms" clamp around them, Alastair disengaged the engine, and silence fell.

Suddenly the sub gave a sharp jerk. He had to grip the chair for support. Claire clung to the wall. Then came the sound of a winch, and the sensation of rising, such as in a lift or ascension chamber. As they were pulled from the water, the late-afternoon sun brightened the interior of the vehicle, casting the impressive visage of the ship in an almost-celestial glow. The relieved expression on Claire's face was rivaled only by her obvious anxiousness to get the hell out of the sub.

The locking system gave a loud thunk, which was followed by a knocking above their heads. Alastair pulled a set of small folding steps from the wall and climbed up to turn the wheel on the door. He pulled it open and moved just in time to avoid a trickle of water that spilled into the chamber. Next he reached up and turned another wheel on a second door that he then pushed up. Gloved hands appeared not far from his, pulling the heavy hatch completely open. Alastair looked up.

A young man in a simple uniform smiled down at him. "Lord Wolfred, I presume?"

"You are correct, sir," Alastair replied with a grin. "Permission to board?"

A woman in a crisp navy jacket and her blond hair tucked beneath a cap joined the crewman. "Permission granted."

Alastair stepped down to the floor. Seconds later, a metal ladder was lowered into the cabin. He guided the feet of it into the slots on the steps that were designed to hold the ladder in place. Then he gestured for Claire to precede him. "You first."

She didn't argue. She merely flashed a grateful smile and practically jumped up the steps. Quickly she climbed up into the chilly ocean air.

Before exiting himself, Alastair handed all their luggage up to the crewmen above. Only then did he turn off the lights so the storage cells wouldn't drain of all power, lock the starting mechanism, engage security protocols, and finally climb the ladder to the outside world.

The wind was bitter despite the sun's warmth, and his cheeks soon stung from it. The deck was devoid of people save for the crew, and he concluded that either they'd been taken aboard in a restricted area, or the passengers were simply too smart to brave being outside.

"I took the liberty of having your lady friend escorted to your cabin," the captain explained to him. "It was too cold out here for her to be standing about." She was a handsome woman, with dark brown eyes that were warm but stern.

"Thank you," he said. "I appreciate your cooperation in this matter."

"It's Crown business. How could I possibly refuse? Besides, I don't much like the idea of such a villain using my girl to escape justice. Come with me, Lord Wolfred. I'll escort you to your cabin." Then, to the crewmen, she said, "See that those bags are brought to his lordship's lodgings immediately."

There was a chorus of "Yes, ma'am" as they walked away.

"What do you need from me and my crew?" The captain walked with her hands clasped behind her back, not the least bit off kilter with the floor gently rolling beneath her feet.

"Cooperation. I ask that anything suspicious be reported to me immediately, and that no one be allowed to leave the ship under any circumstances without my consent."

"We are in the middle of the ocean, my lord. Where would they go?"

He arched a brow. "If I managed to get on, someone else could manage to get off. Just tell your crew to be careful and diligent. We don't want to alarm your passengers, so I'd prefer that no one say a word about this to anyone."

"Of course. We're at your disposal."

He stopped her before she could open the door to the interior of the ship. "I would also appreciate it if your crew kept me apprised of any strange behavior on the part of my companion." It wasn't that he didn't trust Claire. . . . No, it was exactly that he didn't trust her. After watching her with the Doctor earlier, an uneasy suspicion had begun to take hold of his mind. It made sense, given that she'd agreed so easily to help hunt Howard down.

The captain didn't even blink. "Of course, my lord." She opened the door and preceded him through it at his gesture.

Alastair suspected that Claire planned to kill the bastard, either for her own revenge or for the Company, though he was inclined toward the former. In fact, he was rather annoyed with himself for not having thought of it before this. He'd been so caught up in her being a traitor to her agency that he hadn't thought of just how far she'd go for justice—how desperate she truly was.

He couldn't let her do it—not just because of all the information they could get out of Howard, or the number of Warden agents who were being held hostage that he might be traded for, but because if she killed Howard, she would surely be executed, if not by Company operatives, then by the W.O.R. for her betrayal.

A few days ago he hadn't cared if she lived or died,

but then he caught a glimpse of the real her, and that little peek was enough to make him question his own judgment. He was starting to respect her, and that had nothing to do with how attractive he found her— though perhaps it made her even more attractive. Her intense loyalty, her determination and her selflessness were amazing. She had hunted her brother's killer, despite the man's being an incredibly dangerous spy. She had turned her back on her agency without a whimper. She didn't lament her lot in life or whine about it. She acted. Regardless of the goal, if Claire Brooks wanted it, she went for it.

And he knew by the way she looked at him that it wouldn't be long before she gave in and came after him as well. What a mess that would make of things, because he wouldn't stop her.

Yes, he had the worst luck with women, but Claire was no danger to him provided he kept his heart out of it. They had no future—her best-case scenario involved being a W.O.R. prisoner for most of the rest of her life. And he—well, he couldn't afford an alliance with a woman who betrayed her own agency. His father had made certain of that.

In fact, he blamed his father for his lack of judgment. Surely it had to be a hereditary fault. But in all honesty, if the circumstances were different, there'd be nothing to stand in their way. If she was just an American woman and he was just an Englishman, they could be together. The class difference would matter to some, but not to him.

What the hell was wrong with his head? How had

he made the jump from wanting to bed her to thoughts of marriage? Class didn't matter at all in an affair.

"There is a telephone in your suite that has a direct connection to the bridge, and to my own quarters should you require anything," the captain informed him as they walked down a softly lit corridor. It was just wide enough for the two of them to walk side by side. The wood paneling on the walls gleamed, and the carpet beneath his feet sank with every step—and not just because his metal-enforced bones made him weigh more than the average man.

"Excellent. I appreciate the inconvenience this must cost you, Captain . . ."

"Winscott, my lord. Charlotte Winscott." She offered her hand.

Alastair accepted the handshake. "Thank you, Captain Winscott. I won't forget your assistance."

She smiled. "You're not the first Warden my girl's had aboard, sir. I doubt you'll be the last, but you are welcome all the same. Your cabin is just at the end of this corridor. Perhaps you and your companion would care to dine at my table tonight?"

"I'm certain we would enjoy that very much."

Captain Winscott led him to a set of double doors of polished mahogany. "This is the only acceptable suite we had unoccupied for the journey. It's usually taken by newlyweds on their wedding trip, so I think you'll find it comfortable, though I apologize if it's perhaps not quite the image you wish to convey."

Her cheeks were flushed with embarrassment, and Alastair gave her a smile. "That's perfect; I assure you."

"My lord," she said, hesitating at opening the doors, "forgive my impertinence, but is the lady with you Claire Clarke?"

Alastair blinked. "Why, yes."

"I saw her onstage in Boston two years ago. She was magnificent." She turned the handle and opened the door for him. "Here you are. Your baggage will be along directly. Let us know if there's anything we can do to make your stay more comfortable. I will see you tonight at eight for dinner."

He thanked her again and entered the suite, shaking his head. Claire was the only agent he knew of whose talent for acting had actually garnered her admirers. No doubt he would have an excellent seat for tonight's performance once they were amongst the other passengers.

The captain hadn't been joking—the suite was indeed lavish and suited for honeymooning couples. It was papered in soft cream with a delicate damask print. Rich ebony furniture and ivory carpets promised plush comfort. A bottle of champagne chilled in a Cardice-lined bucket sat near the bed—a large four-poster affair that looked as though it could sleep six adults and a couple of dogs quite comfortably.

Claire stood at one of the many windows that overlooked the bow of the ship and the ocean beyond. There was nothing but teal water ahead of them as far as the eye could see.

"Feel better now that you can see wide-open space?"

"Much, thank you." She turned toward him. Her gown was wrinkled and her hair mussed, but she was still one of the most glorious women he'd ever laid eyes on. "I'm sorry for my behavior earlier. I despise irrationality."

He shrugged. "I don't know of anyone who likes it. Don't give it another thought. You need to put all of your attention to finding Howard tonight. I doubt he's traveling with his own face, though there's always a chance."

"I'll know his eyes," she promised. "They were so empty. They reminded me of . . ."

"What?"

She shook her head. "It's not important."

He didn't believe that. "Whom did he remind you of, Claire?"

She waved a hand at him. "Just someone I used to know. It's nothing."

But it wasn't nothing. Alastair was prevented from questioning her further by the arrival of their luggage. Claire immediately began unpacking and sent for a maid to come collect the gown she wished to wear later, and Alastair's evening clothes as well, so they might be pressed and readied for that evening.

He didn't push her further on the subject of Howard. She hadn't pried when he hadn't wanted to discuss the past, so he would give her the same courtesy.

She wasn't cold toward him, but there was a distance between them that hadn't been there before. He wasn't completely without insight where she was concerned, and he knew the reason. He'd seen her vulnerable, out of control, and she didn't like that. He also suspected she was putting a wall between them so it would make it easier to betray his trust and go after Howard on her own.

He wasn't going to let her throw herself away on a bastard like Howard. It didn't matter how many walls she tried to build. He'd tear them down—every last one.

Even if it meant she ended up hating him.

She wanted to throw something in his face.

Claire sat across the captain's table from Alastair and wished it wouldn't be immature of her to break her wineglass over his gorgeous head.

He laughed at some insipid comment made by the old gal sitting next to him. Claire smiled so they wouldn't see her grind her teeth.

First of all, he wasn't the least bit sorry for rendering her unconscious at the docks. Second, he'd been insufferably kind to her when she lost her mind on the submersible, and third, he looked at her as though he knew exactly what she was all about and had her all figured out.

Well, if he could truly see inside her, why the hell was he being so nice? What was wrong with him? If he suspected she was going to betray him, if he thought he understood her at all, why was he being so damn pleasant about it? Or did he enjoy letting people abuse his trust? Did it fulfill some perverse need inside him? Had he no pride? What sort of man was he?

A good one, a voice in her head whispered, and Claire snarled silently at it to shut up. She wasn't so self-ignorant that she didn't know some of these thoughts were fueled by a guilty conscience. But it wouldn't say much for her character, either, if she gave up avenging her brother just because it might hurt Alastair's feelings.

To make matters worse, they were forced to share a suite. Of course, she hadn't expected they would have separate cabins, but separate bedrooms would have been nice. Instead, she was forced to share a horribly romantic setting with the one man to have ever made her stop and wish her life had been different.

Because he seemed to be the one man who liked her despite knowing exactly what she was. Granted, Luke had liked her well enough, but at the time, they had been two cogs in the same machine. Alastair started off seeing her as his enemy. Even so, he had been willing to trust her, and she took full advantage of it.

Either he was very gullible or he didn't see her as much of a threat. Since she knew of his reputation and had seen him dangle the Doctor as if he were nothing more than a rag doll, she was inclined to believe the latter.

She'd known him a matter of days, and he was under her skin like a splinter.

But worse than all that was the fact that he hadn't even commented on how good she looked this evening. She was pretty—she knew this because she'd been told as much her entire life. Men often made idiots of themselves for her attention, and that proved a useful thing many times in her career. Tonight she had sat at a proper vanity table and artfully arranged her hair into a crown of twists and curls, secured with pins that dug into her scalp. She'd painted her face with a subtle blend of cosmetics that brightened her skin, emphasized her eyes and gave a rosy tint to her lips and cheeks. She wore a fashionable gown that was understated and elegant, in a rich chocolate velvet that made her skin look like ivory and darkened the green of her eyes. She'd even laced herself into a tight corset that diminished her waist and made her hips and breasts seem impossibly full and inviting.

Alastair Payne had looked at her, smiled and offered his arm. He hadn't said a damn word except to ask if she was ready. He wasn't her suitor and there was no reason for him to comment on her appearance, but would it have killed him to tell her she looked nice?

And now he sat across from her, with no idea how handsome he was or how lovely he looked when he laughed. Though he needed a haircut, a good night's sleep and to gain a few pounds, she thought he was the most perfect specimen of manhood she'd ever seen.

He had seen her almost at her worst today—when she'd entertained the notion of ripping out the Doctor's eyes. Then he'd seen her at her weakest in the submersible. And she had yet to see him at anything other than his patriotic best.

If only she could loathe him. But loathing him, as easy as it should be, proved to be as difficult as finding Stanton Howard in this glittering crowd.

"Would you like another glass of wine, madam?" a waiter asked from just over her shoulder.

"Why not?" She flashed him her most beguiling smile. His polite expression didn't waver. Perhaps she was losing her touch.

He refilled her glass and went off to serve the rest of the table. The captain dined at the front of the large dining room, where everyone could see her and her guests and she could see all of them in turn. It was the perfect vantage point from which to survey the room.

Not one man—or woman—stood out as someone who could be Stanton Howard. Had she truly thought it would be that easy? That she'd glance around once and spot him instantly? He was a master of disguise. For that matter, he might not even be in the dining room.

It would have been so much easier to find him if he'd brought the Doctor with him as they originally suspected he would. Perhaps that was why he'd left the other man behind, or perhaps he was simply keeping to form and betrayed the Doctor as he betrayed everyone he met.

They had that in common, she and Howard.

"More wine, my lord?"

She glanced over as the waiter spoke to Alastair. The Earl of Wolfred flashed that lopsided, rakish grin of his, and the young man practically melted at his feet. "Of course."

Ugh. Did the man not know how to *not* flirt? All he had to do was turn on that bloody British charm of his and people turned into drooling idiots, panting all over themselves for a scrap of his attention.

"Miss Clarke."

Claire turned her head, grateful for the distraction, and smiled to the woman on her right. She and Alastair had been given the very sought-after seats at the head of the table. "Yes, Captain?"

"I've been wanting to tell you how much I enjoyed seeing you perform in Boston when you appeared in *Much Ado About Nothing*."

Claire almost made a face. Shakespeare, of course. She didn't understand the appeal, but people seemed to like his works, and she'd gotten good reviews as well as a decent paycheck for the role. "Thank you. It's always so lovely to know that one's work has been appreciated. It gives me a feeling of great pride to know I brought a character to life for someone."

She caught Alastair glancing at her out of the corner of her eye. He seemed surprised to hear her talk. She was an actress, by trades both true and false. Did he think she didn't know how to speak in a proper fashion? Or was he surprised to hear such sincerity in her voice? She didn't have to pretend at that. She'd wanted to be an actress long before she ever became a spy.

The Company had been a great, dangerous rehearsal.

Alastair was still staring. She fought the urge to stick her tongue out at him and ignored him instead, keeping her attention focused on the one person who actually seemed impressed with *her*.

The captain continued to talk about various plays and performances, many with which Claire was familiar. They were in the middle of discussing Oscar Wilde, one of Claire's personal favorites, when an older woman, tall and pale with graying red hair and clear gray eyes, approached. She wore a striking gown of russet silk and a matching hat trimmed with dyed ostrich feathers. She was regal and imperious. She was not beautiful, but she was handsome, with the sort of features that begged to be studied and committed to memory.

There was something strangely familiar about her face. . . . "Wolfred? Is that you? Whatever are you doing here?"

Alastair rose to his feet, the color draining from his face. The woman kissed his left cheek, then his right, smiling at him with such adoration that Claire felt guilty for witnessing it.

The woman didn't even seem to notice that he hadn't spoken. He looked as though someone had punched him hard in the stomach. "Darling, you look marvelous. I heard that you had a certain young lady with you, and I had to come see for myself."

Uh-oh. Claire stared at the older woman. She certainly seemed to like Alastair, but there was an expression in her eyes that plainly said this situation could go sour fast—and that Alastair had better tell her what she wanted to hear.

Alastair turned his head to look at her. He looked as though he wanted to apologize. There was also no denying that he expected her to play along. That was when she saw the resemblance.

Oh hell.

He smiled, transforming his expression to one of manly adoration. He was a better actor than she. "Mother, you remember Claire, my . . . fiancée."

Chapter 11

"Claire, darling!"

Alastair could only stand and watch as his mother—Amelia Payne, the dowager Countess Wolfred—engulfed Claire in a rose-scented embrace. To her credit, Claire looked every inch the delighted fiancée, rather than a woman caught in a huge lie.

"Lady Wolfred," she cooed with a smile. "How wonderful to see you again."

"As it is to see you." His mother beamed at Claire. He almost believed they truly knew and adored each other. It was as disconcerting as it was impressive. How was a man to ever know if either of them was lying? "But I am so sorry to interrupt your meal. We shall catch up later, of course?" This was directed at Alastair, and with both of them looking at him with murder in their eyes, he knew he didn't have a choice.

And he knew they weren't lying.

He swallowed. This was the last thing he needed. "Of course, Mother."

She swept away with all the grace of a queen. He drew a breath, and barely had time to plaster a smile on his face before people at the table began congratulating him—and Claire—on their impending nuptials.

"You are a lucky woman, Miss Clarke," Mrs. Neilson, the woman sitting next to him gushed at Claire. If any of them cared about the fact that she was an actress and American, while he was an earl, none of them showed it.

Great liars, all of them. Now he understood what Dhanya had meant when she referred to Britain as a "nation of spies."

Claire smiled. It looked sincere, but it reminded Alastair of a lioness baring her fangs. "Indeed I am." Her gaze shifted, locking with his. He refused to back down. He'd done what he had to do to save both her and his mother any embarrassment, and he refused to apologize for it. The scandal of marrying "beneath" him would be far less than introducing his mother to his supposed mistress.

Though he had no doubt both of them would make him regret it before the night was over.

It would be a small price to pay to have the trip continue on with as little drama as possible. They were there to apprehend Howard, not play at house. Besides, when this was over, he would be the one suffering, as word would get out that he'd been jilted and he'd have to play the part.

And he hadn't his mother's thespian skills.

For the remainder of dinner, they made polite conversation with the rest of the table and put on a good show of being a devoted couple. Afterward, when the ship's orchestra—half a dozen automatons designed to look like beautiful lords and ladies of the previous century—began to play, couples took to the floor to dance.

The machines fascinated him. He liked mechanical things, and this modern age was rife with them, such wonders. The automatons looked like a new design by Les Enfants Magnifiques in France. Each *androide* had a series of slots in its back where punch cards could be inserted. The cards told the automatons how to move, so that they actually played the instruments in front of them. Occasionally one of the lady machines would stop playing and do a little twirl, skirts flaring around her delicate ankles. Their hands and faces looked incredibly lifelike until one got close enough to see hinged fingers and eyes only painted to look real.

"You're more interested in those machines than your fiancée," came a voice beside him.

He turned his head and met Claire's amused gaze. "I am a cad," he replied.

"Indeed, but a clever one."

"It was the only thing I could think of to save both you and my mother from embarrassment."

She smiled a little, full lips curving so invitingly. "I understand all about the English obsession with decorum and propriety. I don't care about me, but I would not want to cause you or your mother any discomfort."

"I appreciate that." It sounded trite, but he couldn't think of anything else to say.

She turned her attention to the musical machines. "They make my flesh creep."

"Really? I think they're wonderful."

"They remind me of corpses."

Alastair frowned. She was right. "Now you've ruined it for me as well."

"Really?" She cast a surprised glance in his direction.

"No." He grinned. "I think they look like big dolls."

"Dangerous dolls. All someone would have to do is tamper with their operational cards or their logic engine, and they could easily become deadly weapons."

He'd seen it happen. "I doubt that will happen here, and those instruments are secured to them. I think it would be deuced difficult to kill someone with a violin bow."

Claire arched a teasing brow. "Clearly you've never been to Berlin."

A chuckle pushed past his lips at the absurd statement. "I think you saw a different side of Berlin than I did."

"I don't doubt that. Are you going to dance with me, or do we let people think you have some infirmity that keeps you from taking your betrothed for a whirl on the floor?"

He held out his hand. "It would be my honor." Her fingers slipped into his, and he escorted her into the middle of the dance floor.

"Do you see him?" he asked after a few moments.

She frowned. "Don't rush me. If he's in this room, he's no doubt in disguise. I haven't seen anyone who even remotely reminded me of him all evening."

He smiled down at her—just like a doting fiancé should. "Keep looking. And try not to frown, will you? We may be watched, and we don't want our cover questioned."

"We are being watched," she retorted with a bright smile—it was more like a baring of teeth. "By your *mother* and everyone else in the room."

"I have faith in your acting abilities, my dear." He twirled her around. "And my mother is not watching us; she's watching out for us. There's a difference."

Arched brows lifted slightly. "Is your mother a Warden?" she asked in a low tone.

Alastair replied just as softly, "Once upon a time, yes."

"So she knows you're on a mission."

"Most likely, yes."

Claire swore. "Is she going to be a problem?"

Alastair slanted his gaze at her. "What do you mean?"

She looked as though the answer should be obvious. "Is she going to interfere with our work?"

"No. She's smart enough not to do that."

"Thank God."

He would not react. He would not snap. "Just what the hell is that supposed to mean? My mother's been doing this since before you could walk. I would be honored to have her assistance in any assignment. She is a countess, an incredibly strong woman, and she has saved more lives than you or I ever will. You will show her the proper respect."

"Or what?" she challenged, eyes glinting.

"You can return to the submersible for the duration of this mission and I'll find Howard on my own."

It was a cruel threat, but one he would follow through on.

"Fine," she snapped, but her cheeks were pink. Obviously she felt chastised. Good.

"I know this is important to you. It's important to me as well, but my family is more important."

Her gaze lifted to his, bright with anger. "It's important because Howard killed the only family I had left."

His heart broke for her, but she didn't want or need his sympathy. "Then stop turning your anger on me and on my mother, and find Howard."

"I would if you'd stop making me behave irrationally."

He almost stumbled over his own feet. She probably had no idea how much she had just revealed to him with that simple, emotional retort. What a fine pair they were. It would have been better if Luke had accompanied her. There'd be none of this foolishness. Luke would have claimed Claire as his sister or some other relation. Hell, Luke could have claimed her as his mistress, not that Alastair wanted to think about that.

He turned her around in time to the music. "Take your time. Look at every face."

That was all the urging she needed. He steered them around the dance floor, making certain they turned at the right time so that she could study every person in the room.

"Nothing," she said finally, shoulders slumping in defeat. It was an odd effect, because she smiled at him as she spoke, keeping up the pretense. "What if he's not on the boat?"

"He is. The Doctor was all too happy to give Howard up. Seems he promised to take the Doctor with him, pay him for his services and keep him out of the Company's reach. Surprise, Howard lied."

"He certainly doesn't seem to care about making enemies."

"Why should he? If what we've heard is true, he plans to have a new face crafted for himself shortly after arriving in America. No one will ever recognize him then."

Their gazes locked. Claire's expression of wonder was a mirror of his own. "A doctor," she said. "If he left one behind, he must have another with him—he wouldn't trust his new face to someone he didn't know."

Alastair nodded. It was a sound assumption, provided Howard hadn't made arrangements with an American doctor. "We need to find out if there are any doctors on board. If Howard wants a new face, he's got to have someone he can trust to do the procedure."

"And tend his wound," she said, eyes widening. "Alastair, I shot him. He's wounded. Unless he had a serum like Dr. Stone's, he should still be in a degree of pain."

"You shot him, and you're just telling me now?"

Chances were that Howard did have access to some healing compounds, but probably not anything like what Evie concocted.

"I forgot." She seemed almost as surprised as he was. "How could I have forgotten?"

"Many people lose bits of the events leading up to an injury. It was weeks before I remembered what happened to me, and even still some of it has never come back."

She didn't look comforted. "Let's find the captain. If she doesn't know whether there's a doctor on board, she'll be able to tell us how to find out."

They returned to the table only to find that the captain had retired for the night. It took all of Alastair's resolve not to kick something in frustration or put his fist through the top of the table. But he held himself in check because he was English and that sort of behavior was rude.

"What now?" Claire asked.

He looked around the room. There were so many rich women and men milling about, so many bored people looking for a fresh face to interrogate. "We mingle. Ask a few discreet questions."

Mingling proved a lesson in futility—and a study in patience. Everyone they spoke to had heard of their "engagement" and had far more interest in asking questions than answering them. No one had met a doctor—of course they didn't get to talk to everyone—or they assumed either Alastair or Claire was under the weather and suggested the ship's doctor. Eventually they had to give up. Even his mother, who had demanded he come by her cabin, told him she'd see him in the morning instead.

He and Claire had no choice but to retire as well.

"That was brilliant," he remarked drily as he removed his cravat in their cabin. "I've never talked about myself so much in my life."

"They all think we're going to be married."

He had wondered how long it would take her to come back to this. "What did you want me to do—tell my mother you were my mistress? That would have humiliated her in front of all those people."

"Don't you think that was what she assumed?"

"If she assumed that, she never would have publicly approached. Mother has more sense than that."

"Too bad you didn't inherit any of it."

They were both exhausted and vexed, and old enough to know better than to have a conversation when what they wanted was a fight.

"Oh, I'm sorry. Did I put you in an uncomfortable situation? Forgive me, Miss Brooks, for not wanting to cause my mother pain. Forgive me for not wanting to embarrass you. When this is over and I have to tell people we're not engaged, I will have to be the one left, you understand. That never looks good for any man, certainly not one with any degree of honor. I will be the one who will have a broken engagement attached to my name, because unlike Claire Clarke, I actually goddamn exist!"

She blinked. "This is the 1890s. Surely no one would have thought twice at your traveling with a lover."

"You're welcome!" he yelled before stomping to the

small bar in the corner of the cabin. He poured himself a measure of scotch and downed it in one fiery gulp. Then he poured another. Christ, he couldn't even get twenty feet away from her.

"Did—did you really not want to embarrass me?"

He scowled at her before taking a drink. "Of course I didn't. No one deserves to be humiliated like that." Like he had been by Sascha and her lover.

She came to him, cupped his face in her hands, and held tight when he tried to pull away. He frowned. "What?"

Claire sighed, looking at him with sad green eyes. "No one has ever cared about my feelings. You are *such* a good man." She came up on her toes and pressed her lips briefly to his.

It wasn't enough, yet it was more than sufficient to make his body stand to attention. "No," he murmured. "I'm not."

Her smooth brow wrinkled. "Why would you say that?"

"Because I wanted to come inside you the first time I saw you. I was determined to despise you, and I still wanted to feel you wrapped around my cock. Good men don't think that way."

A slight smile curved her lips. He thought he saw gooseflesh on her arms. "Of course they do. They just don't act on it." She moved closer, her hips brushing the tops of his thighs. "Did you really wonder what it would feel like to be inside me?"

Alastair shivered. Gooseflesh. This was a dangerous conversation, and they had more important things to worry about. "Yes," he rasped. "God help me, I still do."

Her gaze locked with his, dark lashes a coy veil. "I think about it, too. This attraction between us, it's new to me. I think it's new to you as well. What do we do about it, Alastair?"

This was an invitation if ever he'd been given one. He wanted to bruise her lips with his, wanted to shove his tongue in her mouth, undress her and take her in every position they could try without injuring themselves. He wanted to forget about Stanton Howard and what was going to happen when this was over. He wanted to know how she'd managed to get under his skin so very quickly.

And he wanted to know if she would look into his eyes when he was inside her.

"I'm going to get cleaned up," he said, stepping back and putting distance between them before he did something he'd enjoy but later regret. "The bed's all yours. I'll sleep on the sofa."

And then he walked away.

Alastair Payne was the first man to ever turn her down. This realization kept Claire awake for a good portion of the night, and it was the first thing she thought of when she woke early in the morning.

Damn him for being so good. And damn her for wanting him so much more because of it. Why were things she could never have so damn attractive?

It was obvious he was just as attracted to her— people didn't alternate between friendly banter and all-out verbal war unless there were some high emotions involved.

She stretched, recoiling when her flesh encountered the cold sheets on the other side of the bed. The sun hadn't been up for long, but a bright finger of it shone through the window above her head.

Slowly, quietly, she sat up. Against the wall, beneath a bank of drawn curtains, Alastair slept on a sofa that seemed to struggle to contain the entirety of his impressive self. He'd gone to sleep in those flimsy trousers he seemed to favor, and one pant leg rode up to reveal the entirety of one muscular calf. The blanket had slid from his shoulders, leaving an expanse of skin bare for her viewing pleasure. He was all copper and gold where the morning sun touched him as he lay, so peaceful in his sleep.

She wanted to walk over and dump a bucket of ice water over his head—that, or start kissing various parts of him until he woke up and gave in to her. Then maybe she'd stop thinking about it so damn much. Maybe then she'd be able to concentrate on Howard, because since she met the Earl of Wolfred, she hadn't been able to think about much other than him.

A ridiculous female she was not. Of course she had her moments where sense seemed to abandon her, but she was not one to obsess over a man—unless she planned to kill him. Then along came a man who kissed her as if he were dying of thirst and she were water, who told her he'd rather stick his privates in a rudder than in her, and who then told her he thought about being inside her. . . .

Alastair Payne, she decided, was a man determined to deny their attraction. She supposed he had good reason—his last dalliance with a Company agent hadn't ended well for either of them. And she had to admit, a fling between the two of them wasn't going to end up much better.

Still, she'd like to go on to whatever awaited her in the afterlife, having given a little of herself to a truly decent man. Never mind that sometimes he opened his mouth and was an ass—who wasn't? Everything he said and did—even the mistakes—was because he was trying to do the right thing.

Claire liked to do the right thing as well—the right thing for her.

And right now she had to do right by her brother. That meant getting into the passenger list and seeing if there were any doctors on board. Perhaps she'd get lucky and find one of Howard's known aliases, though the very fact that they were known made it unlikely.

She slipped out of bed and into the bath, where she cleaned up; then she dressed in the clothing she'd laid out the night before. The gown was a dark wine-colored soft wool that would be both warm and fashionable and had shucked any wrinkles during the night. She'd prefer a pair of trousers, but with the number of society dames on board, it wouldn't be a wise idea. And as much as she hated to admit it, she didn't want to embarrass Alastair.

She brushed and pinned her hair up so that a little bit hung around her face, applied a little color to her cheeks and lips, darkened her lashes, and slipped into the gown. It had a corseted bodice that buckled in the front, making it easier for her to manage.

Alastair was still sleeping when she slipped out into the main cabin. She took her room key and her black leather boots, and tiptoed out into the corridor. Outside the door, she tugged on her footwear, tied each boot, and hurried on her way.

An elderly lady and gentleman smiled at her as she breezed past. She wished them a good morning and kept going. She had reached the end of the corridor and was about to enter the main area of the ship when she heard someone call out.

"Claire, darling!"

She closed her eyes. God must truly hate her. Straightening her spine, Claire turned. "Lady Wolfred, good morning."

Now that she knew the woman's identity, the resemblance between her and Alastair was unmistakable. She was a tall woman—a little taller than even Claire herself—and lean. Her coloring was the same as her son's, though her eyes were lighter and her bone structure more delicate. She stood before Claire in an olive green jacket and matching Turkish trousers. A wide-brimmed hat and polished maroon boots completed the ensemble. Lady Wolfred was definitely a woman who marched to the beat of her own drum.

"Where's that dear boy of mine?" She peered over Claire's shoulder as though she expected Alastair to pop up behind her.

"Sleeping, ma'am."

Eyes sharp as a lightning strike locked with Claire's.

Obviously she was where Alastair had gotten his flinty gaze, not the augmentation. "Sneaking out while they're asleep never goes well, my dear. I was just about to scrounge up some breakfast. Join me."

"Actually, I was just on my way—" Her stomach growled, betraying her.

Lady Wolfred smiled—the same lopsided twist her son favored. "It will wait. Come. There's so much for us to discuss."

"Balls," Claire muttered under her breath, following after the woman like a puppy.

The older woman paused and turned with a much more genuine smile on her face. "My mother used to say that when she was vexed."

That would teach her to open her mouth. "I know. Alastair told me."

A pale ginger brow rose. "Did he? Hmm."

Claire didn't know what she meant by that, and she didn't care. She should simply tell the woman she was busy and do what she originally intended, but she couldn't bring herself to be rude to Alastair's mother.

Plus, she was curious as to what sort of woman raised such a man. Snooping could wait. Howard wasn't going anywhere.

Had she really just thought that? She could not lose her focus or stray from her path, not now. She'd given up her freedom for this; she would damn well see it through.

The dining room wasn't nearly as full as it had been the night before, it being still a little too early to be considered "decent" by most of the passengers.

"I do so enjoy this time of morning," Lady Wolfred admitted as she seated herself at a small table near a window. "One has a few hours of quiet before the idiots tumble out of bed. I'm in desperate need of some coffee. You do drink coffee, don't you?"

Claire nodded. She was still thinking on the "idiots" remark. "I did just tell you that your son was still in bed, didn't I?"

The skin around Lady Wolfred's eyes wrinkled. "Oh, my dear, I would never refer to my dear boy as an idiot. A fool, occasionally, but his mind is as sound as the Tower of London. You do realize he's not asleep?"

Claire's heart skipped a beat. She glanced up as a waiter filled their cups with rich, hot coffee, and waited for him to depart before saying, "What do you mean? He was sound asleep when I left."

The older woman poured a generous amount of cream into her cup. "That boy takes after his mama, and he is up early unless he has good reason not to be. Second, if the two of you are sharing a cabin, which I can only assume you are—shockingly scandalous, you know!—then he most certainly is awake, because he has that blasted ear of his. I thought he overheard things he shouldn't as a child, but he never misses anything now."

Claire stared at her. "His ear?"

The lady nodded, looking entirely too pleased with herself. Still, Claire liked her. Or, at least she thought she did. "Some new Warden technology. They augmented his hearing. He's had so much done, sometimes I wonder if he's more machine than man, but then he smiles and I know he's still my boy."

"He's not a machine," Claire retorted, depositing far too much sugar into her cup and not caring one whit. "He has too much feeling to be a machine." Augmented hearing? And here she thought she'd been so quiet sneaking out. How long before he came and found her? He probably had a heightened sense of smell as well and could track her like a damn bloodhound.

Lady Wolfred watched her over the rim of her cup, like a cat watching a plump little bird through a window.

"You're not a Warden, are you?"

"No, ma'am. I'm not."

"You're not Company, either." It was a statement, not a question.

Claire hesitated, just a split second. "No."

Lady Wolfred studied her with an unblinking gaze. "But you used to be, and now here you are, worrying not that my son might wonder what you're up to, but whether or not he was hurt when you sneaked out."

Claire's head snapped up. "I am not worried about either of those things! Now I see where your son gets his infuriating tendency to think he knows everything." Damn. So much for not wishing to be rude.

But now she also knew where Alastair got his ability to read her like a dime novel.

To her surprise, the older woman laughed—loudly. The handful of passengers in the dining room glanced at them curiously.

"Smile, darling. Wouldn't want them to speculate as

to why you're glaring daggers at your future mama-in-law."

Claire flashed a grin so bright, she hoped it blinded the woman.

Lady Wolfred gave her an assessing look. "Yes, you'll do nicely, but if you're not Warden and you're not Company, then you'll need to decide just where your loyalties lie, my dear, if you want my son."

"My loyalty is with myself. What makes you think I want your son?" She should have just denied it outright, but she was curious. At least she knew why Alastair confused her so much; he'd obviously been raised by a madwoman.

"Please. If you are half as bright as you appear, you're smart enough to know a good catch when you see one."

"Yes, well, perhaps your son is smart enough to know a bad choice when he sees one." That revealed a little more than she was comfortable with, but it was out there now. No taking it back.

"Yes," Lady Wolfred slowly agreed, setting her cup on its saucer. "I would hope that he is indeed. Tell me, Claire, what is it you and my son are after? Or should I ask, whom?"

She obviously knew what sort of work her son did. In fact, she talked like a woman who had spent a great deal of her life on the fringe of one sort of intrigue or another. Hadn't Alastair said she had been involved with the Wardens along with his father? Perhaps the lady might be of some assistance.

"We're looking for a man who can change his ap-

pearance with little effort. We think he's probably traveling with a doctor or a man with some medical experience.
If you've spent a great deal of time around agents, then
you know the type. They won't sit with their back to a
door. They watch everyone. They'll lead conversation
but never add to it."

Lady Wolfred took a sip of her coffee. "I know exactly who you want. His friend is Dr. George Stephens.
They came on board with all of us yesterday morning,
joined some of us for luncheon, but were absent during
dinner. Friendly boys, but quiet. His friend's name is
Richard. No, Randolph. No, wait."

The woman had already given her more than
enough, but Claire was on the edge of her seat, trembling with anticipation despite having barely touched
her coffee. "Yes?"

"Robert!" Lady Wolfred grinned triumphantly. "His
name is Robert Brooks."

Chapter 12

Alastair waited a few minutes before peeling himself off the torture device that was the sofa. Claire was still gone—either having breakfast or doing her own investigation. Whatever, it didn't matter. She obviously wanted time alone, and he wasn't going to chase after her like some pathetic child or love-struck suitor.

The shower-bath was a gleaming brass contraption that ran water heated by the same boilers that powered the ship's engines. He stood under the hot spray for a long time, letting it relax his muscles and clear his mind. Afterward, he put special drops in his eyes that he had to use once a month to keep the augmentation sharp, shaved and dressed in a gray merino suit, pulled on his shoes, and left the room in search of breakfast.

He found his mother instead, sitting alone in the dining room.

"Good morning, Mother." He kissed her cheek. "You look lovely this morning."

"Flatterer. Will you join your old mum for breakfast?"

He surveyed the table. "It looks as though you've already eaten."

"I can still watch you—make certain you're eating enough."

Alastair rolled his eyes, but he joined her anyway. The only person who didn't seem to want to fatten him up was Claire. Though, to be fair, she probably didn't care how much he weighed.

The waiter brought him coffee, and he ordered eggs, sausage, toast, potatoes and a pot of strawberry jam. That was when he noticed the third coffee cup on the table. His mother had entertained another guest before him.

"I'm glad to see you're eating," she told him. "For a while there I was worried you might waste to nothing but skin and bone."

Alastair arched a brow as he fixed his coffee. "So worried you decided to journey to America straightaway. If I hadn't stolen away upon this ship, I wouldn't see you for another two months." There was no judgment in his tone, only good-natured ribbing.

"Such a cheeky boy. You get that from your father."

"Mmm." He chuckled and took a sip from his cup. "Lucky that's all I got."

She clucked her tongue, but otherwise didn't rise to the bait. Instead, she talked about her friend, Buella, with whom she was traveling to New York. Buella's husband had taken up with a burlesque dancer less than half his age in Paris and was making a fool of himself across the entire Continent. So Buella had taken it into her head to go to America and perhaps take up with some businessman or an actor much younger than she was herself as well.

Alastair listened like the dutiful son, his gaze scanning the room the entire time, following each new person—anyone who might seem just a little bit off. Detached. Stanton Howard was a top-notch agent and actor, but he was also mad, and oftentimes mad people behaved in ways otherwise "normal" people did not.

His breakfast came, and he ate as he watched. His mother continued to talk as he worked, only now she talked about the trip they'd taken to New York as a family when he'd been down from school one summer. His father had called it a vacation, but he'd been there on Warden business.

"You're so much like him," his mother mused, her tone both dry and proud. "Always working. Even now you're working. Couldn't bear to sit with your back to the door, could you?"

Alastair wiped his mouth with his napkin. "I'm nothing like him at all." He was loyal to his agency, for one thing. He knew his duty.

"I remember a time when you wanted nothing more than to be exactly like him. You couldn't wait to sign up with the Wardens. You fretted for weeks that they might find fault with you and not take you. You and Lucas Grey were mad as a bag of cats until you were accepted."

"People change, Mama. I changed. Father changed. If I work hard, it's to atone for the mistakes he made."

She regarded him a moment before dropping her gaze to her cup. He thought he spied a tremor in her fingers. "Your father wasn't a double agent, dearest."

"What was he, then?" And how the hell did she even know about that? She'd never said anything to him, not even when she had to know her son's opinion of the man had been ruined by the papers he found in his father's office and the things he'd heard from other W.O.R. agents.

"A good man trying to protect the woman he loved."

Alastair frowned. Then it all became very clear. Damn it all to hell. "You?"

She nodded, suddenly looking her age. "I got myself into a spot of trouble. You know I did a bit of work for the Wardens myself in my youth."

"Of course I know. That's how you and Father met."

His mother smiled. "Yes. And some time into our relationship—both professional and personal—I trusted the wrong person. I have no desire to give you particulars over breakfast in such a public place, but your father took a great risk to keep me from coming to harm, and the price he paid for that was the suspicion of his fellow agents. I never forgave him for choosing me over his own integrity, but I loved him so very fiercely for it."

Alastair stared at her, dumbfounded. "I didn't know that you had any part in it. I didn't even know that you knew."

She patted his hand. "I was a coward. I didn't want you to know the truth about me. I feared it might change how you thought of me, but it's time you knew the truth. I don't want you to resent your father for my mistakes any longer. It's been the great shame of my life."

"Why are you telling me this now?"

"Because that young woman you have with you is a good girl in a very bad spot, I think. And she needs someone like you by her side if she's to get through it."

His heart gave a hard thump. "Mother, what are you talking about?"

"Claire. I had breakfast with her just before you arrived. She didn't give me specific details—she didn't have to. I know what a woman in danger of doing the wrong thing looks like. If you care about her, you need to help her."

He tried to force a chuckle, but it sounded like a cough. "Care about her? I've known her only a few days."

"I fell in love with your father the moment I laid eyes on him."

"I don't love Claire." It was impossible. He liked her . . . sort of. Respected her, even, but love? No. He couldn't love someone he couldn't trust wholeheartedly, especially not after such a brief acquaintance.

"Maybe not yet, but you might, and wouldn't you rather she be alive when you figure that out?"

His heart went cold in his chest. She *had* talked to Claire. "Tell me what happened."

"She asked if I knew of any passenger traveling with a doctor. I told her I did."

Sweet Jesus. "Howard," he whispered.

"Howard? No, that wasn't the name he used."

"Did you give her the name?"

"Yes. It was Robert Brooks."

Only a few times in his life had Alastair truly felt the blood rush from his head—this was one of them. He could feel it pooling in his feet. "The bastard's using her brother's name."

"I assume from your tone and expression that this villain most certainly killed her brother before assuming his identity?"

He nodded. "I have to find her. She'll kill him. Do you know where she went?"

"She said she needed some air. And to hit something."

He wouldn't put it past her to find Howard's room and take his eyes out. He jumped to his feet. "I have to go." Then, almost as an afterthought, he kissed her on the forehead. "Love you." Because he did love her, and because confessing to him couldn't have been easy on her.

And because she restored his faith in his father. They'd talk about it in more depth at another time, but for now it was enough to know his father wasn't a traitor.

That his father had been a *good man*.

As he took off in pursuit of Claire, the "woman in danger of doing a bad thing," he realized that maybe he really was like his father after all.

Robert Brooks. The name stared up at Claire, mocking her with its neat loops and precise corners. The person who'd written this passenger list had lovely handwriting, and if he stood in front of her at this moment, she'd make him eat the damn list before she reached down his throat and pulled it and his guts out.

It wasn't as though anyone who worked on the ship could know that Howard was traveling under her brother's name. It would be simple enough to get acceptable identification, false as it was. But this . . . *insult* felt personal—as though Howard had known they'd come for him, and he wanted to rub a little extra salt in her already-raw wounds.

She was not going to kill him quickly.

"I suspected I'd find you here."

Despite all else, the sound of Alastair's voice brought an unexpected smile to her lips. "That doesn't surprise me." Her smile faded as she raised her gaze to his. They were all alone in the captain's office. The woman had handed over the passenger list without hesitation. It was amazing what people would do when they thought you were one of the good ones. "The bastard's using my brother's name."

He didn't look surprised. "I know. I spoke to my mother. She told me." There was just the right amount of sympathy in his tone. "Do you have his stateroom number?"

She could lie and tell him no, so that she could sneak off later by herself, but it would be as easy as glancing at the page in front of her to see the truth. "Yes. He's in first class. Number A18."

He didn't remark on the fact that it was not too far from their own cabin. "The captain's hosting a party tonight in the ballroom. If Howard's there, we can search his cabin and hopefully discover what he's up to."

She frowned at him. "He's a Company agent. What else do you need?"

"He's on this ship for a reason. A man that gifted with disguise doesn't permanently alter his face unless he's done something so vile, he'll have practically every agency in the world after him. Howard is up to something, and I want to know what it is before we make a move against him. He could have more than one associate on board, and that increases the danger to all the other guests."

Claire returned her focus to the passenger log so he couldn't see the impotent rage in her eyes.

"We'll get him, Claire. There's nowhere he can run to in the middle of the ocean."

"Not unless he has a submersible like we do. Hell, he could steal yours, Alastair."

"For his sake, I hope not. It's programmed to lock down if anyone tries to take it. No one can get in or out except for me."

Of course not. It must be nice to think of everything. She used to be like that. At one time she would have also planned to search Howard's room and gather as much information as they could. Now she just wanted him to die a slow and torturous death. Everything else paled next to her desire for revenge. At this moment, it didn't even matter if Alastair hated her afterward.

She closed the leather-bound book. She knew the cabin number, and staring at her brother's name for much longer was going to surely drive her insane.

"Your mother is a very interesting woman."

His lips quirked. "That's a remarkably polite way to put it. She's quite something, yes. I hope she didn't give you too much trouble."

"She did—a bit." Claire frowned. "I think she likes me."

"Oh, she does. She wouldn't pretend if she did not. You're a little bit like her, you know."

"Complimenting a woman by saying she reminds you of your mother is a good way to remain single for the rest of your life, my lord." She rose to her feet as she spoke.

Alastair chuckled. "In this case I'm not entirely certain it's a compliment."

"That's good to know." She wasn't the least bit insulted that his comparison between herself and his mother wasn't entirely complimentary. It would be a little too disconcerting if it was, especially since he claimed he wanted to sleep with her.

Now, that would be a pleasant way to spend the rest of the day. Forget all about Howard, and her fear that he was going to win after all. Even if—when—they caught him, it wouldn't bring Robert back.

In fact, at that moment, she didn't even understand her need for revenge. She hadn't seen Robert in a long time. He was always busy or gone on a mission. They hadn't been close since shortly after they joined the Company, perhaps even before. He used to pick on her something terrible at times. He had spent as much time as he could away from home, away from their father, with whom he often clashed.

He held out his hand. "Come."

Entwining her fingers with his felt as natural as breathing. "Where?"

"For a walk."

"Is that really what we should do right now? We should plan; we should follow Dr. George Stephens."

"The last thing we want to do is call too much attention to ourselves," he reminded her. "Let's go for a walk and see who we can run into." As soon as the words left his mouth, a female crew member ran into the room.

"Where's Captain Winscott?" she demanded, her cheeks pale, eyes big as horseshoes.

"She was going to the bridge," Claire informed her. The poor thing looked as though she might be ill at any moment.

Alastair's brow knit in concern. "What's happened?"

"There's been an accident in the cargo hold," the woman informed them in a voice that was both sob and gasp. "A steam carriage fell off its rigging."

"Is anyone hurt?" Alastair demanded, stepping closer and bringing Claire with him.

A tear trickled down the woman's cheek. "A man. It fell on a man."

Alastair ran so fast, Claire couldn't keep up with him. Her strong but normal legs were no match for his augmented ones. He seemed to know where he was going, so she pushed on, keeping him in sight even when her lungs began to labor and her muscles burn.

She followed him down staircases, along long corridors, around sharp corners, and down even farther, into the low recesses of the ship. At the bottom of the stairs, just outside the cargo hold, she stopped and braced a hand against the wall, gasping for air. Damn corset.

Claire paused only for a moment, then followed after Alastair. It was easy enough to locate him; she just followed the panic—and the screaming.

A small crowd of people had already gathered—mostly crew. Some wore uniforms that bespoke of a position abovedecks, while others were grimy, coal dusted, and obviously worked down here, rarely seeing daylight, like dwarves in underground mines. Artificial light filled the cavernous space, casting shadows over passenger belongings and transport items.

The carriage that had fallen from its moorings was a bright red Daimler with cream-colored wheels and brass fittings. It didn't look to be too damaged by the fall. Of course the man beneath it couldn't say the same.

His screams had diminished since she arrived, and they were now more like anguished cries. She understood only bits of what he said. Her Russian wasn't as good as it ought to be, though she had spent some time in St. Petersburg a few years ago.

The crew members tried to lift the carriage, with little success. Every time they tried to move the vehicle, the screams began anew—hoarse, tortuous sounds that made her stomach roil.

Alastair pushed closer. "You there, take the side. And you, help him." He pointed at where he wanted them to be. Then to the others, he said, "I'm going to lift the back, and when I do, I want you two to pull him out. Understood?"

"You can't lift that thing, mate," one of the crew cried. "The four of us couldn't budge it."

His face was grim, and his gaze the color of cold steel. "When I lift, you pull. Am. I. Understood?"

The man nodded. "Perfectly, sir."

Claire put her hand on his arm. "Alastair."

"Stand back," he told her. "The carriage might slip. Do you have any medical training?"

"Of course. I'll see if I can find a hospital kit." There would have to be one somewhere—all ships like this were expected to be equipped with necessary medical items should an accident occur. She spotted it on the wall near the door where she'd come in, and went to grab it.

When she returned, Alastair had removed his coat and tossed it over a battered black trunk. He rolled up his sleeves, revealing the defined lines of his forearms.

Her chest tightened as he approached the carriage. The man beneath it looked up at him with shock-widened eyes and said something in Russian. Blood trickled from his mouth.

Alastair responded in the same language, his voice taking an even rougher edge. Then he bent his legs and reached beneath the vehicle with both hands.

Claire's heart began to pound hard against her ribs. *Be careful*, she thought. *Please be careful*. She held her breath as he began to lift. She could see the muscles of his thighs straining beneath his trousers. His forearms were nothing but muscle and sinew as he slowly straightened, bringing the carriage with him.

Her mouth dropped. He was lifting the damn thing. Granted, he had help, but he was doing what four couldn't do before. The strain of the task showed in his face. The pinned man screamed as the weight eased off him, but Alastair kept lifting.

"Get in there and pull him out!" Claire shouted at the crew who just stood there, staring. Alastair wouldn't be able to hold the thing forever, and if it slipped, more people were going to get hurt.

The men did as she commanded, and pulled the screaming Russian out from under the carriage.

Once he saw the man was clear, Alastair set the carriage down. It hit the floor of the bay with a thud that vibrated beneath Claire's feet. She moved to his side. "Are you all right?"

"I'm fine." As he spoke, he clenched and unclenched his fists. "Give me the kit."

She'd almost forgotten about the medical case. She handed it over as he went to the injured Russian's side. He crouched beside the man. One look at his injuries and Claire knew he wasn't long for this world. She swallowed hard. He looked like a rag doll—boneless and covered in blood.

Alastair spoke in Russian—asking who had done this to him. The dying man responded in broken sentences. Of course this wasn't an accident. Touring carriages didn't just fall from secure moorings. And even if they did, passengers weren't allowed down here. When she heard the Russian groan, "Brooks," she knew she was right.

Stanton Howard was behind this.

Rage cut through her, pushing her to act. She knelt on the other side of the man, then took the bandages and pads that Alastair gave her. They couldn't save this man, but they could make him comfortable. She took the sealed syringe of laudanum from the box as well.

The man reached up and took Alastair's hand. His voice was getting weaker. It was harder for her to pick out familiar words as blood bubbled on his lips.

She looked at Alastair. He was white-faced, angry and sad. He nodded at her, and she pierced the man's arm with the needle and injected the entirety of it into his veins. Then she took his other hand and held it until she felt his muscles let go.

"He's dead," Alastair said. Then, to the crew members, "Take him to the morgue." He rose to his feet. Claire followed him as he retrieved his coat and left the cargo bay.

"Alastair?"

"In a minute," he replied.

She fell silent, and she remained so until they reached their cabin, where he tossed his coat on a chair and sat down on the bed, his bloodstained fingers dangling between his knees, his head bowed.

He was shaking.

Damn it, how could she not have realized sooner what effect this might have on him? The man had been crushed by a carriage himself. This must have brought back horrible memories for him, yet he had tried to save the man.

She knelt on the carpet in front of him and placed her hands on either side of his face. The blood on her fingers was little more than dried, rusty smudges almost the same color as his hair.

"I'm fine," he muttered.

"No, you're not, but if you don't want to talk about it, that's all right." She pressed her lips to his forehead. If only she could take whatever he was feeling away from him. She'd gladly suffer it herself if it meant he didn't have to.

His fingers came up to close over her wrists, but he didn't pull her hands away. "I told the man I was a Warden, and he told me Howard did that to him. He released the locking mechanism holding the carriage in place. The man was a Russian spy on board to sell information to Howard. Howard was supposed to give him the plans to a Company weapon in return."

"Howard killed him instead, not only getting the information but keeping the plans as well."

"God knows how many other buyers he has lined up. The ship could be crawling with spies."

"You need to send word to the Wardens." She tried not to think about just how badly this could go.

He nodded. "I'll telegraph the director. We need to find out just what Howard's selling and whom else he plans to meet with. At this point he doesn't know I talked to the Russian. I'm sure he thought the carriage would kill him outright."

"Or, as with me, Howard's getting sloppy," she remarked. "He didn't check to make sure I was dead, either."

Alastair's gaze locked with hers. "No, and I think tonight is the perfect time to let him see that you're still alive."

Chapter 13

Alastair was fine after a few minutes. The unpleasant memories and feelings caused by seeing the Russian spy crushed by the carriage had passed, leaving him feeling nothing but sympathy for the poor man for having to die like that.

Still, there was a part of him that wondered if Howard had intentionally killed the Russian that way, knowing Alastair would hear about it, if not see it firsthand. He'd been a Warden too long to believe it a complete coincidence.

He took his portable telegraph machine out of its case and quickly sent word to Dhanya about what they'd found out so far. She didn't respond immediately for a face-to-face chat, so he knew she was out of the office. Damn. Hopefully she'd get back to him soon.

He'd known this wasn't going to be an easy job when he took the assignment, but it was looking more and more like it was going to become a colossal knob up. Grabbing Howard was going to be difficult enough without having to worry about his associates coming for them—or him. At best he had Stephens, the surgeon, and one other foreign agent on board. At worst the number might be multiplied by many.

What was Claire's part in all of this? Was he a fool for actually believing she knew nothing about the Russians? Was he stupid for wanting to think she was exactly as she appeared? Luke had insisted she was trustworthy and he had laughed in his friend's face. Now—well, now he understood the effect Claire Brooks could have on a man.

He wanted to trust her. He wanted to believe the best of her.

After sending the message to Dhanya, he gathered up a small scatter pistol and ammunition to give to his mother. There'd be no telling her to stay in her cabin while there was a party going on, especially not a party that was sure to be full of intrigue. Besides, as it stood, she was the only person who could point out Howard in his current disguise. They couldn't afford to be blind tonight. His mother would point Howard out and keep watch while Alastair searched the bastard's cabin. Hopefully his mother would be able to keep an eye on Claire as well.

The best choice of action would be to keep Claire with him, but his mind warned him that she might not be as trustworthy as he wanted to believe. Leaving her free to go after Howard wasn't a good idea. He didn't for one moment suspect her of being in league with the bastard—her hatred was too real—but she would at-

tempt to kill him if she could. He just had to hope that
he could stop her in time, or that maybe she'd change
her mind.

There was a better chance of the sun not rising.

He glanced at her. She was curled up on the bed
sound asleep. How she could nap after the morning
they'd had eluded him, but he smiled regardless. She
looked so harmless asleep—peaceful and unburdened
by life as an operative.

The Wardens had better treat her well when they
imprisoned her. Maybe they'd offer her a deal of
some kind—a shorter sentence for information. Of
course, the Company would be gunning for her, so
unless she went into hiding, she wouldn't have much
of a future.

He could give her one. The thought stopped him
cold. After he took Howard into custody, he could always let her go. He could say she overpowered him.
Drugged him. Hell, he could tell them just about anything. They'd have Howard and his doctor. They'd have
the Russian's information. Dhanya would be happy
with that. She might not care that Claire got away.

He'd known her only a few days; yet here he sat,
contemplating betraying his agency for her, betraying
everything he believed in. The woman was a witch.

The kiss they'd shared at the inn was still fresh in his
mind. He had her taste in the back of his mouth—like
a memory that came easily to mind but was shrouded
in fog. It had been a long time since he'd felt a want
that deep for a woman.

It was because he couldn't have her—that was the

appeal. When this was over, he'd walk away and leave her to her fate, and gradually he'd stop thinking about her so much. Once the spell she'd woven around him faded, he'd realize there really hadn't been anything special about her.

His telegraph machine began to click and clack, drawing his attention away from the woman sleeping on the bed. She didn't even stir at the sound. Either she'd never developed an operative's habit of sleeping lightly, or she felt safe enough in his presence to allow herself to truly sleep. He should be flattered, but it could just as easily be that she didn't think of him as enough of a threat to be concerned.

What would she think if he climbed onto that bed and showed her just how much of a threat he could be? She wasn't the only one who knew how to use seduction as a weapon. As armor. As comfort.

But he didn't go to the bed. He watched the letters being printed on the paper fed from a roll in the telegraph instead. Being a "good" and "honorable" man was sometimes a pain in the arse.

OBTAIN INFORMATION ON HOWARD'S PLANS AND OBTAIN ALL DOCUMENTS. ASCERTAIN DEGREE OF FOREIGN OPERATIVE INVOLVEMENT. DO NOT ALLOW HOWARD TO ESCAPE. CAPTURE OTHER AGENTS IF POSSIBLE. W.O.R. OPERATIVES EN ROUTE TO ASSIST. BE CAREFUL.

Be careful. He snorted. It wasn't as though he planned to run up to Howard, slap him in the forehead and cry, *You're it!* Ever since Sascha, Dhanya seemed to think he had a suicide wish.

At least she was sending extra agents. By early morning this should be over. He turned in his chair and looked at the woman on the bed. Once this was done, he would probably never see her again.

He stood and walked over to the bed where he sat down on the coverlet. Seeing the Russian die earlier had made him realize how close he had come, made him realize for the umpteenth time just how fragile human life truly was. Giving in to his attraction to Claire was not the right thing to do. Maybe there was something wrong with him in that he was attracted to the wrong women, but at that moment he didn't care.

Right now he was alone with the most incredible woman he'd ever met—a woman who could drive him to distraction and break his heart simply with a few words. Yes, it was wrong, but after tonight, it wouldn't matter. She'd be gone, and he would have nothing but this. If he didn't listen to his foolish heart, he would regret it more than listening to his head.

He was four and thirty years of age. He shouldn't have as many regrets as he did. He certainly didn't want to acquire any more.

Alastair reached out and brushed the side of her face with his fingers. Her skin was like velvet, warm and soft. She shifted in her sleep, turning her face toward him.

He trailed his fingers down her jaw, to the slender line of her neck. A bit of hair had come free from her pins—a brush of silk against the back of his hand.

Slowly, he lowered his face toward her. He braced his other hand on the pillow beside her. A faint voice in his head insisted that there was still time to cease this madness, that he could get up and walk away.

He ignored it. He couldn't trust his own judgment. The voice that had told him to trust Sascha was the same telling him to run away from Claire. It was the voice of a scared boy who didn't want to get hurt again, but Sascha had not been worth the risk. He had known that then, just as he now knew that Claire was.

Alastair brushed his lips across hers. Full and damp, they parted easily for him, and he caught her lower lip between his and gently sucked.

"Mmm." Claire stirred. He released her lip and reared up a bit—enough so that he could look into her eyes when they fluttered open. A tiny frown puckered her brow. "Alastair?"

Perhaps this was a mistake. Perhaps she didn't want him after all. He pulled back, but she caught him with a hand behind his neck. She was strong, tugging his head back to hers, and he hadn't the inclination to fight her.

"You're not going to run away," she whispered, her gaze locked with his. "Not this time."

She kissed him, and when her tongue flicked over his lips, he opened his mouth, letting her inside and tasting her in turn. She was hot and wet, vaguely sweet and potent as fine whiskey. His heart thumped hard against his ribs as a rush of longing raced through his veins. Claire's fingers curved over the back of his skull, weaving through his hair as he slid his hand down to cup her breast. Full and firm, she filled his palm, the tightened bud of her nipple hard beneath her gown.

The only sound in the room, mixed with the faint hum of the ship's engines, was their combined breaths—shallow and humid. His fingers squeezed, thumb and forefinger rolling her tightened flesh until she moaned against his lips.

Alastair shuddered. He wanted to taste her skin; he wanted to hear more of those little moans of pleasure as he claimed every inch of her body—and her soul.

When she tugged on him, he went readily. She hooked him with one leg and turned. He rolled and landed on his back on the bed with her sprawled on top of him. She sat up, calves hugging his thighs, and began struggling with the buttons on her dress. "Damn thing," she muttered. Then she grabbed the gaping fabric with both hands and pulled. Buttons flew in all directions—one bounced off Alastair's cheek.

He laughed and reached up to help pull the bodice off her shoulders. She pulled her arms free with a grin and then fell forward, bracing a palm on either side of his head and leaning down to nibble on his lips. She rolled her hips, pushing the warmth between her legs down on the hardness between his. Alastair groaned and reached for the strings of her corset, untying and loosening them with quick, deft fingers. He threw the lacing across the room, then did the same to the garment itself.

"You're wearing too many clothes," she chided, unbuttoning his waistcoat.

"So are you." He pulled at her chemise, but she pulled away and slipped off the bed to stand beside it.

Alastair watched, his mouth dry, as she slid the damaged gown over her hips to fall in a froth at her feet. She reached down and grabbed the skirt of her chemise, pulling it up to reveal shapely calves in silk stockings, suspenders and garters. Short little bloomers of pale pink were revealed next. Between the legs of them was slightly darker—damp. His cock hardened even further.

She pulled the delicate linen over her head and stood before him, loose bits of hair tumbling around her pale naked shoulders, breasts standing high and firm, pink nipples tightly puckered.

"You're bloody perfect," he told her.

She actually flushed as she brought her hands to the tie on her drawers. She plucked at the string, and then pushed the flimsy fabric down, letting it fall into the pile of gown.

She left the stockings on.

Alastair rose from the bed and went to her, sliding eager hands over the curve of her hips. "Perfect," he repeated.

"Your turn," she said, pushing the open waistcoat over his shoulders.

He didn't hesitate. First he toed off his boots as she tugged on his shirt, pulling it up and over his head. Her soft palms stroked his shoulders, down his chest. One skimmed down farther and rubbed the eager bulge in his trousers. He hissed.

Claire smiled. "Why, Lord Wolfred, is that for me?"

His lips tilted as their gazes met. "If you want it."

"Oh"—her fingers squeezed—"I do."

Quickly he unfastened the buttons. His trousers fell to the floor and were immediately followed by his small clothes and stockings. Naked, he stood before her, pride and other parts swelling at the obvious desire in her green eyes.

"You're perfect," she told him. "The most beautiful man I've ever seen. I want you inside me."

He swept her off her feet and into his arms, turning to place her on the mattress and kneel between her spread legs. He kissed her mouth, her jaw and throat. He took each nipple into his mouth and sucked until her back arched and she cried out. Then he slid lower, twirling his tongue around the dip of her navel, and down farther until he found the soft hair between her thighs.

She smelled of heat and arousal, and when he parted her with his fingers, he found her pink flesh glistening with moisture. He held her open as his tongue stroked the hardened crest of flesh there. Claire gasped and arched her hips. One of her hands came down on the back of his head, pushing down in a silent plea for more.

He gave it to her, lapping at her salty slickness, pushing his tongue inside her, sucking and licking until her body lifted, tight as a bowstring, and a hoarse cry tore from her lips.

He came up and guided himself into her, feeling the tight warmth of her body yield to him. Her wide green eyes were open, and her gaze locked with his, so bright and trusting. At that moment he understood what she'd said about a woman looking into the eyes of a man she wanted to be with. Whatever else might happen between them, *this* was what he would take away with him.

Claire wrapped her legs around Alastair's hips as her body opened to him. He filled her; he became part of her. The things she saw in his stormy eyes scared her as much as they thrilled her. As a spy he could hide his emotions, but as a man he was as open as a window on a perfect summer day.

He began to move inside her, a sweet friction that sent shudders of delight coursing through her entire body. She set the rhythm of her hips to match his, undulating beneath him. Every inch of her was aware of him—even the places they didn't touch. A glance down and she could see where they were joined—the gold of his skin against her paler flesh. She gripped his arms, braced tight on either side of her, and arched her neck as he plunged even deeper into her.

And all the while, he never stopped watching her. It was as though the secrets of the universe were hidden in her eyes and he was determined to learn them all. She'd been with other men, and some of those times had been quick and ferocious, rough and frenetic. She'd also been made love to sweetly, gently.

Being with Alastair was like nothing she'd ever experienced before. He was neither fierce nor gentle, fast nor slow, but this was without a doubt the most intense encounter she'd ever experienced. She could feel his muscles tremble beneath her hands, and she knew he was holding back. So was she.

Her resolve didn't last for long. Alastair shifted his hips, changing his thrust so that the friction between them increased. Between her legs she pulsed, ached. The sensation grew, tightening into a pressure that begged to be released. She arched her hips, shoving her pelvis against his. The tension grew, edging closer and closer to what felt like the edge of the world.

She was close, so close. It was more and more difficult to look him in the eye as her lids kept wanting to close tight. Her neck arched, her skull pressing into the pillow as she hurtled toward that imaginary edge.

"Look at me," he commanded, the rough growl of his voice sending a tremor down her spine.

Claire forced her eyes open as the first shudder rocked her body. An explosion of pleasure rocketed outward from the part of her wrapped so tight around him. Violent and unexpected, it tore through her, bringing a wail of release from her lips. He didn't try to silence her; he just kept watching, his eyes darkening as she came. The lines of his face tightened as he thrust faster and faster. And then he stiffened. His eyes fluttered shut, squeezed tight.

"Look at me," she demanded. She let him see everything; now she wanted the same.

Alastair's eyes opened, and in them she saw terrible and beautiful things. A hoarse cry tore from his throat as he came. She gripped him tight with her sex and her legs, holding him inside her as he filled her with warmth.

His head bowed, and she reached up to touch the russet silk of his hair. His arms—his entire body—

trembled. He lowered onto his forearms, and she wrapped her arms around his torso. He was so warm and hard against her.

After a few moments, he rolled off her, leaving her cold. When he left the bed, it was like a slap to the face. No man had ever left her so quickly, though she'd been guilty of it herself. Shame crawled over her skin like something oily and dark and unexpected. She would never have thought him capable of being so callous.

Then he returned with a washcloth. She could only stare at him as he came back to the bed, nudged her thighs apart and began to gently clean the tender flesh there. What the hell? No man had ever cleaned her before. It felt slightly odd—courtly even. And it was strangely sweet—considerate.

"I shouldn't have lost control like that," he told her. "I'm sorry."

"I believe I was a willing participant," she informed him a little peevishly. "You don't have to get all righteous and regretful on me."

His gaze lifted to hers. "I meant I didn't intend to come inside you. I should have had more control of myself."

"Oh."

The side of his mouth lifted, deepening the groove there. "I'm neither righteous nor regretful, Claire. Were I eighteen again, I'd prove to you just how little regret I have."

Much to her embarrassment, she actually blushed. "Good. There's no need to apologize. I have an A.C.D." The copper ring, or Anti-Conception Device, was mandatory for every female field agent. It was an understood fact that many female agents used their feminine charms to get close to a target, which made the protection necessary. Unfortunately, it was also understood that female agents were occasionally the victims of sexual violence, which also made the device necessary.

"Good to know," he remarked. He gave the inside of her thigh one more wipe with the warm, wet cloth, then left again. This time when he returned, he pulled back the covers on the bed. "Get in."

Her naked skin was chilled, so he didn't have to tell her twice. He slid in beside her, pulling her against his side. He was warm and smelled of spice. She'd never smell cardamom again without thinking of him.

"What now?" she asked, unable to help herself. Why did she have to ruin the moment by asking such a ridiculous question?

"Now we wait," he replied, running his fingers over her shoulder.

"For what?"

"Until I can do it again." He smiled at her. She grinned back and cupped his face with one hand so she could kiss him. He rolled toward her, meeting her halfway. The hair on his chest tickled her breasts and rubbed softly against her ribs.

He wasn't content to kiss her mouth. He had to kiss her eyes, her cheeks, her shoulders, her hips and the back of her knees. He kissed her in places that no man had ever touched, let alone kissed, and when he was done, and she was a tingling jumble of sensations, he pressed his chest against her back, drew her leg up to hook over the back of his thigh and slid inside her once again. His hand went between her thighs, stroking and teasing her sweet spot as he thrust inside her, until she came again.

This time he didn't get up immediately to clean her. Instead, he held her tight against him so she could feel the beat of his heart against her back, his warm breath against her neck. Claire knew the exact moment he fell asleep. Her own body was languid and heavy, her mind darkening as slumber pressed down upon her.

A tear trickled from her eye, left a hot trail across her temple and then disappeared into her hair. She'd never been the sort of woman to have many regrets, but the last thought to cross her mind before she fell asleep was that all that was about to change.

After tonight, regret was all she was going to have.

Chapter 14

Alastair and Claire stayed in bed until it was time to dress for dinner, and he didn't regret a single moment of it. It wasn't as though there was much they could do at that point. Knock on doors and ask for Robert Brooks?

They barely spoke to each other, but the silence was a comfortable one. They didn't need to talk, and words would only further complicate a situation that didn't need anything else heaped upon it.

Their evening clothing had been sent out for pressing after the unfortunate incident involving the Russian and had been returned just a few moments ago.

"Of all the amenities on board, you'd think they'd have a steam closet," Claire remarked as she fluffed the skirts of the gown hanging on a hook in front of her.

"They hadn't been invented when the ship was built," he told her as he sorted through his belongings for a suitable cravat. It would be terribly convenient to have one, however. One simply hung wrinkled cloth-ing in the ingenious contraption, closed the door and filled the tank with water. A push of a button to start the gas flame that heated the tank, and when the cloth-ing was finally removed a short time later, it was wrin-kle free. It was not entirely ideal if a crisp pleat was required, but he had to think it was a welcome inven-tion when it came to ladies' gowns.

"How do you know that?"

He shrugged. "I know when the ship was built, and it was three years before the first steam closet. Not sure how I know that, but I do. What? I wager you have some useless information tucked away in that sharp mind of yours."

She turned to face him, a surprised expression on her face. "You think I'm sharp?"

"Well, yes." He frowned. "Surely that's not a sur-prise?"

She went back to fussing with her gown. Damn it, he'd embarrassed her. "Most men comment on my face, not my mind."

"I'm not most men."

"No. You're not." Judging from her expression, he didn't know if that was a compliment or not. He wasn't going to think on it much.

He pressed his lips together, debating whether or not to speak. "I'm going to search Howard's room to-night. I need you to keep him occupied."

Claire stilled. "I can do that." There was a flatness to her tone that sent a shiver of trepidation down his spine. He was taking a big chance on her, trusting her not to do anything stupid, but stopping Howard and seizing as much information as they could was more important than bringing the bastard in alive, where he could be used as a bargaining chip.

"Good. By morning this should all be over."

"And I'll return to Warden custody."

He swallowed. "Yes."

She smoothed her hands over the hips of her dressing gown as she turned toward him. Her tongue slipped out to moisten her full lower lip. "I just want to thank you."

"What the devil for?" If she said for the sex, he'd explode.

"For treating me like a partner rather than a prisoner. I know you were determined not to like me when this began, but you treated me with respect. I appreciate that."

He thought of some of the things he'd said to her and cringed. "Not always, I didn't."

She tilted her head. "I'm guilty as well. Anyway, I just wanted to thank you in case . . . in case I don't get a chance to later."

Hell and damnation. "I should thank you, too."

"For what?"

He would have chuckled at her incredulous tone had the situation been different. "For reminding me that 'Company agent' is not synonymous with 'villain.' I was feeling pretty jaded before I met you. Are you crying?"

"Of course not!" She turned her back to him. "You're welcome."

Silence fell between them then. What else was there say? Nothing that would make any of this easier. They dressed a few feet away from each other—turned away and each consumed by his or her own thoughts.

When they were done, he was dressed in traditional stark black and white. His cravat was ivory silk—a color he was told was more flattering to his complexion than white. Claire stood before him in a gown of stunning wine-colored satin. The rich color made her eyes stand out like jewels in her face. She looked incredible—breasts lifted but not indecently so, waist nipped. Her skirts were full but not so much that she wouldn't have freedom of movement. The bustle was a froth of fabric, but not the large kind that often made women look as though they had a table beneath their gown. Her hair was pinned up in an artful style on top of her head that looked as though it might tumble free at any moment—seductress hair.

"You're beautiful," he blurted.

This she seemed more comfortable hearing. She smiled. "Thank you. There's actually a pocket for my pistol beneath the bustle. Look." She turned and showed him the secret compartment. "You Wardens think of everything."

Not everything. He had yet to think of a way to get her out of this.

He handed her the weapon. "See if it fits."

It did, and with the bustle in place, it was unnoticeable.

She slipped on a pair of black gloves that matched her boots and gathered up her reticule, which held a selection of gadgets from Arden and her fan—a lethal-looking thing he was glad she'd never pointed at him.

"Shall we?" It was quarter of eight. They were to dine at the captain's table again.

Claire took the arm he offered. "Of course."

It was so easy to pretend that they were truly a couple on their way to an enjoyable dinner. He could almost tell himself that the rest of it didn't exist, but there was a dead man in the ship's morgue that was evidence to the contrary—a reminder of just how dangerous this mission really was.

When they arrived in the dining room, the space was filled with guests. Jewels glittered like the crystals in the chandeliers, and conversation filled the air. They were the last ones to be seated at the table.

His mother smiled at him from farther down the long table. He smiled back.

"Lord Wolfred. Miss Clarke." The captain rose to her feet to welcome them. "I'm so glad you could join us after the harrowing events of today."

"You've provided a welcome distraction, Captain Winscott," Alastair replied, pushing in Claire's chair. He waited for the captain to sit before seating himself.

"What events?" his mother asked.

He really should have sent her a note. Hindsight was about to give him a huge kick in the arse.

"A man was mortally injured in the cargo hold earlier today, my lady. Your son tried to save him. You've become quite the hero to my crew, Lord Wolfred."

Alastair smiled self-consciously. Beneath the table, Claire gave his leg a reassuring squeeze. His mother, however, had gone pale. She was not a stupid woman. She had to suspect it wasn't a simple accident.

"If you don't mind my asking, my lord, just how did you attempt to save the man?"

His gaze fell on the fellow who spoke—a man in his thirties, perhaps, with thick dark hair, muttonchops and round spectacles. There was nothing special about him, except his eyes. He had eyes like a shark.

Stanton Howard. He knew it without a doubt. Claire's fingers biting into his leg only added to his certainty.

"I assisted in lifting a carriage off the man, Mr. . . . ?"

"Brooks. That is quite heroic indeed."

"Not heroic enough. The man still died."

"What a shame." Howard's tone would have sounded perfectly sincere to someone untrained. Alastair caught the mocking edge. He also caught how Claire's fingernails threatened to puncture his trousers at the sound of her last name on the bastard's tongue.

"It is," he agreed. His gaze locked with Howard's, unflinching and direct. "Fortunately I speak Russian, so I was able to give the man a little comfort."

He didn't miss the slight gasp that came from a man farther down the table. He might not have heard it over the din at all had it not been for his augmented hearing. Dr. Stephens, he presumed.

"How very fortunate for the poor man that you happened along." Howard raised his wineglass. "To Lord Wolfred."

The rest of the table joined in the toast—even Claire. There was a reason she was hailed as an incomparable actress as Claire Clarke. She smiled as if he were her personal hero, acting for all the world as though the man who killed her brother wasn't sitting just a few feet away.

Alastair thanked them and drank when the others did, but his gaze never left Howard's. He did, however, manage a small smile.

The game was now afoot.

The only thing stopping Claire from tearing across the table and plunging a fork deep into Stanton Howard's eye was Alastair—and perhaps the disapproval of Lady Wolfred.

And the fact that she wouldn't have time to make him beg for his life.

Several times during the dinner, she'd felt Alastair's hand—either on her leg or covering her own fingers. His touch gave her patience and strength. It made her tingle. She did not want her legacy to be the headline LUNATIC AMERICAN ACTRESS KILLS MAN WITH FORK.

No, when she killed him, she wanted to savor it. It would not be quick. And before the life drained out of him, he would tell her why Robert had to die.

The real insult wasn't just that he now used Robert's name, but that he'd even affected a little bit of her brother's mannerisms and ways of speaking into this current disguise. It was disturbingly familiar—both sickening and heartbreaking to see bits of her brother in this bastard.

And the way he looked at her. She wanted to kick the smug look off his face. When they'd been introduced, she had the pleasure of seeing his façade slip just a little. Now he looked as though they shared some kind of private joke.

How long could a man stay alive with his privates sliced off and shoved down his throat?

After dinner came dessert and coffee. And then the automaton orchestra began to play as the remains of the meal were whisked away from the tables.

Several of the men left to go enjoy a cigar before the entertainment truly got under way. Howard was one of them. Alastair was not. Neither was Dr. Stephens. Claire fingered the bracelet on her wrist. She could go after Howard and garrote him. But then she wouldn't see his face.

"Why don't you go with them, my dear?" she asked the man beside her, sweetness dripping from her tongue.

He gave her a charming smile. "And leave you vulnerable to the attentions of other men? I think not."

She could kick him, but he wasn't the one who kindled her anger. He was simply the one keeping her from cornering Stephens and demanding information.

Alastair leaned closer and whispered in her ear, "Howard left Stephens behind to watch us."

She didn't glance at the young man who was doing a horrible job of pretending not to watch them. "Perhaps you'd take a turn with me then?"

"Delighted." He stood and offered her his hand, which she took and squeezed as hard as she could to let him know what she thought of the situation. He only smiled.

"You'd better hope I don't decide to squeeze back," he warned her playfully.

She wasn't intimidated. That hand had been all over her earlier—inside her—and she knew how gentle it could be.

They excused themselves to the captain and made their way into the center of the dining room. Word had gotten around of Alastair's attempt to save the Russian earlier that day, and several people stopped him to praise his heroics. He handled the whole thing with grace and aplomb while Claire twitched next to him. She was all agitated energy—not a good look for her.

And it wasn't good for Alastair's plan. She drew a deep breath, slowly exhaled and concentrated on being calm, keeping her eyes open and appearing as though she hadn't a care in the world. She could take a page from Lady Wolfred. The woman obviously wanted to know what had happened with the Russian and what was going on now; yet she sat at the captain's table, chatting with the other ladies as though nothing were amiss. Only once did Claire catch her watching her son with an expression of concern.

Claire went through the motions, playing what had to be the role of her lifetime, it so went against everything she felt. She laughed and made conversation, charmed and flirted as the situation required.

In other words, she did her damn job.

"Well done, Agent Brooks," Alastair whispered into her ear a little while later, when they were finally alone, no one trying to curry his favor or flirt with a hero.

She sighed. "Thank you. Has he come back yet?"

"Twenty minutes ago," he replied.

Claire started. "I didn't notice. How could I have not noticed?"

"It was when Mr. Williams complimented you on your cleavage."

"He commented on the detailed rosette work on my gown."

"Right along the neckline of your gown. Really, Claire. You didn't notice that the man practically had his face buried in your tits?"

She glanced down. She wasn't showing any more chest than any other lady in the room. Less than some. Besides, she knew when a man was flirting with her, and Mr. Williams had not been flirting with her. He had, however, flirted with Alastair. "No. Listen to you, Lord Wolfred, using such coarse language. One might think you were jealous."

"And if I were?"

Claire swallowed. Her throat was suddenly very tight and dry. She took a sip of the wine Alastair had procured for her earlier. "What's the point? After tonight we'll never see each other again." Hell, that hurt more than it ought to.

"The night's not over yet, and for the remainder of it you're mine."

A shiver curled down her spine. Hesitantly she lifted her gaze to his. This was what women meant when they said a man made their insides melt. One look into Alastair's rainy-day eyes and she was a candle with a too-long wick. Images flashed through her mind of the two of them entwined, moving together like they were one creature. He'd made sure she climaxed every time—and more. Her pleasure seemed to be more important than his own.

Any minute now she'd be nothing but a satin-wrapped puddle on the floor.

"All right," she replied, so softly only his augmented ear would ever hear her. "I'm yours. And you are mine."

He took her free hand in his and raised it to his mouth. His warm lips pressed hard against her knuckles. Claire blinked. Never mind melting; she was going to dissolve in a puddle of tears. Damn the man. Why did she have to meet him now, when her path was laid out before her? It was life's last cruel joke that she would find the one man she might adore above all others when there wasn't any future for them.

Then again, if not for Howard, she might not have met Alastair at all.

His declaration put everything in perspective for her and allowed her to actually focus on the task at hand. She would enjoy what time they had left, but she would also concentrate on what needed to be done. She would get information out of Howard before she killed him. Her gift to Alastair, other than giving him reason to despise her, would be that information.

Better that he hate her than wonder what might have been. She told herself it was true. She told herself to believe it.

A little while later, Alastair took her hand and led her out onto the center of the floor, which had been cleared for dancing to avoid having to move everyone to the ballroom.

Claire kept her eye on the room as they went through the various steps and figures of the dance. It was a little bit of fun for the both of them while they took turns keeping an eye on Howard and the doctor. They weren't the only ones watching. Another woman—dressed in the height of French fashion, wearing a very good blond wig—watched the pair as well.

"Is that La Bohème?" she asked Alastair as they circled each other.

"Sophie Chevalier," he replied. "I don't know why she chose that awful name."

She arched brow as a smile threatened. "Yes, it's so silly compared to Dove or Reynard."

He made a face that made her chuckle. "Touché. Yes, that is she. I wonder if she is the other agent Howard plans to meet."

"If she is, her life is in danger." Part of her honestly didn't care. She'd had enough run-ins with the French during some of her missions to think of them all as a giant butter-drenched pain in her ass. But the woman was only doing her job, same as Alastair. Same as that poor Russian.

The same as Robert had been. Chevalier didn't deserve to die because Howard was a dishonorable bastard.

Alastair turned his attention away from the French woman. "Keep an eye on her. We don't want her turning on us, but we may convince her to turn on Howard."

"Agreed." Of course she wasn't going to argue with him. One way or another, she'd handle Chevalier—

even if it meant knocking the woman out and locking her in a closet. No one was going to stand between her and Howard. If she was going to spend the rest of her life in a Warden prison, or die at the hands of a Warden executioner or Company assassin, then she was going to make certain it was worth it.

"Stephens is approaching her," she said, barely moving her lips as she watched the doctor weave through the tables and bodies toward the woman.

"Howard's using him to make contact. He probably doesn't know that we're aware of his connection to the doctor."

If it weren't for his mother, they probably still wouldn't know, and Dr. Stephens would just be a gentleman interested in a pretty woman he met on a trip to America.

They finished their dance, continuing to watch Dr. Stephens and his companion. A few minutes later, he made his way to the other side of the room, where he stood drinking a glass of champagne. Finally Howard joined him.

"Think they're setting up a meet?" she asked, taking a sip from her own glass as they stood, their shoulders to the wall so they could each watch the unfolding intrigue.

"Most likely he's confirming that Chevalier will meet Howard at some previously determined time and location. As soon as it looks as though they're about to get together, I'm going to head to Howard's stateroom. Whatever he's peddling, he doesn't have it on him."

"How can you tell?" She couldn't look at him for fear he'd see her intentions in her eyes.

"He's far too relaxed. He's got it hidden somewhere secure."

Claire had told herself she was going to enjoy the evening as much as she could since it would be her last in the free world—her last with Alastair—but enjoyment was the last thing she experienced. She was agitated and anxious, and she was wishing Howard had never managed to overtake her on that roof. If she'd just been a little smarter, a little quicker, none of this would have happened.

But she never would have met Alastair.

Alastair stepped in front of her. Her eyes began to burn. Hell's bells. She would not cry. She would not.

"Are you all right?" he asked. "You look pale."

"I'm fine," she replied. "Just a little antsy. Don't worry, I can do the job."

He smiled. "I know you can." For a moment she thought she saw something in his eyes, but it had to be her guilty conscience playing with her mind. In that moment she could have sworn that he knew what she was up to, that he knew exactly what she intended to do.

But then he brushed a stray strand of hair back from her face. Something hard pushed into her ear. "It's a communication device," he murmured. "It uses aetheric waves, and it is specifically attuned with my ear."

"Yes, I've used one before." She pretended she was also smoothing her hair and adjusted the little metal gadget so that it fit snugly.

"Of course you have." He looked at her as if she were a temperamental child, but he didn't chastise her.

She wanted to kick him or punch him—force him to anger so he'd feel just a fraction of her agitation. "He's moving." Out of the corner of her eye, she watched Howard straighten his cuffs and set off across the dining room.

Alastair didn't even look. "Right. I'm off. If anything happens, or if it looks as though Howard is returning to his room, give me as much warning as possible."

"I will."

He reached down and squeezed her hand, then left the dining room. Alone, Claire turned her gaze toward her prey. Howard nodded to Chevalier as he walked past her, and then set off in the direction of the doors to the deck.

Claire set her jaw as he slipped outside. She waited a few seconds and then approached Chevalier.

"Sophie," she said.

The woman looked at her blankly. "Pardon?"

Claire rolled her eyes. "Don't bother, sweetheart. Or should I call you La Bohème?"

The woman's blue eyes darkened. "Who are you?"

"The Dove," she replied without cringing. "The man you're about to meet is going to double-cross you."

"I am supposed to believe you? Go away. You know nothing."

Ah, French charm. It was legendary. "I know he was behind that Russian's death this morning."

Chevalier went still, her eyes narrowing. "You are certain?"

Claire stepped closer. "The Wardens are closing in on him. You do not want to get caught in this."

One penciled brow rose. "As you have?"

She didn't respond, just stared at the woman until she sighed. "Fine. I suppose I should thank you."

"Thank me by walking away."

The woman bowed her head. "As you wish." And then she turned on one sharp little heel and did just that.

A click sounded in her ear. It was followed by Alastair's low, rough voice urging her to be careful. Howard was most likely armed.

"You, too," she replied, lowering her head so no one could hear. "Find what you need and get out of there."

Claire turned to the exit. How long she stood there she didn't know. Beyond the glass it was dark. Was Howard out there, watching? Waiting? There was only one way to find out.

She opened the door and walked out into the night.

Chapter 15

Alastair didn't have much time. Any minute now he expected his mother's voice to crackle in his ear telling him that Claire had gone after Howard. That was when the trouble would start. His first priority had to be finding the information Howard was selling, but his anxiety focused solely on Claire.

He'd run all the way to stateroom A18. It took him only a few seconds at full speed. He should have brought Claire with him, but they needed to keep watch, and one of them had to approach Chevalier. In no conceivable scenario would he ask his mother to do that. She was already more involved than he liked.

If Claire was going to kill Howard, she was going to do it. He couldn't stop her. He might delay her, but she would find a way to do it. Either he trusted her or he didn't.

He *wanted* to trust her, but if the situation were reversed, he would kill Howard, and trust had nothing to do with it.

From inside his jacket he withdrew a thin piece of metal about the size of a playing card, with a woven pattern of thin lengths of metal in its center and a square aetheric battery on one end. He inserted the thin part into the punch card reader on the door's locking mechanism. The metal card was a lock-picking device that quickly sorted through the different combinations of punches by manipulating the woven bits of metal so that they either allowed a punch or didn't, until the device found the correct one. The block on the end contained a small engine that sped up the process.

Locks like these weren't terribly complex, but picking them without such a device was very difficult and time-consuming, and some punch locks were very intricate indeed—like the one on his house. These sorts of machines were not available to the public. Arden had made this one, and it had done its job in the length of time it took him to remember the look on Claire's face when they'd shagged earlier.

Shag. That sounded so crude, but "making love" sounded ridiculous. He didn't know what to call what they had done, other than bloody marvelous. Even that was a tad flowery for his liking.

He plucked the device from the lock and slipped it back into his coat with one hand as he opened the door with the other. Now was not the time to be distracted by thoughts of Claire. Like she said, whatever there was between them, it would be over after tonight. There was nothing either of them could do about it.

Howard's room was shrouded in darkness, but lights on the ship's exterior, and the moon high in the sky, provided more than enough for him to see by. His eyes didn't need much illumination. If anyone walked in, he'd most likely scare the person half to death.

The room was neat—tidy to the point of obsession. Obviously Howard had a place for everything and demanded everything be in its place.

The closet contained several suits and shirts, as well as two small trunks. Alastair opened both to find cosmetics and appliances for disguise—false noses, wigs and facial hair, rubbery bits for warts and moles, padding for the face and mouth. There were even special filaments that fit over a person's eye to change the color of the iris, and things to put in shoes to change the way he walked and stood. The man was obviously a master.

Next he looked under the bed, eyes adjusting to the dimmer light accordingly, and found another trunk—one that looked like a salesman's sample case. In that he found a collection of blades, pistols and other weapons that no ordinary gentleman would ever need. There were two empty spaces in the case, so he could only assume Howard had them.

"If you can hear me," he murmured, pressing the switch to activate his communicator, "Howard is armed. Be careful, Claire."

"Don't worry about me," she replied. Her words did little to alleviate his concern. "Careful" and "Claire" were not synonymous. There was something in her tone that made him wonder whether she was already on the move.

Alastair slid the weapon case back underneath the bed and inspected the underside of the mattress, as well as under the blankets and the pillows. Nothing. He went through the dressers and nightstands, and was headed for the bath when he heard his mother say, "Claire just went out onto the deck after your man."

"Did she speak to anyone?"

"A blond woman."

Chevalier. At least she warned the woman. She probably saved her life. "I'll be there as soon as I can."

"Do you want me to follow her?"

Damnation, that was the last thing he wanted or needed. "Mother, you stay exactly where you are."

She harrumphed but didn't argue, for which he was grateful. He had to work fast if he had any hope of stopping Claire and apprehending Howard. She wouldn't kill the bastard right away. She'd want answers. And she'd want to kill him slowly in revenge for her brother. Plus, her conscience would be bothering her right about now, and she'd probably try to get as much information out of Howard as she could—for him.

Little fool.

He peeled back the rugs and peered beneath the chairs. Finally, beneath the writing desk, stuck to the underside, he found a small packet, about the size of a ledger. Alastair inspected it first, to make certain it wasn't booby trapped, and then carefully removed it from the desk.

Inside he found not only Russian documents, but Turkish and Spanish as well. There were even bits of sensitive information about two Warden operations going on in India at the moment, as well as several pages of detailed Company secrets—and the plans for what appeared to be some sort of narrow cannon. His gaze skimmed over the device until he saw the words "Centralized Aetheric Death Beam."

The machine appeared to have borrowed from the research and designs of not only Nikola Tesla but also Frederick Chillingham—Arden's father. Combining their research resulted in a device that could gather aetheric energy, route it into a single stream, and direct it at a target, resulting in mechanical failure, physical destruction and death. The cannon would be easily transported, and it could be used in conjunction with several such devices for an even more powerful strike. It was like an aether pistol, but easily several hundred times more deadly.

"Damn it all," he whispered. No wonder Howard had meetings with so many agencies. Such a weapon would command a fortune. Had the blackguard approached the Wardens? he wondered.

He paused, an unpleasant thought taking hold. Did Dhanya already know about this? Was he on Howard's trail to prevent him from selling this device, or was he there to procure it for the W.O.R. so they didn't have to make an offer for it?

It didn't matter. The important thing was keeping this out of dangerous hands. He closed the packet and slipped it inside his jacket. Then he left the cabin and went to his mother's stateroom, where he hid the packet inside the false bottom of a hatbox.

"Alastair?" It was his mother. "Where are you?"

"Second location," he replied, choosing to be cryptic because hearing from her again meant something was wrong. "Why?"

"Dr. Stephens and that lovely blond woman just left the party."

Claire was supposed to have warned Chevalier off. Had the Frenchwoman told Stephens about Claire? Or was Stephens plotting to sell her the plans himself? No, Howard would never have revealed his hiding spot. The most likely scenario was that Stephens had been assigned to "deal" with Chevalier—get the payment from her and then kill her.

He couldn't let the woman die, but he had to get to Claire.

Jaw set, he took off running down the corridor. Doors whizzed by. His hair blew back from his face, he ran so fast. When he spotted Stephens and Chevalier about to enter another stateroom, he intercepted them. Stephens pulled a pistol from his coat. Chevalier drew back, going for her own weapon.

Alastair struck, using the speed of his own body for momentum, and punched Stephens in the jaw. He had to hold back so as not to kill the man, but he felt the bones of Stephens's face crack under the force of the blow.

The doctor made a strangled, guttural sound, then fell to the carpet, unconscious.

"W.O.R. agents will be here soon," he told Chevalier. "They may offer leniency in exchange for information."

She smiled coyly. "Don't worry your pretty little head about me, chéri. I won't be here when they arrive."

Alastair really didn't care one way or another. He nodded at her and then bolted for the nearest deck door. He had to find Claire and Howard.

Hopefully he wouldn't be too late.

"Miss *Clarke*, I didn't expect to see you out here." If mockery were a sauce, it would have been running down Howard's chin.

Claire stopped a few feet away from where he leaned against the deck rail. The ship's lanterns cast him in sinister relief, but she was strangely calm as she faced him. "Of course you did, Howard. I should probably thank you for making it as easy for me as you have."

"I had hoped our paths might cross again one day." He flashed an indolent smirk. "You look surprisingly well for someone who was shot and then fell off a building."

"You don't look half bad yourself. I assume you had some help with that."

"Indeed. Very similar to your own treatment, I wager." He reached into his jacket, and Claire's hand went to the holster in her bustle, every muscle tensed. . . .

He withdrew a silver cheroot case and opened it. "Care for one?"

When she was younger, Claire occasionally smoked

with Robert. She never quite got the appeal of it, but it was a happy memory and she would never besmirch it. "No."

Howard shrugged. "Suit yourself." A match struck, flared and lit the tip of the thin cigar as he held it between his teeth. He shook the match until the flame died and flicked it over the rail. He'd even stolen the way her brother flicked his wrist. "So what now? You put a bullet between my eyes? Maybe carve me up with that wicked fan of yours?"

How did he know about her fan? "Maybe. What are you up to, Howard? Why all the deals and double crosses?"

Exhaling a stream of smoke, the spy laughed. It was Robert's laughter—the bastard. "You don't really think I'm just going to confess to you, do you? Good lord, woman, have you lost your wits? Here's what I'd like to know—when did you start fucking Wardens? I could forgive you Huntley because you didn't know, but that ginger Reynard? Have you no pride?"

He sounded sincerely perplexed—and angry. She hadn't expected him to confess. She might have to torture him for that. More's the pity. Claire kept her fingers curled around the handle of her pistol beneath the bustle of her gown. "What is it to you?

He shrugged. "Just looking out for you."

"Don't. You killed the only man who ever had that responsibility."

"Did I?" Surely he wasn't going to play that game with her? "Are you quite certain?"

Claire pulled her pistol free and pointed it at Howard. "I've had enough of your games. You killed my brother, and I'm going to make certain you pay for it."

He didn't seem the least bit perturbed by having a pistol drawn on him, though she thought there was perhaps a pinch of wariness around his eyes. He looked at her as if she were a joke. She'd seen the same look often enough on her father's face, when he'd hit the bottom of a bottle, before he'd tell her how useless she was or took a swing at Robert.

This wasn't the first time she'd compared him to her father. She'd never seen him in any enemy before, so what was it about Howard that made her think of him?

"Careful with that thing, Claire-a-bell. You might hurt someone."

Claire stiffened, her blood turning to ice and freezing her in place. "What did you just call me?"

"Claire-a-bell. That was what your brother called you, wasn't it?"

She pulled back the hammer, aiming at his right shin. "You don't get to talk about him."

A thin stream of fragrant smoke drifted from his lips. "No? Don't you want to know what happened that night? Wouldn't you like to know about your brother's last moments?"

She would. He was toying with her. "You're just stalling."

"We're in the middle of the ocean. What difference will a few minutes make? Or would you rather I spent the time waiting for your fox to arrive telling you all those boring secrets I've been collecting?" He smiled coldly as he raised the cheroot. "Come now, I'll tell you all about the night I killed Robert Brooks."

She pulled the trigger. In the dark, the aetheric stream looked like a bolt of lightning. Howard screamed as it struck his shin, burning his trouser leg and the flesh beneath, cauterizing its own wound. His cheroot flew over the rail.

Claire braced herself for the smell. "I don't care how you killed him. I just want to know why."

"You bitch!" he cried. "You fucking shot me."

She raised the pistol, this time pointing it at his right shoulder. "And I'll do it again if you don't tell me what I want to know."

"All of this for Robert Brooks?" Disbelief colored the words he ground between his teeth.

"My brother."

He started to laugh, leaning hard on the rail. His trouser leg had stopped smoking and it now flapped around the scorched skin of his leg in the breeze. The cold tried to permeate her skin, but rage kept her warm.

"There's nothing amusing about this situation," she reminded him.

"Sure there is. You're out here making barbecue out of me over a useless twat who didn't even remember your last birthday."

"He was still my brother." Now she was the one grinding her teeth. "And how the hell do you know that he missed my birthday?" Why was she listening to any of this? Alastair would be here soon, and it would be so much better if Howard was already dead when he arrived.

He was still chuckling, only now he slid down into the chair bolted to the deck beside him. He reached up and tugged at his hair—it came off in his hand, revealing light brown, slicked-back hair. He pulled off his eyebrows as well—revealing others beneath.

It was the perfect time to kill him, but Claire couldn't bring herself to pull the trigger. She could only stand there like an idiot as he took thin, gelatin-like lenses from his eyes, removed a false nose and muttonchops, and pulled padding from his mouth along with a set of teeth. All of these things he placed on the length of deck chair beside his wounded leg, until he finally turned to her, his true face revealed.

"Robert," she whispered—it came out like a sob, squeezed from her tight throat. Good God. Stanton Howard hadn't just been pretending to be her brother. He *was* her brother.

Her brother stared at her. "Not any more. Robert Brooks died in an explosion caused by Stanton Howard. Soon Stanton Howard will disappear as well."

"Why?" It was the only thought to pierce the clamor in her mind as she moved toward him, still not quite believing her eyes. The hand holding the pistol trembled, but she didn't lower it completely. Her mind didn't completely trust what her eyes had just seen.

He smiled. "Because I was tired of being someone's puppet. I want to be the one pulling the strings."

"But . . . you didn't tell me."

"Of course I didn't." He made a face indicating he thought she was stupid to think otherwise. "I couldn't tell anyone. I really didn't think you'd come looking for revenge."

"How could you not know I'd want to avenge you?"

He looked almost sympathetic through his pain. "We haven't spoken in what, six months? It's not as though we've been close these last few years. Honestly, Sis, I don't think I would have done this for you."

His words cut her to the bone. "I betrayed my agency for you. I resigned myself to dying to avenge you. For nothing."

There must have been something in her tone or in her face, because he gave her a loving glance—one that came far too easily. "I couldn't tell you, Claire-a-bell. It was too dangerous."

He had always been the better actor of the two of them. It took this to make her realize just how much of a willing audience she had been. If not for her chasing Stanton Howard, he never would have revealed to her that he still lived. He would have let her go on thinking he was dead. He wouldn't have cared.

"You shot me," she said. It was an idiotic statement given the scope of his crimes, but it encapsulated so much of how she felt.

"You shot me!" He lifted his injured leg. "Twice!"

"I didn't know it was you! You knew when you pulled the trigger just who you were aiming at."

"Why do you think you're still alive? Anyone else and you would have died that night." His expression softened. "But now that you know, you can join me. We can be a team again."

"Join you? And what, run away, change my face and

my name and become *your* puppet? No, Robert." He didn't mean it anyway. He was just playing her, as she imagined he'd always played her.

Robert's jaw tightened. No wonder "Howard" had reminded her of her father. Why had she never realized that Robert had grown up to be an even bigger monster? There was no warmth of feeling in him at all. Perhaps their father was to blame for some of that, the Company for a share as well, but her brother was rotten to the core, and she hadn't seen it. This was the cruelest joke of all.

"I can't have you telling my secret, Claire."

She didn't quite hear him. "The way you killed that poor Russian . . ."

He lunged suddenly—so fast she couldn't react—and snatched the pistol from her hand. He turned his arm and torso. "Will be nothing compared to the way I'm going to kill your lover."

Claire's gaze followed the length of his arm. Her heart leaped at the sight of Alastair. How long had he been standing there? His rugged face was void of expression, and his attention was focused on Robert. "You can't run, Brooks."

Robert chuckled. "Of course I can. You think I didn't notice that lovely little submersible attached to the ship. I assume it's yours? I'll take that—and my sister."

"You won't get very far." As if on cue, the bright light of a dirigible washed over the deck, the soft engines whirring high above them. Beneath that was the sound of smaller craft—sparrows, as they were called, tiny personal flying machines that were used for landing in tight spots or flanking an enemy. They looked like big fireflies, Claire thought.

"They'll be so busy trying to save you, they won't worry about me." Robert grinned. "You lose."

He pulled the trigger.

Chapter 16

The blast caught Alastair in the chest, knocking him off his feet and into the wall behind him. For a second, his entire torso seemed to be engulfed in flame—which died just as quickly as it flared.

Claire didn't think; she just moved. She pulled her fan from her reticule and tossed the ridiculous bag aside. As she lunged, she flicked her wrist, opening the fan with a sharp "snick". Robert pivoted, the smile draining from his face as he spotted her. He whipped his arm around to shoot her, but she lashed out before he could fire—the pistol hadn't quite recharged. The gregorite razors of her fan sliced through his wrist as though it were no more substantial than butter.

Hot blood struck the side of her face. Her brother grasped at his arm and fell screaming to the deck. Claire grabbed the pistol from where it had slid as two sparrows landed on the deck, the wind from their blades stirring up the cool air. The sounds of excited voices filled the night, coming from passengers, curious and excited; from W.O.R. agents arriving on the scene; and from her brother's screams. Claire ignored them all—even the ones yelling at her—and ran to Alastair's side.

"Alastair?" She fell to her knees. He was so still. "Alastair?"

He was breathing. He was alive, thank God.

"You bitch!" She turned to see her brother coming at her. He'd somehow managed to incapacitate a Warden and steal the woman's weapon. He ran toward her, slipping in his own blood as it poured down his front from the stump of his wrist and limping from the burn on his leg.

He could kill her if he wanted, but he was not going to touch Alastair. Not again. She raised the pistol, aimed and fired. By some manner of grace she managed to shoot him in the hand holding the weapon. He collapsed to the deck, whimpering. If he'd screamed one more time, she would have gone for his throat.

The next few minutes unfolded terribly fast. Wardens claimed her brother as more came for her. They seized her by the arms and pulled her to her feet.

"I can't leave him!" she cried. "You have to help him."

"We'll look after Lord Wolfred, ma'am," one of the male agents informed her, "but now you have to come with us."

She didn't fight them—it would do her no good, and only prevent as many agents as possible helping Alastair. She kept her gaze focused on him as they dragged her away, toward one of the sparrows.

They took her weapons and strapped her into the small backseat of the largest of the sparrow ships—most weren't designed to carry more than one rider. Buckles and straps secured a volans canopy to her person. The canopy was a dome of silk that would deploy should she fall from the flier or should there be some sort of malfunction that resulted in falling from a great height, and carry her safely to the ground, or in this case, the ocean. The pilot had a folding metal partition behind her head to prevent Claire from attacking her, and to save Claire from being restrained. These safety measures had been implemented by many agencies after both agents and prisoners had died as the result of aircraft-related incidents.

The same agent who buckled her in draped a blanket over her to keep her from getting chilled.

She watched over the side of the small craft as it lifted off the deck, its whirling blades blocking out almost any other sound. Agents surrounded her brother and Alastair. She didn't want her brother to die, but he was not her concern—Alastair was. How much of her conversation with Robert had he heard? Would he live? And if so, would she ever see him again?

Why couldn't Robert have shot her instead? It wouldn't have hurt any more than realizing he hadn't cared about her the same way she had about him. He'd not only betrayed the Company; he betrayed her as well, by turning into such a beast their father would be proud to call son.

Slowly the sparrow ascended. Alastair grew smaller and smaller until there was nothing but the ship and its lights below her, and even those were becoming tiny and distant.

She didn't cry. The wind stung her eyes and made them water a bit, but that was the extent of tearing. Even when the sparrow docked in the lower decks of a large Warden dirigible, her eyes remained dry. The pack containing the canopy was removed from her person and her hands were bound with what appeared to be garters. They were the ones she'd been given before the mission—the ones that had a multitude of uses. Obviously someone had retrieved her reticule from the deck.

Her pistol had been taken from her when they nabbed her on the ship, as had her fan, leaving her defenseless—not that she was of the mind to defend herself. She was too . . . shocked for that.

Robert, the one person she thought she had in this world, the person she had depended on, who had looked after her, was not what she thought he was. Maybe as a young man he had loved her and wanted to do what was best for her, but the life he'd led as a Company agent had destroyed the boy who used to rescue her from the closet. He used to stand up to their father, and now he had become him—or something even worse.

The truly awful part was that she wasn't even completely surprised by it. Part of her had known he wasn't the hero she made him out to be. Hell, she'd almost killed her own brother. She would have killed him if she had had to.

To save Alastair. And now he was gone, too. Perhaps even for good if that wound got the best of him. Ah, the thought of a world without him in it proved that her tear ducts still worked. She blinked the tears away. Men like Alastair didn't die without a fight, and if they got him to Dr. Stone in time, she would save him. If anyone could save him, it was Evelyn.

"Where do you want me to put her, Captain MacRae?" the guard asked a tall, well-built man with sandy brown hair and dark blue eyes.

The captain looked at her, the blood on her hands and face, the state of her gown. "Put her in my cabin."

"Sir?" The guard sounded just as astounded as Claire was.

MacRae's features hardened. "She just cut off a man's hand and shot the son of a bitch to save one of ours. Give her my damn cabin. Never mind—I'll take her myself. And get those restraints off her."

"As a Warden, I can't do that, sir."

"Then get the hell out of my sight." MacRae took her by the elbow. "This way, Miss Brooks."

"How do you know my name?" Claire asked.

"When I intercepted the Wardens' call for a ship, they told me it was you I'd be picking up. You're the Dove, right?"

"Yes." It hardly mattered now. "Are you going to kill me?"

He shot her a frown as he led her down a set of narrow steps, belowdecks. "Hadn't occurred to me, no. My job's to return you safe and sound to the Wardens."

"You're not British." Inane, but it was what came to mind. She should ask why he was being so nice to her, but she could assume only that it was a lie or he was getting paid a lot to deliver her.

"No, ma'am. My father was Scottish, my mother American, and I grew up in Canada, Australia and China and other parts of the world. My father's business didn't exactly lend itself to living in one place for very long, if you take my meaning."

Claire smiled. "I believe I do. You don't have to give me your cabin. Just put me in a cell if you have one."

He steered her left at the bottom of the stairs, toward the back of the ship. "I'm putting you where you'll be safe, and my room's the safest I've got."

As they passed by a door, it opened and a gentleman stuck his head out. "Everything all right, Mac?"

The captain waved at him. "Brief detour, Theo. Don't worry, I'll have you where you need to be on time."

The man smiled, his relief almost palpable. He gave a nod to Claire before he closed the door. She caught a glimpse of an attractive blond woman in the room as well. It was none of her business, so she didn't ask.

Captain MacRae slipped a punch card into the lock of the last room at the end of the corridor and opened the door. He stood back so she could enter first.

The room was large, with dark wood and richly colored fabrics. It was neat—for a man—and smelled of sandalwood and leather.

"Make yourself comfortable," he said. "We'll be in London in less than two hours." He withdrew a wicked-looking blade from the sheath at his waist. "Let me get those restraints off you."

Claire extended her arms. MacRae slipped the tip of the blade into a small notch on the clip of the garter and turned. There was a soft click, and the bonds slid open, releasing their bite on her wrists.

"Thank you."

He took the deceptively strong piece of ribbon and tucked it in his pocket. "You're welcome. There's whiskey if you want, some shortbread in the box on the desk and a few books on the shelf. If you need anything, just ring."

"Just like Evelyn," she murmured as she looked around the room.

"What was that?" MacRae asked. His tone was clipped, his shoulders suddenly very straight.

"Nothing," Claire replied, stunned by his sudden change in demeanor. "Just that you're being so kind. The only other Warden to show me such concern was Dr. Stone."

"I'm not a Warden," he informed her coolly. "And I'm not like Dr. Stone. I keep my promises. Make yourself at home." With that, he closed the door to the cabin, leaving her alone and locked in—if the sound of the punch lock was any indication. Obviously he didn't want her wandering around on her own or escaping. Chivalry went just so far.

It was only then that Claire allowed her spine to sag. A wave of weariness washed over her, driving her to the bed, where she sat down on the soft mattress. She looked up and caught sight of herself in the mirror.

Damn. She looked like something out of a nightmare. Blood smeared her face, dappled her gown and stained her hands.

Her brother's blood. The memory of slicing through his flesh rolled her stomach, but she would have slit his throat if it meant saving Alastair. Robert had betrayed her deeper than anyone else—betrayed everything he swore allegiance to. How could she have loved him? Believed he loved her? Perhaps he had once, but he'd changed into something hard and selfish—and insane.

Had she become that as well? Almost. She'd been willing to put her own desire for vengeance ahead of capturing a vicious spy, above saving the lives of many. The Wardens would manage to get secrets out of Robert. She'd heard they had some sort of device that could literally suck memories out of a person's head. Perhaps they'd use it on her and take away the moments she'd spent with Alastair.

Of course, the thought of him brought all those moments rushing to the front of her mind. Claire rose from the bed and crossed to a narrow door that opened as soon as she turned the handle. It was a small water closet with a shower-bath stall and a small sink. She washed her hands and face with cool water, scrubbing as best she could so she didn't leave rusty stains on the towel.

It was because of Alastair alone that she hadn't killed her own brother. Even before she knew his true identity and still thought of him as Howard, she hadn't pulled the trigger because Alastair wanted him alive.

She might have actually done the deed, but now she would never know for certain. It had been a selfless moment—something she hadn't experienced in a long time. Hell, she'd had sex with him out of purely selfish reasons, and now he was wounded—maybe even dead—because he had protected a friend and ended up stuck with her instead.

If Alastair died, his blood would be on her hands as surely as Robert's had been. And that . . . That would be one regret she couldn't bear to live with.

She made it back to the bed before the tears started. Then she curled up on the quilt and let them come. For the first time since her mother's death Claire allowed herself to truly cry—not just a few hot tears, but great, gulping sobs wrenched from the bottom of her soul.

By the time the ship docked in London, Claire had pulled herself together, though her eyes were still scratchy and a little red. She was taken from the cabin by Captain MacRae and escorted to the deck where she was handed over into Warden custody. A woman of obvious Indian descent met her. The moonlight turned the woman's hair almost blue and added a surreal element to the scene.

"Miss Brooks, I am director of the W.O.R. Thank you for your assistance in apprehending Stanton Howard. Given the circumstances, you have the sincere appreciation of the entire Warden agency."

So the Wardens knew Howard was really Robert. Of course they did. Nice of her not to refer to him by his proper name. "Is Alastair all right?"

The woman's face tightened. "He's in Dr. Stone's care now. We have every confidence that he will make a full recovery."

Claire's weary gaze lifted. "Meaning you have no idea whether he'll live or not."

She pursed her full lips. "You'll be taken back to your accommodations at our headquarters. I will meet with you tomorrow for a debriefing." Then to the captain she said, "Thank you for your assistance, Mac."

He merely nodded before turning his back on them both and walking away. The guards led Claire to the other side of the boarding plank where the director waited—with another two guards, both heavily armed. Did they think she'd try to escape?

Then she heard it—the subtle click of an aether pistol being primed.

"Get down!" one of the guards shouted. He shoved Claire toward the other woman, using his own body to shield them. Claire watched in horror as his body stiffened and his eyes rolled back into his head as the smell of burned flesh rent the air. The guard crumpled to the ground.

Claire didn't think; she just acted. She yanked open the door to the waiting carriage and shoved the woman inside, quickly jumping in behind her. Another aether blast scorched the door panel—she felt the heat of it against her skin.

"I assume that welcoming party was for me?" she demanded.

The dark-haired woman shot her an arch look as she shoved scatter shot into a pistol. "Do you? How very astute you are." She passed the gun to Claire and began loading another. Then she banged on the roof with a fist. "Go!"

The carriage lunged into motion. Thank God it was a steam carriage and not dependent on horses, which would run wild at the sound of gunfire. There was a loud boom, and the vehicle took off like mad.

Another blast hit the roof—they were firing at the driver. The back window shattered as a finger of lightning-like energy struck it. The other woman cried out, shielding her face from the shards. Then with a strange synchronized motion, the two of them rose up and returned fire out the destroyed window.

Claire grinned as the man in the road fell to the ground. Wardens converged on him as the carriage carried her and her companion farther away.

"Good shot," the woman commented, a little breathless.

Claire offered her the pistol. "I think you might have been the one to get him."

The woman stared at the pistol as she took it from Claire's hand. "This would be a perfect opportunity for you to try to escape."

"I'm done running," Claire responded, using her skirt to brush glass from the leather seat. "Besides, I have a lot of information in my head that you might find useful, and I can tell you how to get to my brother. Pain won't work on him, but spiders will."

Dark brows rose. "So you have no plans to escape?"

"No. I'm done. I'll give you everything you want. I would like something in return, though."

The woman didn't look surprised. "I'm not sure what I can . . ."

"Please, you're the head of the Wardens. You can do whatever you want."

A droll expression took hold of her exotic features. "What are your demands?"

"No demands. I'll be much less a madwoman if you can keep me in a cell with a view of some sort, and I would like to be kept updated on Lord Wolfred's recovery."

After a moment of silence the woman raised a brow. "That's it?"

"One other thing."

"Of course."

Claire almost smiled at her. "Should Lord Wolfred recover and ever want to see me, I want you to forbid it. He's never to see me again. Do we have an agreement?"

The woman looked stunned, mixed with a healthy measure of curiosity. Then all that melted into resolution. She offered her hand, and Claire took it.

"We do, Miss Brooks. We do."

They told him he was lucky to be alive. They told him that if Brooks had aimed just a little bit to the left, he would have been killed. They told him Claire had damn near sliced her own brother's hand off to save him—and then shot the bastard herself.

And when he asked about her, all anyone would tell him was that she was in custody, cooperating with the Wardens, and being well treated.

That had been over a fortnight ago.

Alastair was almost completely healed now, thanks to Evelyn and her miracle elixir. The burn on his chest from the aether blast had shrunk and was a healthy pink scar that he had to rub special oils on every day to promote healing. The skin felt almost perfectly normal—no pain at all, despite having to heal from the inside out. The scar would last, but it wouldn't be of much significance.

Evelyn visited his home every day to check on his progress, and she usually took tea with him and his mother, who had canceled her trip to America the night he'd been shot and returned to England with him. She'd even hand-delivered the information he'd hidden in her hatbox to Dhanya. And God love her, she took care of putting out the rumor that he'd suffered an injury whilst hunting, so people wouldn't ask unanswerable questions. It wouldn't do for people to find out the Earl of Wolfred had been shot. They might ask why, or better yet, speculate on whether or not it had anything to do with the shooting on board that steamship where they captured a spy. . . . The Wardens had made certain the ship's passengers and crew were well contained, but it wouldn't take much to start tongues wagging.

He'd asked Evelyn about Claire only twice. The first time she told him she was doing well. The second time she said, "She's asked me not to tell you about her."

Those words—however reluctantly spoken—were like a punch to the throat. "Ah" was all he could think to say in response. He felt like a proper twat. It couldn't have all been pretend, could it?

Or did she blame him for having to injure her own brother? He should have been the one to do it. Instead, he stood there, listening as they spoke and needing to hear that she was as shocked as he was—that she hadn't known her brother was Howard all along and that she hadn't meant to double-cross the W.O.R.

No, it hadn't all been pretend, because he had seen the look on Claire's face when her brother turned the pistol on him. He would never forget it, because that was the awful moment when he realized he was in love with her. It was reckless and foolish and positively juvenile of him and he didn't care. He'd fallen in love with the wrong woman—again. Only this time . . . This time he knew it was wrong, and he didn't care.

This time, even though he knew it was over, he kept trying to figure out a way to have her. He hadn't done that with either Arden or Sascha.

On the day Dhanya came to check up on him, he was in his study, going over the accounts for his country estates. On the desk beside him was one of his father's journals. His mother had given them to him, with the suggestion that the volumes might help him better understand the man he'd mistaken for a traitor. Some of it was difficult reading, as there were private thoughts about Alastair's mother and even Alastair himself in them. However, his mother had been right, as she usually was. He did feel closer to his father, and to his mother as well.

Oddly enough, reading about his mother and father's relationship made him feel closer to Claire, too. Like his mother, Claire had simply aligned herself with the wrong people, and she paid a price for it. Except his mother had had his father to protect her. Claire had no one.

"You look hale and hearty," the director commented from the doorway.

Alastair glanced up and smiled. "As do you. Come in. Would you like a glass of something?"

"Brandy if you have it." She crossed the threshold, closing the door behind her. "How are you, my friend?"

"Hale and hearty, as you guessed," he replied, rising to give her a hug. Then he crossed to the small cabinet where he kept his spirits and withdrew two crystal snifters and a bottle. He poured a measure for them both and returned to his desk. He handed her a glass. "Come to check on me, have you?"

"I've been checking on you ever since you were brought back," she informed him. "But yes, I wanted to see you for myself. I also wished to speak to you."

He resumed his seat behind the desk and leaned back in his chair. "About what?"

"About breaking my word."

Alastair frowned at her over the rim of his snifter. "What do you mean?"

Dhanya crossed one of her long trouser-clad legs over the other, a small frown puckering the skin between her brows. "Claire Brooks told me she would do whatever the W.O.R. required of her with a few flimsy conditions. One of them was that you not be allowed to visit her if you tried."

This time it felt like a kick to the gut. "Yes, I heard she wasn't keen to see me."

"See, that's my dilemma. She is keen to see you, Alastair. She's been driving both Evie and me mad asking about you. Oh, she thinks she's being wily, but really . . . Women know these things."

Alastair's heart—that most foolish of organs— fluttered against his ribs. "What has she been asking?"

Dhanya took a sip from her glass. "How you are, of course. If you've recovered. If you've asked about her—and then of course she reminds us that she won't see you. Sometimes she asks about your mother, but it's clear she really wants to know about you. Occasionally she'll say she feels responsible for your injury, given that Howard turned out to be her brother."

"Yes, that was a surprise indeed. Have you gotten much out of him?"

"A fair bit, yes. That's not why I'm here."

"Why are you here?"

She took another drink. "Because I want you to go see Claire. I don't care if you want to see her or not. The woman barely eats. She just stares out the window. . . ."

"She has a window?"

"Yes. Given her terror of small spaces, I gave her a cell with a view. Not like she's going to escape. I don't think she'd try even if I gave her a hammer and a chisel."

Now he was the one who wore a frown. "Why wouldn't she?"

"My best guess? Because this is where you are." When he opened his mouth to speak, she held up her hand. "I don't care what happened between the two of you during those few days you were together, and I really do *not* wish to know. However, it obviously affected the woman. If you have any compassion for her at all, you'll see her."

Compassion? He had a hell of a lot more than just compassion. He didn't know what it was, but he missed her. He'd gone from despising what she was and all she stood for to respecting and liking her in a matter of a day. From there he'd come to find her the most attractive and intriguing woman of his acquaintance. She saved his life.

He would have betrayed the Wardens for her and actually helped her escape, effectively repeating the past and proving himself more like his father than he ever thought. He wouldn't have regretted it at all.

"I'll see her." Dhanya looked relieved. "What is going to happen to her?"

"There's going to be a trial," she confided. "A conclave of Wardens will gather to review her file and weigh it against the service that she's done for us. They will decide whether she's locked away for life or whether she's eventually set free."

His stomach lurched. "If you let her go, there's a good chance the Company will try to kill her." That was usually the case when the Wardens turned a prisoner free. It was almost expected. They didn't make it public knowledge, but word always got out.

"They already have." She relayed to him what happened the night he was shot, when Claire returned to London.

It was as if a giant hand wrapped around his internal organs and squeezed. "She was unharmed?"

"Not a scratch. Killed the bastard, too. She's quite the shot."

"Better than her brother." Absently he rubbed the scar on his chest through his shirt. If Claire had been the one doing the shooting, he'd be dead.

"You could always turn her," he suggested. It was better than just cutting her loose. He didn't know if even he could protect her if that happened.

Dhanya's sharp, amber gaze locked with his. Her nostrils flared slightly as she drew a deep breath. "We could. You know what's required for that to happen."

"I do."

"You would be willing to do that?"

"Without a second thought."

"It won't be easy."

"Nothing worthwhile ever is."

"Ah." Dhanya nodded, a slight smile curving her lips. "That's the way of it, then."

Alastair allowed himself a reluctant smile as well. "I'm afraid so."

She took a sip of brandy. "You know that normally I would be against such an alliance. I would be against your doing anything that might injure you or the Wardens in any way."

"But?"

"You've given so much of yourself to this agency, Alastair. Literally. I cannot help but feel that it owes you something in return."

His heart jumped. "You'll support me?"

Dhanya drained her glass. "Go see Claire. If you still feel this way after that, we'll talk. I will do whatever I can to help you. Be certain this is what you want, my friend. You know the consequences should you fail."

Alastair nodded, allowing the grimness of the situation to temper his hope ever so slightly. "At best I'll be ruined. At worst I'll die."

Chapter 17

Claire picked at the food on her plate. It wasn't that it wasn't tasty—for English fare it was quite good—and it wasn't that she was nervous about her upcoming trial, though she should have been.

No, her lack of appetite—and the subsequent loosening of her clothing—was because she missed Alastair. She refused to admit it aloud because it seemed too entirely foolish, but she could admit it to herself in the privacy of her cell when no one was watching.

She hadn't seen him since that night on the ship two and a half weeks ago when her heart decided he was more important than her own brother. To be honest, that hadn't been a difficult decision. Still, there were moments when she felt almost guilty for it. Some small part of her continued to cling to love for Robert, even though he no longer deserved it. But then, she was beginning to realize that her heart wasn't the smartest of organs when it came to deciding to whom to give itself.

She took a drink of the wine that accompanied her supper. It was good—slightly sweet—and dulled the ache of self-pity in her chest all the faster with barely any food in her belly. She needn't worry about rotting in Warden custody; she'd just waste away at this rate.

He hadn't tried to see her. What did she expect? She'd told them she didn't want to see him. Did she think he'd scale the side of the building, pull the bars off her window and risk his life and his future to whisk her away? Of course she didn't, but a girl could dream. It was a foolish, romantic dream, but she couldn't seem to help it.

Claire drained the glass in one long swallow and filled it again with what was left in the decanter. What a horrible life this was, being a prisoner of the Wardens. Wine every night, crystal and silverware. A window through which to view the world, books to read and company on occasion. Evie—she was no longer Dr. Stone in her mind—came to visit every few days, bringing news and sometimes a treat, such as chocolate or tea.

She hadn't been tortured; she hadn't been mistreated. Perhaps this would continue only so long as she proved useful. After all, she had so much information to give about the Company, its spies and practices. The information she had on her own brother was enough to keep her in comfort for a few more months at least. She hadn't asked about her brother. She didn't want to know. Perhaps he was dining on steak and wine right now as well. God willing, he'd choke.

Robert's betrayal scored her to the bone, proving that trust was not something lightly given or assumed simply because of blood. Alastair had been the last person she thought she could trust; yet he ended up being the most trustworthy man she'd ever known.

And none of it mattered because she'd given up her life—or at least her freedom—for a man who did not deserve her sacrifice. What a fool she was.

She thought about Alastair often—every few moments during the day, and some during the night. She remembered his scent, his smile. She missed the grooves around his mouth. She missed how his eyes flashed like a cat's.

The locks on her cell door disengaged with a now-familiar clink-whir-clink-thunk. It wasn't Evie's usual time to visit, and she hadn't been told that the director would be coming by. She took another drink from her glass as she turned to face the guard. Was it time to fetch her tray already?

But it wasn't a guard who crossed the threshold. No guard had the ability to rob her of breath and reason, or the power to stop her heart in midbeat.

Alastair.

The glass dropped from her hand, landing with a dull thud on the carpet. The sturdy crystal didn't break, but there was wine everywhere.

Claire didn't give a rat's ass. Her every sense was attuned to him. He was all that mattered.

He wasn't wearing a hat, and the thick waves of his hair shone with copper in the lamplight. He looked tired but gorgeous, his eyes the color of a rainy afternoon. He wore a long gray greatcoat over a black jacket and putty-colored trousers. He was whole. Healthy. Alive.

Tears threatened, burning the back of her eyes, but Claire held them at bay. It took every ounce of her strength not to fall to the floor in a sobbing heap. She didn't trust herself to speak.

It was so good to see him. It was like feeling rain on her face after days roasting in a desert.

The door shut, locking him in the cell with her. He removed his long coat and tossed it over the footboard of the bed, walking toward her with slow, measured steps. He was all grace and control, that intense gaze never leaving her face. She stood, trembling—weak in the knees—as he drew closer. His scent—cardamom and man—filled her senses and flooded her chest. Claire closed her eyes, wet heat greeting her lashes.

Strong hands cupped her face. She opened her eyes again, unable to prevent a tear from slipping free; a fat drop of regret that burned her cheek. Alastair caught it with his thumb.

"Don't ever say you don't want to see me." His voice was a silken rasp. "Don't start lying to me now, Claire. Not after all we've been through."

"I'm sorry." Tears made a blur of his face, and she blinked them away. She didn't want to miss looking at him. Her hands gripped the lapels of his jacket. "I thought it would be easier if I turned you away."

"I won't let you," he vowed. "I refuse to let you go."

He would have to. Surely he knew that? There was no future for them, but at that moment, Claire didn't care. She couldn't think of it. All that mattered was that he was there with her.

Warm, firm lips came down on hers. Her heart thumped hard against her ribs as she kissed him back, opening her mouth to his, tasting him and the salt of her own tears.

She was not a woman who cried often. She was not a woman who considered herself weak, but with this man she didn't care. Let him see what effect he had on her. So much of her life had been about subterfuge and hiding her true feelings. Not any more. She would not be ashamed to cry in sheer joy of seeing him.

Pins scattered as Alastair slid his fingers into her hair. The knot slid free, sending the heavy mass tumbling around her shoulders and down her back. Claire's own hands moved down his chest, across the plane of his stomach and beneath his jacket to press against his back. She could feel the heat of him through his clothes, and it seeped into her fingers, relieving a chill she hadn't even felt until then.

He kissed her eyelids, her forehead and cheeks, brushing his lips against her skin with a tenderness that made her chest ache.

When he began removing her clothing, she didn't fight. Why would she when she wanted this as much as he? Her own fingers went to work divesting him of the layers of cloth that kept her from being able to feel his skin against hers.

Finally they stood face-to-face, naked. Alastair's gaze traveled the length of her with a possessive glint that brought a shiver trickling down her spine. He didn't comment that she had lost weight, even though she knew he noticed. It was as though he found her perfect regardless.

The scar on his chest from where Robert had shot him was the size of a silver dollar. Pale pink, it marred the golden perfection of his skin. She pressed her lips to the light dusting of freckles around it, and finally against the scar itself, infusing the kiss with every ounce of regret that memories of that night wrought.

His arms came around her, engulfing her in warm strength. He was so strong. So tender. When she raised her head, his mouth found hers again, and for a moment she thought she tasted wet salt on his lips.

He reached down and hooked one arm beneath her knees, sweeping her off her feet like a damsel in a novel. He carried her the few feet to the bed and placed her on the quilt before settling his larger frame beside her. The bed gave a little under his augmented weight but held firm.

Warm fingers brushed her face, her throat, breasts, belly and lower. Claire opened her legs to him, letting him slip those incredibly talented fingers inside where she wanted them most. She sighed into his hair as his mouth closed over one of her nipples, laving the puckered flesh with the warm lash of his tongue. She slid one of her hands down between their bodies and closed her fingers around the length of his cock, moving them up and down. Alastair groaned against her breast, changing the tempo of his fingers inside her so that she gasped.

They caressed each other and tasted each other for

what felt like hours. He brought her to climax with firm, unhurried strokes of his tongue, and she took him into her own mouth until he pulled her hair and begged her to stop. And then he pushed her back on the mattress as he knelt before her, lifted her bottom so that it rested on the top of his thighs, and slid inside her with one smooth thrust of his hips. Claire cried out in delight.

He held her like that, for a moment, until she opened her eyes and met his gaze. Only then did he lean forward, supporting his weight first on his hands, then his elbows, so that they were pressed together from chest to foot. His pelvis pressed against hers, every rolling thrust stroking not only the sensitive recesses of her body but the aching, greedy knot that his tongue had sweetly tortured just minutes before.

His breath fanned her cheek, warm and moist, as his stormy gaze locked with hers. No man had ever looked at her with such unabashed longing or sexual confidence. He knew exactly what he did to her body and how much she liked it, just as she knew the effect she had on him. The muscles in his back trembled beneath her hands as she dug her fingers into his flesh, urging him deeper inside her. He teased them both with slow, measured thrusts that slowly drove the tension between them higher and higher. And all the while, he looked into her eyes and let her see everything he felt. How much of her emotions could he see?

How could he have brought her to this? She had no shame, no pride where he was concerned. She didn't even know his middle name or his favorite color. Hell, she didn't even know if he had siblings, and here she was offering her heart on a platter. She would kill for him. She would die for him.

She came then—a great shudder of pleasure that took her by surprise. He just kept moving inside her as every nerve in her body lit up at once. She thought he might have gasped, or said something, but she didn't hear the words. And when the last of the sparks subsided, she opened her eyes to find him still watching. She wrapped her legs around his hips and arched up, forcing him as deep as he could go.

His pace quickened then. Claire gasped as her sensitive flesh ignited once more. He made her climax a second time before his own body stiffened, his groans of release mingling with her own cries.

For a while they stayed as they were, reluctant to break apart. Eventually he left her long enough to lie down on the bed, then pulled her close. Claire stroked the strong curve of his shoulder.

"Why are you here, Alastair?"

"I couldn't go without seeing you any longer."

Her heart swelled at his words, even as it ached. "You shouldn't have come. This is just going to make it harder to say good-bye." She started to rise, but couldn't break free of his grip.

"I've no intention of saying good-bye."

The lines around his eyes and mouth were deeper than she remembered—that was her fault. "There's no future for us. What are you going to do? Move into this cell with me?"

"Let me worry about that."

"No." She pushed against his chest, wriggling so that they were eye to eye. "You can't do that to me. I won't let you give me false hope, because I'll cling to it. Life will go on for you and you'll move on, but I'll still be here, hoping for something I can never have."

His gaze never wavered. "I'm not going to just let you go."

"You have to."

"No. I don't. And neither do you. You have to have faith."

She laughed humorlessly. She would have never thought him capable of being so cruel. "In what? In you? I have faith in you, but even you can't fix this. I am an enemy of your government."

"Do you care about me?"

She stared at him. "How can you even ask me that?"

"Tell me."

"Yes. I care for you." She couldn't help but add, "More than I should."

"I care about you, too. It doesn't make sense, and yes, it's inconvenient as hell, but I'm not just going to sit back and let you go, not after you saved my life."

"What you feel is gratitude."

"You're not stupid, Claire. Don't pretend to be now."

She came up on her elbow. "If not gratitude, then what, Alastair? Love?" She held her breath.

"Maybe," he replied. "It could be."

Claire sighed. Her heart seemed to crack. "You're not stupid, Alastair," she said, throwing his words back at him.

He turned his back to her and sat up, reaching for

his discarded clothing. He grabbed his trousers and stood up, pulling them on with quick, jerky movements. Claire watched as he did so, unembarrassed by her nudity and wishing she could enjoy his.

"Don't leave like this," she entreated.

He pulled his shirt over his head and jammed the tails into his trousers. "How would you have me leave, Claire? You obviously wanted to piss me off, push me away. Now that you've succeeded, you wish to take it back?"

"I . . ." She didn't know what the hell to say. He was right, and she felt like a damn idiot for it. "I don't know. I don't want you to be angry with me, but surely you can see that this situation will only lead to heartache—for both of us."

Alastair tugged on his boots. "I'm not going to give up that easily."

Hell's bells, he broke her heart. "What can you do? They're not going to let me go, Alastair. And even if they did, it wouldn't be long before the Company sent an assassin after me. You have to let me go."

He turned to face her, dropping to a crouch in front of where she sat on the side of the bed so that they were eye to eye. She was chilled, but she didn't move—she was pinned by that thundercloud gaze of his.

"If the Wardens did let you go, would you want to be with me?"

She shook her head. He was a stubborn fool. "Alastair . . ."

He caught her face in his hands, forcing her to meet his gaze. "I don't care if you think it's a lost cause, or foolish. I don't care that we've spent only a handful of days in each other's company. Tell me honestly. If you were free, would you choose to be with me?"

"Yes," she whispered, her throat so tight she could scarcely draw breath. She had to be insane to admit it, but God help her, she couldn't lie. And what harm was the truth when it could never be? "Yes, I would choose to be with you."

The smile that lit his face was so bright, it hurt to look upon, and it changed him from a weary man to an exuberant boy in a split second. Claire's eyes burned at the sight of it. He kissed her then, hard and relentless— a branding of his lips upon hers.

"I will see you tomorrow," he informed her when he lifted his head.

Claire stared at him, dazed, as he rose to his feet and snatched his greatcoat from the footboard. She pulled the quilt up around her shoulders. "Tomorrow?" He was going to come back? What point did that serve but to torture them both?

He pounded on the door for the guard. "I'm a stubborn man, Claire, especially when I want something. And make no mistake, I want you."

The door opened, and he swept through it, flashing her a triumphant grin over his shoulder. She could only stare at him, a sharp pain under her breastbone. It was hope, and it hurt like hell.

Alastair made good on his promise. He did come back the next day—just in time for lunch. He brought her chocolate-dipped cherries and fed them to her as they played cards on the bed. As they played, he told her stories about his childhood and asked about hers. She told him the happy memories she had, and about her mother. She did not speak of Robert or her father.

On the second day he came in the afternoon, and he had tea brought in. They had tiny little sandwiches with no crusts and scones with strawberry preserves and clotted cream. He told her about how he met Luke and about becoming a Warden. She told him about her and Robert's being recruited by the Company after their parents' death when a high-ranking agent saw them both in a tiny stage production. It was a story few people knew. And he was certainly one of the few people who knew how poor she and Robert had been, sharing a room above a seamstress's shop.

On the third day, he came for dinner and brought her flowers and a cylinder-playing Victrola. They danced the waltz in her cell and had sex on the windowsill. Afterward, he confided how he'd felt about his father when he thought the man was a traitor, and he told her how the truth had made him see his mother in a different light. She had gotten tangled up in an intrigue with a person she hadn't known was a double agent until it was too late. His father had done what he had to in order to protect her, and he had allowed his own reputation to be questioned—for love.

She told him about her father and why she was afraid of small spaces. And she told him that she had promised herself she would never be caged again.

He'd looked at her then. "I was going to let you escape."

She went completely still. Only her heart continued to move, pounding violently against her ribs. "I beg your pardon?"

"That night on the ship. I was going to tell them you got away. I thought I'd give you the submersible, or find a place for you to hide until the ship reached New York."

He had planned to betray his agency—his country. For her. She didn't deserve such devotion. "I was going to kill him, you know. Stanton Howard. Robert. I never intended to let the Wardens have him."

Alastair nodded. "I know. I wouldn't have blamed you for ending him."

"But I would have ruined your mission."

"The Wardens would have been happy enough with the information I found in his room. We had the Doctor after all. I would have told them I had to kill him."

Claire was actually shaking. "I wouldn't have let you do that."

His smile was sad. "Doesn't really matter now, anyway."

That was a subdued night for both of them after that. But still he came back the next day, and the day after that. He was with her when Evie came to check on her and when the director came to question her about yet more Company secrets. He asked his own questions as well, and all of her answers were recorded by a machine that etched the sound of her voice into a brass cylinder. She talked until she was hoarse, and then they came back the next day and asked even more questions. It was as though they gleaned every detail of her life in the Company from her.

And then they came with Lady Huntley with them— Luke's wife. She had a strange helmet in a box that had wires and knobs attached to it. "It stores memories," she explained to Claire. "We'd like you to wear it while you tell us about a few important events."

Claire turned to Alastair, who smiled. Was it her imagination, or did he seem suddenly very tired? "It will be all right. Lady Huntley's machines almost always work as they ought."

Claire started. Lady Huntley shot him a filthy look. "Your faith in me is astounding." Then to Claire, she said, "There is no danger to you, I swear."

The woman reminded her of a schoolteacher she'd once had, so dry and clipped. She glanced at Alastair. He nodded, a slight smile curving his lips. "You'll be fine."

His assurance was the only reason she let them put the damn thing on her. They asked several questions about Robert—some of them painful to answer. She didn't know when her brother had lost his sense of decency, but she told them what she did know. It was strange thinking the memories of those moments were being lifted from her mind as she thought of them. Not stolen, but . . . borrowed.

They also asked her to talk again about how she came to join the Company, and she explained that they had approached Robert first. He refused to go without her. She recounted as much as she could remember about the few times they worked together, and about how she'd been led to believe that the Company was behind his "death."

"I realize now that Robert wanted it to look like the Company had betrayed him by hiring a killer. Senior officers would be too busy looking for who gave the order to look too closely at his 'death.' And no one would be surprised when Stanton Howard disappeared. They'd assume he either was in hiding or had been killed by the people who hired him."

"And he would have gotten away with it—and sold Company secrets as well as sensitive information from other agencies if you hadn't gone after him," Alastair remarked. The director shot him a pointed gaze, which he met with a slightly smug smile. What was he playing at?

"Why these marathon interrogations?" she asked. "And why now? You people didn't hound me this hard when you first caught me."

The director cleared her throat. Between her, Lady Huntley and Evie, Claire was beginning to feel as pretty and intelligent as swamp water. "Next week you will appear before the upper echelon of Warden officers, who will listen to all the evidence you've given us, plus ask you questions of their own. They will decide whether or not you remain a prisoner here, or whether you are set free."

The thought of freedom flipped her heart like a hotcake on a grill. "Toss me to the wolves, will you?" They all knew what would happen to her if she was set free. The Company would be on her before she made it to the street. Odd, but a few weeks ago that thought wouldn't have bothered her at all. Now she found death wasn't so appealing, and it was all because of the man sitting a few feet away, watching her as though he would trade places with her if he could.

She loved him for that. The realization hit her hard. Love?

"No," Alastair said in a tone that brooked no refusal. "You will not be tossed to the wolves. Trust me."

And she did. That was the cruelest part of all. She trusted him with her life, even her heart. But she couldn't say these things in front of the director and Luke's wife, so she only nodded, letting her faith in him smother the fear in her heart. He was only going to be disappointed. Or worse. If the Company came for her, they would come for him as well, and she couldn't bear the thought of his death—it robbed all breath from her lungs.

He stayed for a few minutes after the women left. He took both of her hands in his and met her gaze with his own unflinching one. "I have to go away for a few days. I'll be back in time for the trial; I promise."

Was this the moment where he finally recovered his wits and walked away from her? No, he wouldn't be that smart, or cruel. He was going to stay with her until the bitter end; she knew that. She was even reconciled to it.

"Where are you going?"

"Paris."

"You poor thing," she drawled. "What a hardship for you to have to go to such an exciting city." She was only a little jealous that he could just up and leave whenever he wanted. She would probably never see Paris again. And she would so like to see it with him. That was what really bothered her—that he was going to the city of love and she wouldn't be able to share it with him.

One corner of his mouth lifted, deepening the groove in his cheek. She adored that little smile, halfhearted as it was. "We all have to make sacrifices."

"You don't. I don't want you to sacrifice anything for me. You've already done so much. . . ."

He cut her off with a kiss. "I do those things because I want to. Now, be a good girl and say good-bye to me properly. I'll be back before you know it."

So she did. She said good-bye with her mouth and hands and body. They didn't even remove all of their clothing—just the necessary items. She straddled him as he sat in the chair and took him inside with a fierce shove of her hips. It was fast and frenzied, and entirely too fraught with emotion, but he didn't seem to mind. In fact, he seemed just as desperate for her as she was for him. And when he finally left her, Claire told herself she would see him again. He would come back for her.

But not even all that damn hope he had given her could make her believe it.

Chapter 18

He promised Claire he'd be back in time for the trial, and Alastair intended to keep that promise even if it killed him.

It almost did.

"Damn it, man," Luke snarled when he met him at the docks. Alastair had just climbed out of the submersible. The little thing was proving to be worth every penny he paid for it. "Promise me that after this you'll go a full year without almost dying."

"I promise," Alastair replied, clapping his friend on the shoulder.

It hadn't been that close a call, and for that he was grateful. In Paris he'd gone into a social club known as a Company favorite. A couple of young bucks had thought they'd make themselves a name by killing him. One pulled a gun; the other a knife. At the end of it, the one with the gun had been shot in the foot and the one with the blade had a broken wrist and a shattered jaw. Not bad, considering what he could have done to them, but he'd let them live in a gesture of good faith, and it had earned him a little respect from the man he'd gone to that club to see.

"Were you successful at least?" Luke asked as they walked, timbers creaking beneath their feet.

"Yes." Alastair patted the left side of his jacket, the lining of which concealed a packet of papers. "Very successful."

"I am glad to hear it. I hope to hell you know what you're doing."

It was said with just enough humor that Alastair grinned. "So do I, my friend. How much time do we have?"

Luke consulted his pocket watch—it was one of Arden's designs, so lord only knew what else the bloody thing did. It probably turned into a carriage if looked at the right way. "Proceedings start in thirty minutes."

"No going home to change first, then. Do I look all right?"

His friend glanced at him and chuckled. "You look like a man who just walked into the lion's den and lived to tell the tale, as I'm certain you're well aware. You should make quite an impression, on the conclave as well as on Claire. She won't thank you for this; you know that."

Alastair nodded. It was a cool, foggy morning, and he pulled the collar of his greatcoat closer. He could use a coffee. "I don't want her gratitude."

"No, and that's a good thing in this situation." Luke

shot him a sideways glance. "Do you have any idea what you're doing or getting yourself into?"

"Yes, and I'm jumping in with both feet regardless."

Luke shrugged a shoulder. "I felt the same way when I met Arden again. Didn't matter if it was right or not. In the end I couldn't stop myself."

"You don't think it's odd that I've known her only a couple of weeks at best?"

"What did I tell you the night I first met Arden?"

Alastair frowned. "I don't remember."

"I do." And that was a miracle unto itself, as much of Luke's memory had yet to return. "I told you she was the girl I intended to marry. So no, I don't think all this fuss is odd at all. A tad dramatic, perhaps . . ." His words trailed off into a grin.

Alastair smiled back. At the end of the dock sat two Velocycles—Luke's and his own.

"How did you get it here?" he asked.

"Carried it over my shoulder." Luke chuckled at Alastair's dry glance. "I drove it. She drove mine."

As if on cue, Arden popped up from behind one of the machines. "Hello, Alastair. I was just looking at some of the modifications you've made. I'm impressed."

"Praise indeed," he replied lightly, and gave her a kiss on the cheek. She looked tired, but she had that glow about her that happy expectant mothers tended to have. "I'm surprised your husband let you ride."

"You try telling her no," Luke shot back. "You'd better get going if you intend to be at Downing Street in time."

Alastair swung one leg over the Velocycle. "Thank you both for your help."

Arden put her hand on his as he gripped the steering bars. "I'm so happy for you, dearest. I hope it all turns out as you want."

He looked into her wide brown eyes and was touched by the depth of sincerity he saw there. She was such a love. He felt only friendship for her now. He brought her hand to his mouth and kissed it—even though she had a smear of dirt on her glove from fiddling with his Velocycle. "Thank you."

He pulled on his goggles, kicked the stability bar up, revved the engine and took off toward the exit of the dockyards. The damp wind sliced through his hair and stung his cheeks. Half circles of moisture beaded on the inside of his goggles, but they didn't interfere with his vision, so he didn't care. Bent low over the steering bars, he whipped the two-wheeled vehicle in and out of traffic, weaving around steam carriages and omnibuses, horses and wagons—both mechanical and organic.

Traffic thinned slightly the farther west he went. While shops and businesses were open for business— their automaton employees sweeping steps and washing windows—it was still a little early for those who lived in the west end to be up and about, and then many of the aristocracy were in the country.

He arrived at number 13 Downing Street with six minutes to spare. He parked the Velocycle in the concealed underground lot that was explicitly for official Warden use, then made his way into the building from a secret stairwell that only he and a few others knew about. It was one of the director's private entrances. There was another off street level for agents, but he hadn't time to run up there. Fortunately, the lift came almost immediately after he pressed the button for it. He rode it up two floors, practically tearing the gate off its hinges in his hurry to get to his destination.

Punch cards gave him access to the doors. At the final one he had to prick his finger on a spindle. He wasn't quite certain of how the device sorted one person's blood from another's, but somehow it knew his when it tasted it, and that was all that mattered. He inserted his card into the lock, and the door slid open.

The conclave—of which he sometimes was a part— met in a subterranean chamber just one level below ground, in one of the vast sections of number 13 that spread beneath the street. It was a large chamber with a long ebony table around which conclave members sat. Chosen from senior agents and officials, they generally met in numbers of seven or greater. Today, given the gravity of the matter, there were thirteen members gathered around the table. He would not be one of them, given his involvement in the proceedings.

Dhanya sat at the head of the table. She shot him a sharp glance as he walked in, chastising him for his last-moment arrival. He shrugged, then seated himself in the small box used to house agents who were to give testimony during the trial. He was astounded when Luke entered the room a moment after him and joined him in the box.

"What the hell are you doing here?" Alastair demanded.

Luke shrugged. "We were about to leave the docks when Arden received a wireless communication from Dhanya requesting my presence. I suppose they want to ask me about Claire's involvement in the Company."

Every curse Alastair knew sprang to his lips. This was not going to be good. And there was nothing he could do about it now. He glared at Dhanya. She'd known about this and hadn't warned him.

The director stared back at him, thin brow arched, as though she had no idea what had him so pissed.

Evie joined them in the box. They both stood at her arrival but hardly had time to say hello—again—before the clock on the wall chimed the hour, and Dhanya called the trial to order.

"My fellow Wardens. Today you are here to decide the fate of Claire Brooks, the former Company operative known as the Dove." Low murmurs greeted the code name. "I ask that you put all personal bias behind you and base your decision solely on the information provided at this trial. Do you swear?"

Every Warden at the table raised his or her right hand and said, "Aye." That was when Alastair noticed a familiar face at the table—too familiar. It was his mother. What the hell was she doing there? In that moment he forgot his anger at Dhanya. She'd purposefully put his mother on the conclave. He could kiss her.

"Bring the prisoner in," Dhanya instructed the guards.

Alastair's breath seized in his chest as the door in the back of the chamber opened. Claire came into the room, flanked by two guards. She wore a pair of black trousers, tucked into high black boots, and a violet shirt under a black waistcoat; her hair was pinned up in a loose knot. She looked thin and tired, but she was still so beautiful, the sight of her shoved his heart into his throat. Her large green eyes looked up, widening when they caught sight of him. Had she thought he'd lied? That he wouldn't come?

The flicker of hope in her expression cut him to the quick. This had to work. He'd break her out of the damn place if he had to. He'd dig her out with a spoon and a butter knife if need be.

Claire was put in a chair separate from the conclave table. A metal man stood on either side of her, but she wasn't restrained. That was a good sign—he hoped. The automatons were standard human-sized models with visual sensors set around their heads, and a voice box. They weren't sentient—thank God—but they were programmed so meticulously, and by such incredible minds, that they unsettled many people with their humanlike behavior.

The proceedings began with Dhanya addressing Claire. "Miss Brooks, you understand that this meeting has been called to decide whether or not you are to remain in Warden custody or be set free, yes?"

Claire nodded. "I do."

"Then you understand the importance of truth during this trial? And you swear to give it?" One of the guards held a Bible in front of Claire's chest as the other clamped a leather and brass glove over her hand and wrist. The glove was attached to a box that looked like the bottom of a phonograph, but it held a large pad of paper rather than a brass cylinder.

"That's one of mine," Arden whispered. She might as well have been yelling, so close was she to Alastair's augmented ear. "It detects changes in body chemistry and pulse rate to determine if a person is lying or telling the truth."

Alastair glanced at her, trying not to grin at her excited expression. The machine was already scratching on the paper. "I know." It would help their case if the conclave had proof of Claire's truthfulness.

God help them if she lied.

Claire placed her hand on the Bible. "I swear." The machine drew another series of arcs on the pad.

"Good. Then we can begin. Miss Brooks, how long have you been a Company operative?"

"My brother and I were recruited when I was fifteen years old. Thirteen years ago."

Fifteen. And Alastair's father had told him that seventeen was too young.

"Did you want to join the Company?" Dhanya asked.

Claire shrugged. "We were poor and had no family. Robert—my brother—said we'd be taken care of, that it would be like being onstage all the time. I didn't care what we did so long as we ate."

It was easy to tell how uncomfortable she was being so candid in front of these strangers, and Alastair could have kissed her for it. Dhanya asked a few more questions, the answers to which all painted Claire in a sympathetic light.

"How many Wardens have you killed, Miss Brooks?" asked Lord Ashford, the man who had stood in as director while Dhanya was gone. He was a crusty old Whig who looked as though he'd died five years ago but hadn't had the courtesy to leave his body. Bastard.

"I don't know," Claire replied calmly. "I've never counted."

Ashford lifted his hooked nose and stared down it at her.

Alastair clenched his jaw, feeling the weight of Luke's gaze upon him. He didn't dare glance at his friend. Instead, he looked at Claire.

"I'm told the count is somewhere between six and a dozen, Miss Brooks." Ashford sniffed. All that disdain must have been clogging his nasal passages.

"I'm sure I'd remember killing that many people, my lord, and I don't."

"Their deaths may have been caused by your actions."

Claire kept her gaze on the old man, her expression blank. "And in your day, sir, how many people died because of your doing what you considered your duty?"

Ashford's lips tightened, but he didn't ask any more questions. Claire had made her point, but Ashford had done his damage as well.

The questioning of Claire went on for an hour, culminating with the events that had brought her and Alastair together. They were a long way from finished, but Claire looked ready to drop. Dhanya noticed as well, because she instructed one of the guards to bring her some tea. Then the trial resumed.

"Miss Brooks," Dhanya asked, "what did you plan to do to Stanton Howard when you found him?"

"I was going to kill him," Claire replied. "I blamed him for the murder of my brother, and I wanted revenge. I chased him to London, but he shot me and pulled me off a building. Then I was captured by the Wardens."

"He tried to kill you, even though he knew what you did not—that you were his sister?"

A flicker of pain crossed Claire's face. "Yes."

Evie made a soft sound of sympathy, and Alastair gave her hand a squeeze. She squeezed back.

Dhanya continued. "You volunteered to lead our agents to Howard and Reginald DeVane, the man known as the Doctor?"

"Yes. I knew they were headed north to a house party. I wanted to see them both pay for what they'd done."

"Because you thought they had killed your brother?"

"Yes." Claire glanced at Luke. "And because the Doctor had harmed a friend of mine."

Out of the corner of his eye Alastair saw Luke smile slightly at Claire. Under different circumstances, he would have been tempted to punch him for it, but there was no place for jealousy here.

The questioning went on to Claire's and Alastair's setting off to find Robert Brooks. Fortunately, no questions were asked in regards to their relationship.

Dhanya managed to be thorough without bringing that up. "You seriously injured Stanton Howard on board the *Mary Katherine*, even though you knew at that point he was your brother. Why?"

Color bloomed in Claire's pale cheeks, but she didn't look at him. "He had injured Lord Wolfred and was going to kill him. I couldn't let him do that."

Dhanya turned to the table. "I would like the conclave to take note that not only did Miss Brooks injure her own brother, but that she risked her life to save that of Lord Wolfred. Her part in that operation yielded valuable information, and it recovered sensitive secrets that could have been disastrous had they fallen into the wrong hands. Upon her return to Warden custody, Miss Brooks has given her full cooperation and spent many hours answering questions concerning her years as a Company operative. She has made it perfectly clear that she no longer holds any allegiance to that agency or its operatives."

"And you believe her, Madam Director?" It was Alastair's own mother who asked this, but he wasn't surprised. In fact, he was rather impressed. Forcing Dhanya to give her own opinion would certainly carry weight with the rest of the conclave.

Dhanya's gaze drifted from one Warden to the next. "I do."

A silent, joyous cheer sounded in Alastair's mind.

The focus shifted now to witnesses. Dhanya called Evie first, who testified to Claire's behavior when she was first brought into custody. She related that Claire never tried to escape or attempted to harm anyone.

"What observations did you make concerning Miss Brooks?" Dhanya asked.

Evie cast an apologetic glance at Claire. "I thought it sad that she seemed so surprised that I might be kind to her. It seemed to me that she hadn't known much kindness in her life, or joy. She'd been an agent for almost half her life, and she knew no other way."

Claire glanced away, but not before Alastair saw the sheen of tears in her eyes. It broke his heart. He had become an agent because he wanted to, but she hadn't had much choice, not if she wanted to stay with the one person she had left—the person who should have protected her but who was little more than a child himself.

Two of the conclave members asked Evie their own questions—nothing of much import. Then she was dismissed. Luke was called next.

"Lord Huntley, you knew Miss Brooks from the time you spent under Company control. Can you describe the nature of your relationship, please?"

Alastair clenched his jaw, feeling the weight of Luke's gaze upon him. He didn't dare glance at his friend. Instead, he looked at Claire, whose attention was directed at him, not at Luke. There was something in her eyes—an emotion just for him—that eased the tension in his shoulders. If she didn't care that they all knew about her and Luke, he wouldn't care, either.

"We sometimes worked together," Luke explained. "We were friends."

"Is that all you were?" Ashford asked with a slight sneer.

Luke turned to the older man. "I don't know about

you, Ashford, but I regard friendship as a very intimate relationship. Friendship requires a degree of caring and respect. Claire Brooks was my friend."

"Would you say you trusted her with your life?" Dhanya asked, cutting off whatever else Ashford might have to say.

"I would," Luke replied. "And she saved it on at least one occasion. Claire was one of the few agents I met—Warden or Company or whatever—who genuinely believed she was doing something to make the world a better place."

"Stick to answering the questions, Huntley," Ashford commanded.

Luke glared at the old man, but it was Dhanya who answered. "Lord Huntley was called here to give testimony as to the measure of Miss Brooks's character. His statement will go on record, and you, Lord Ashford, will remember that in this room, *I* decide what a witness can and cannot say."

Alastair's teeth clenched so tight, his head began to ache. Was any of this making any sort of difference to any of them? If they all thought as Ashford, they'd surely vote to keep her locked up.

His hand went to the packet in his coat. Those papers were probably the only chance Claire had of freedom. It was all up to him.

Luke was told he could leave the witness box. He shot Ashford a dark glance as he stood. Alastair might have smiled had he not been grinding his teeth in anxiety.

Dhanya's gaze met his. The attention of the entire

table turned toward him. "I call upon Alastair Payne, Lord Wolfred. Please stand, my lord."

Alastair rose, aware of Claire's gaze upon him, so full of hope. He could not fail her.

He wouldn't.

When Alastair stood, Claire's heart jumped into her throat. She hadn't seen him for days, and he looked in sorry need of a bath, a bed and a clean change of clothes. Still, he was the most gorgeous, incredible man she'd ever laid eyes on. She knew his disheveled appearance was all because of her, and she loved him for it. Whatever the outcome of this trial, she would spend the rest of her days knowing that he had cared more than anyone in her life.

Then it struck her just how pathetically sad that was. A man who had known her but a handful of days had changed her life so incredibly much. She would never forget that.

The director questioned Alastair about the mission that had put the two of them together, and he answered honestly. He didn't look at her as he spoke, however; he kept his gaze on the conclave. That was probably wise, but she could use a look from him—just a glance—to let her know nothing had changed between them.

She didn't expect this trial to end in her favor, but it would be easier to accept that if she knew he was on her side.

"I have something to say to the conclave, if I may," he said after telling them how she'd stopped Robert from killing him on the ship.

"What is it?" the director asked. Claire frowned. The woman looked as though she already knew the answer.

From inside his coat, Alastair withdrew a string-tied packet. "I would like to formally request that Claire Brooks be recruited into the Wardens of the Realm."

A great uproar sounded at the table—mostly from the old man named Ashford and a couple of his cronies. Lady Wolfred scowled at them. "Oh, do shut up!"

The director banged the gavel at her right. "Order!" she cried. The men—the ones who hadn't heeded his mother—quieted. "Continue, Lord Wolfred."

Alastair cleared his throat. "Claire Brooks not only volunteered to help us locate the Doctor and Stanton Howard, but she aided in the capture of both and saved my life. She has proved herself a capable and worthy asset to this organization." He held up the packet. "I have here papers signed by the director of the Company stating that he will relinquish all hold on Miss Brooks, as well as retract any orders to do her harm, if Robert Brooks is turned over to Company custody."

Angry voices rose again. "Are you serious?" asked a man whose name Claire didn't know. "This woman is hardly worth the information we can get out of her brother!"

That might have stung had he not been correct. Claire turned her attention back to Alastair. What the hell was he doing?

"We've already gotten everything we can out of Robert Brooks," Alastair informed them. "The information he's given us is invaluable. Claire Brooks has given us intelligence that is almost as good, and she can continue to be of service to this organization. If we hand over Robert Brooks, alias Stanton Howard, into Company custody, not only is it a gesture of goodwill between our agencies, but the director has also agreed to share information on several mutual enemies. We've not had such an accord between our agencies since banding together to rid the Continent of Napoleon."

"How do you know all of this?" Ashford demanded. "And how did such papers fall into your hands?"

Alastair straightened. "I met with the Company director myself in Paris two days ago."

Claire's heart seized as blood rushed to her feet. Alastair met with the director? In Paris? Dear God, that meant he had gone to Le Chat Froid—the Company watering hole in that city. For him to walk in there alone . . .

She stared at him. The damn fool had risked his life. For her. What kind of man took that sort of reckless, stupid chance?

A man in love. It hit her like a sack of bricks. Alastair Payne loved her.

"You what?" Ashford cried. "Behind our backs? I'll have you taken into custody."

"You'll do no such thing," the director informed him. "Lord Wolfred had my permission to go to Paris and meet with the Company's leader. He is right that this is a tremendous opportunity to forge a little peace between our two agencies. Robert Brooks is of no more use to us. Claire Brooks is. And by combining our information with the Company's, we could help to bring down several enemy operations in Europe.

Britain has her share of enemies. It is a chance we cannot ignore."

Ashford looked as though he might have a stroke. "And just who will take responsibility for this woman if we do accept her?"

"I will," Alastair said. "I will accept full responsibility." Now he looked at her. There was such determination in those gray eyes. Such love. Claire blinked back tears. Hell, she'd become a weeping idiot since meeting him.

"No," Ashford said. "I won't support this." His cronies nodded in agreement.

"I will support it," Lady Wolfred said, and three others agreed with her. Still, Ashford had more supporters.

Alastair's shoulders straightened. "If you do not support my motion to enter into this agreement with the Company, I will resign from the Wardens."

"No." Claire tried to stand up, but the automatons pushed her back down into her seat. "Alastair, you can't do that!"

Evie rose to her feet as well. "I too will resign."

Claire stared at the woman, who turned and gave her a supportive smile. This time, there was no stopping the tears that filled her eyes.

Luke stood beside them, as did Arden. "And you'll never get anything out of me or any more inventions from my wife."

Ashford glared at them all before turning to the director. "What are you going to do about this, woman? I demand you take action!"

The director smiled. "I am for the agreement, and if

this conclave doesn't agree to it, you will have my resignation as well."

The old man sputtered. "You're doing this for her?" He gestured at Claire.

The director barely glanced at her. Instead, she nodded at Alastair. "I'm doing it for him. For all he's done for this organization and this country, we owe him. I trust him entirely, and if he says this is something we need to do, then by God we *will* do it." She sat back in her chair. "Now, shall we take a vote? All those in favor of recruiting Claire Brooks and entering into an accord with the Company say aye."

Several hands rose—more than half. "Aye," came the chorus of voices.

The gavel came down. The director turned to Claire. "Congratulations, Miss Brooks. You are now a Warden, and a free woman."

A sob tore from Claire's throat. She hadn't expected this. She hadn't thought . . . Suddenly she was caught up in a hug that smelled slightly of amber. It was Evie. She wrapped her arms around the other woman and hugged her fiercely.

"Thank you," she whispered.

Evie drew back with a wide grin. "I'm so happy for you." She stepped back.

Luke was there next. He gave her a smile and a hug before moving aside for the director. "Welcome to the Wardens," she said. "I look forward to working with you. You will be released into Alastair's custody after all the necessary paperwork is filled out."

The guards took her by the arms and led her from the room. She craned her neck to look over her shoulder. "Alastair?"

He looked up and smiled at her. That was the last thing she saw before the door slammed shut.

Chapter 19

An hour later, Claire was brought to Dhanya's office. Alastair had just finished signing the papers that made Claire his responsibility. Basically he was to be a guardian of sorts, and the person on whom all the blame would fall should she betray the Wardens. All that was left was for her to sign as well.

Her eyes were red, but she walked with a straight spine. He'd never seen her look so uncertain before. It was oddly humbling. He'd thought she was unshakeable.

Dhanya handed her a fountain pen. "If you'll sign these papers, Miss Brooks, you can go on your way."

Claire's fingers shook as she accepted the pen. She looked at Alastair. "Are you certain you want to do this?"

His lips curved slightly. He'd been expecting this. "Give us a second, will you, Dhanya?"

His friend and superior nodded. "Of course. I'll be just outside."

When the door clicked shut, Alastair turned to Claire. "What's the matter?"

She stared at him as though he were mad. Perhaps he was. "Alastair, think about what you're doing."

He shoved a hand through his hair. "I've done nothing *but* think about it for days, Claire. It was my idea to offer you a place in the Wardens so you wouldn't be a target for other agencies. I was the one who worked out the details of trading Robert for you. I was the one who went to Paris and sat down with the Company director—who didn't try to take my head off, I'm pleased to say. So don't you dare ask me to think about it any further. It's done."

"This is a big risk you're taking," she informed him. "What if six months from now you decide I'm not worth the effort?"

"That won't happen."

"What if it does?" Her eyes were round, like saucers.

He understood what this was. She was afraid. His brave, foolish Claire, who had faced dangers that would turn most men to gelatin, was afraid of love—afraid that maybe she wasn't worth it. He brought his hands down on her shoulders.

"I love you," he confessed—not that she hadn't figured that out already. "It hit me fast and hard, and I've tried to think my way out of it a dozen times, but that doesn't change that I do indeed love you. I love everything about you—even the things I don't know yet. I'm not naive enough to suppose we'll never have troubles, but I do know that I would have never forgiven myself if I didn't do everything in my power to give us the chance to try. Maybe it won't last, but, Claire, what if it *does*?"

As speeches went, it wasn't his most eloquent, but she didn't seem to mind. Tears welled up on her lashes and spilled onto her cheeks. "I don't know what to say."

Alastair smiled and wiped away her tears with the backs of his fingers. "Yes, you do."

She stared at him, and his grin widened. "Do it," he commanded, as she had to him that morning not so long ago in the little Scottish inn.

Her lips parted. "I—I love you," she whispered.

He laughed. "Louder."

"I love you," she repeated, her lips curving into a smile. "It's insane, isn't it?"

"Yes," he agreed, wrapping his arms around her. "It is insane, and I don't care. You're stuck with me, Claire Brooks, for as long as you like."

Her arms came up around his neck. "For the rest of my life."

"Agreed."

She pulled back and shoved her hands against his chest, knocking him back a step. "But don't you *ever* take such a foolish, dangerous risk for me again! I won't stand for it, do you hear me?"

Alastair laughed. Not even her ire could dull the joy he felt at that moment. "Of course, you would never take such a risk yourself?"

Her smile faded as she lifted her hand to his face. Her palm pressed gently against his cheek. "I'd rather rot in a Warden prison than live a life without you in it."

He swallowed, a sudden thickness in his throat. "No foolish risks. I promise."

"Then so do I." Her breasts pressed against his torso as he pulled her close once more. "You really want to do this?"

"I do. You?"

She nodded, pulling his head down to hers. "I do. I really do."

And then they kissed, and nothing else mattered.

Six months later

"Amazing performance, Miss Clarke. You are the best Tatiana I've ever witnessed."

Claire smiled as she accepted the bouquet of lilies the older gentleman offered her. "That's very kind of you. Thank you so much." She turned and gave the flowers to a girl who worked for the theater, who took them away to put them in water like the six such offerings that had come before.

She worked her way through the small crowd of theatergoers who had attended that night's performance until finally she was alone in the dressing room. With a weary sigh, she dropped onto the stool in front of her vanity.

Shakespeare. Of all the plays she had to perform and win accolades for, why did it have to be Shakespeare? Fate had a rather ironic sense of humor, it seemed.

She opened a jar of cream to remove the heavy greasepaint from her face—the smell still reminded her of Robert/Howard—and heard a soft noise. She turned her head.

There was someone in her closet.

Her heart bounced off her ribs, but she kept her breathing calm as she reached into the case that contained her makeup and pulled out her new aether pistol. It was much smaller than her original gun, and twice as powerful. Adjustable settings allowed her to control just how much damage she did to her target. She set the switch to DIS—discombobulate. God love Arden and her gadgets.

She slowly rose to her feet and moved toward the closet, approaching from the hinged side in case her intruder thought to peek out. A floorboard creaked faintly beneath her heel, and she cringed. She halted, waiting with bated breath. Nothing.

Once she felt safe to move again, she reached out and closed her hand around the doorknob, then yanked the door open as she brought the pistol up to firing height.

The man in her closet grinned at her over a bouquet of white roses—her favorite. Of course he knew that. Alastair knew almost everything there was to know about her—sometimes without having to be told, the bounder.

"You wouldn't shoot an innocent man, would you?"

"There's nothing innocent about you," she replied, lowering her arm. "Are those for me?"

"Of course." He extended the fragrant blooms to her. "I even paid for them."

She accepted them with a broad smile and breathed

in their sweetness. "They're gorgeous. I hope you brought me something else, though."

He pulled a small tube from inside his coat with a flourish. "Of course. Had to pretend I was drunk to get it, though. Hope you don't mind if tomorrow's papers comment on how inebriated I was tonight."

"I think I can live with the New York society pages thinking you can't hold your liquor." She lifted the tube to the light. "So this contains information on what the French are up to, does it?"

"Supposedly. We'll find out when we're back in London. You need to hide that somewhere safe."

She went to the vanity, where she set the pistol, took a perfume atomizer from her cosmetic case and popped the false bottom off it. She slipped the tube inside and reattached the bottom.

"Arden?" he asked.

Claire nodded. "The woman comes up with the most interesting things. I don't know how Luke can stand living with someone who is always thinking."

"He likes it." Strong arms slipped around her, pulling her back against his chest. Their gazes met in the vanity mirror. "By the way, you were wonderful tonight."

Her foolish heart gave a little leap. "You actually saw some of the performance?"

"I make sure I see part of every one; you know that."

She did. No matter where the W.O.R. sent them or where she performed, Alastair always made certain he watched her. If he couldn't stay for the whole play, he made sure he at least saw some of it, even though such performances were part of their cover.

"Warden business always comes second to you," he added, and brushed his lips along the side of her neck.

Claire shivered. They'd been together months now, and his touch still made her weak in the knees. "I never thought I'd enjoy Shakespeare."

"You're a perfect fairy queen. You have a lot in common with Tatiana."

"Such as?"

"Well, she fell in love with an ass."

She laughed and turned in his arms. "But that wasn't real. Oberon was her real love—and her husband."

Something changed in his gaze—it darkened and made her breath catch. "About that."

"Yes?"

"I was thinking about all these admirers of yours that come sniffing around after every performance. I don't like it."

Her heart was pounding now. "No?"

"Not a bit. I don't like them thinking they stand a chance of charming their way into your bed."

"It would be a very full bed, what with you already in it."

"Exactly." His fingers found the ties on the front of her dressing gown and tugged. "I think I need to stake my claim on your affections once and for all."

She gasped when he kissed the naked flesh of her shoulder. She wore only a chemise and corset beneath the robe. "How do you intend to do that?"

His fingers slid beneath the chemise, up her naked thigh. "How long do we have before our dirigible sails?"

"Ninety minutes."

"Plenty of time." He nudged her thighs apart and slid a finger inside her. Her body clenched in response, every nerve igniting.

"This is certainly one way to claim my affections," she said, breathless. "Though, unless you plan to do this onstage, I'm not sure how much of a public declaration it will be."

His other hand freed one of her breasts from her corset. He lowered his head and flicked the hot, wet tip of his tongue across her nipple. "It would pack the house," he murmured. Her nipple tightened under his breath. "But I had something less burlesque in mind."

The finger inside her curved and stroked a spot deep inside that made her knees turn to water. "Ah! Oh?"

Alastair lifted his head, eyes like pewter as he smiled that seductive little smile of his. The ball of his hand rubbed against her sex in the most delicious manner. He seemed to love these little trysts after a mission, whether it was his, hers or the two of them working together. They went everywhere together, no matter which one of them was working. They were always there in case one of them needed the other.

She needed him now, and she was greedy enough to let him go ahead and give her what she wanted.

"Are you close?" he asked, his voice a whisper as he placed his lips against her ear.

"Yes." So very, very close. She arched her hips. She heard buttons releasing and felt his other hand brush against her leg as he unfastened his trousers. The hot, hard length of him sprang free. She moaned, then shoved herself down on his fingers.

"Do you want me?" His stubble rasped against her neck.

"Yes." Two more strokes and she was going to explode.

Suddenly he pulled his finger from her and replaced it with his cock. He thrust hard and deep, shoving the dressing table against the wall. "Marry me."

His words reverberated through her skull as the first wave of orgasm washed over her.

"Marry me, Claire."

Her head flew back as she came. His words unlocked something inside her, intensifying her climax to a degree she'd never felt before. "Yes!" she cried. "I'll marry you. I'll marry you."

Her words had a similar effect on him. Two more thrusts and he stiffened, groaning her name against her hair.

They stayed locked together for some time, until Claire glanced up at the clock on the wall. "Alastair, we have to go. We're going to miss our flight."

He withdrew from her and fastened his trousers, then turned his attention to helping her dress. She didn't even have time to remove her greasepaint, now smeared. Laughing, she wiped a smudge from his cheek. She grabbed some clothes and wiped her face as clean as she could as he threw the rest of her belongings in a valise. The remainder of their luggage would already be on board the dirigible.

Claire tugged on a simple gown of rose-colored silk.

Alastair fastened the buttons in the back as she packed up the cosmetic case and locked it. Then, hand in hand, they fled the dressing room, through the corridor that was fortunately not nearly as packed as it had been earlier.

The spring night was cool as they ran down the steps of the theater to where a line of steam cabs sat waiting for clients. They jumped into the first one, and Alastair shouted for the driver to go.

They raced through the streets of Manhattan toward the Central Park dirigible yard—a small section of turf on the lower eastern half of the huge park. With a few minutes to spare, they boarded the ship and took their belongings to their stateroom. They were on the deck watching the city disappear when Alastair offered her an emerald-cut sapphire set in a simple golden band. "It was my mother's."

Claire stared at it, then at him. "You were serious."

He chuckled. "Well, yes. Weren't you?"

She opened her mouth, about to question him—them. Was this the right thing? The right time? Was it too soon? What if he regretted it later? Then she closed her jaw. There was nothing to question, at least not in her heart. She had decided months ago, on the deck of a steamship, that he was the most important thing in all her world. That hadn't changed. She thought about what they knew about his parents, how his father had done everything to protect the woman he loved. She and Alastair had already proved their love for each other, even if they hadn't been aware of it at the time.

"You're the only woman for me, Claire. The only risk

I ever took that was worth it, no matter the consequences."

Of all the things she'd done in her life, nothing felt as right as this.

"Yes," she said. She raised her gaze to his. "I will marry you, Alastair Payne. I will marry you and take whatever risks life has to offer."

He grinned and took her hand, holding the ring over her finger. "Ready?"

She took a deep breath. "Ready."

He slid the ring onto her finger. It fit perfectly, of course. She wouldn't have expected anything less. Then he pulled her into his arms and kissed her. And as they left one adventure behind, Claire knew their biggest adventure was yet to come.

ACKNOWLEDGMENTS

Books are a joint project, no matter what any author might say. Of course, we would all like to write a perfect first draft, but it doesn't usually happen that way. I need to thank my agent, Miriam, for her support, enthusiasm, ability to deal with my craziness, and all-around fabulosity; my editor, Danielle, for her patience and being just so wonderfully easy to work with (also, thanks for all the chats about *Sons of Anarchy*, *Supernatural* and other TV); my friends for being understanding when I can't come out and play; and my husband, Steve, for listening to me talk about characters and plot, and for wearing a top hat when the occasion calls for it. Finally, thank you to the readers who have taken the time to e-mail me or tweet about how much you enjoyed the first book in this series. Knowing that my books have given a few hours of entertainment makes things like revisions and copy edits all worthwhile. ☺

Don't miss the next exciting novel
in the Clockwork Agents series,

BREATH OF IRON

Coming in summer 2013 from Signet Eclipse

Evelyn Stone literally held a man's heart in her hands before tossing it into a bucket at her feet. She would examine it and its defects later. Right now she had a patient to fix.

The young surgeon assisting her watched in fascination as she took the mechanical heart he offered and introduced it into the gaping chest cavity. She had very little time to put the device in place and connect it to the circulatory system before the man would die.

It would not look good for her, or for the Wardens of the Realm, if the director of Germany's Schatten Ritters, or "Shadow Knights," died under her care. She was supposed to be the best in her field.

She was also pretty much the only one in her field, except for some bloke in America. No one else in Europe that she knew of had made quite the same strides as she where organ replacement was concerned.

Quickly, Evelyn attached the man's remaining tissue to the mechanical pump and checked the seal. She set aside the part that would fit over the front of his chest like a shield, not only protecting the artificial organ, but providing a convenient port for maintenance.

Once the heart was in place she could relax a little. That was the hardest part. Still, she worked as fast and efficiently as she could, and when the man's new heart began to beat in a steady rhythm, she breathed a sigh of relief. A person's heart could only be stopped for so long before lack of circulation did irreparable damage to the brain and tissue.

Above her head she could hear the polite but enthusiastic applauding of her audience. This was the first time she'd performed this sort of operation with spectators watching her every move, evaluating and assessing.

She set her patient's chest back to rights and fitted the panel for his new heart in place. Later she showed the young surgeon—Dr. Franz Adler—how to properly care for the device, ensuring that it—and the man in possession of it—continued to function at optimum capacity for many years to come.

After the demonstration, Dr. Adler asked her to dinner, just as she'd expected he might.

He began talking about the surgery, the work they did within their respective agencies, and about himself—also as she thought he might—but after a couple of bottles of good German wine, he began to rhapsodize about her "exotic looks," "considerable intellect" and finally, the beauty of her eyes. That was when she knew it was time to take him home.

"I have never seen anything like that," Adler told her much later as they lay in bed. "You are a genius. An artist. Your gift is squandered with the Wardens."

Evelyn smiled. He was handsome and fit and had a delicious German accent that she loved to listen to as he complimented her. Of course, he seemed rather enamored with the sound of his voice as well, but she was sated and such languidness of muscle and spirit gave her patience. Normally she avoided such encounters with peers, especially those also in service to their country, but she'd accomplished something extraordinary that day and she needed to celebrate.

If she weren't enjoying Franz's company she would be alone, probably reliving every last detail of the first organ replacement she had performed. She'd no doubt be very deep in her cups as well, vomiting red wine into the toilet's porcelain bowl. Sex was so much more relaxing and usually required less clean up—and didn't leave behind a taste that made her wonder whether something had died in her mouth.

"I cannot believe you are going to leave in a few days," Franz lamented with a charming pout that emphasized his full lower lip. He was gorgeous, blond and blue-eyed, with a body that ought to be immortalized in marble. He was seven years her junior and thought she was a goddess. She could have done much worse.

She *had* done worse.

"I have to return to London," she explained. "Besides, you are going to be very busy now that you are taking over the SR's medical department."

Long, nimble fingers trailed over her bare arm. "You could always stay and we could run it together."

Of course, with the understanding that he would be the one in charge. No, thank you. "The Wardens would be lost without me. I cannot turn my back on them." That was only half bravado. The Wardens would miss her, but that wasn't what made her go back. What made her go back was that she was good at her job— very good at it—and she wanted to do it where she could do the most good. And, if she admitted it to no one but herself, she wanted to be where she could occasionally hear the latest account of Captain Mac's daring adventures.

She had no business wanting to hear about him. She had given up that right. She didn't remain in London just for him; that would be pathetic. She had friends there, a home and a cat. She was important to the Wardens. She would not be so important to handsome Franz, and she refused to be mistress to a man's career. She had tried that once and it had ended badly.

If she was honest, she would acknowledge that most men would come second to her own work. She really couldn't fault Franz for having a similar mind-set.

"Bah," he said. "The Wardens have no idea how fortunate they are to have such an angel in their employ."

Now he was being grandiose. Perhaps she should give his mouth a new occupation so he would stop talking. Or . . .

"I should go," she said, throwing back the blankets and slipping out of the bed naked. She had no shame of her body, but neither was she overly proud. She had long, strong legs, a soft belly, good hips and full breasts, which, while not gravity defying, still managed a good degree of pertness. Most men found her appealing because of her mixed heritage. She'd been born in Jamaica, several months after her wealthy Irish-Canadian father decided to marry the granddaughter of a woman who had been a slave and the man who had bought her freedom. Unfortunately, he had neglected to buy his bride a ticket when he sailed back to England. Evelyn's mother insisted her grandfather had been an earl (sometimes he was a duke) who had been unable to marry her grandmother because of family obligations. Evie had no problem allowing her mother to hang on to that silly thought if it made her happy.

"Where are you going?" Franz demanded, sliding out of bed. The French safe she made him use dangled from his flaccid penis like a little handkerchief poised to wave in surrender. "It is still dark."

"I'm returning to my hotel," she told him, pulling on her trousers. "I want to check on your director in the morning and I'm having a breakfast meeting with an old school friend." It was such a familiar lie that it rolled easily off her tongue. Although this time it was partially true. She was meeting an old friend, just not from school.

"Surely you can stay a little longer?" He graced her with a seductive smile, reaching out to stroke her bare breast.

Evie grimaced. That cajoling tone might work on some naive chit straight out of the nursery, but not with her. He should know the polite and honorable way to play this game. This was why she often went home with her chosen partners rather than taking them back to her rooms. She had learned some time ago that it was easier to do the leaving than to try to show a stubborn lover the door.

She pulled on her shirt, knocking his hand away from her. "No, I can't." She tucked the tail into her trousers.

Franz blinked. "But I want you to stay."

"And I told you I can't." She shrugged into her corseted waistcoat. "Thank you for a lovely evening." She kissed his cheek as an added gesture.

The younger man raked a hand through his already disheveled hair. "Unbelievable. So we make love and now you leave like I am a whore."

He was difficult to take seriously when he was na-

ked and had a condom hanging from his limp cock. She
sat down on a nearby trunk to pull on her boots. "I'm
sorry, did I mislead you into thinking I wanted something else? Did you hope that tonight would be the beginning of a long and loving relationship? Do you want
to marry me?"

"No, of course not." Too late he realized his mistake,
and his distaste quickly turned to panic. "I mean, I had
hoped that we could enjoy each other's company for a
little while longer and see how things develop."

She had two choices—roll her eyes or smile sympa-
thetically. She chose the smile. "That's very sweet, and
please don't think that I don't appreciate the sentiment,
but I really do have to go." With that, she grabbed her
coat and rose to her feet.

Franz chuckled humorlessly. "I'd heard you were a
cold bitch, and now I believe it."

Evie didn't pause. She shoved her arm into one coat
sleeve. "What's the matter? Angry I'm leaving before
you have the chance to kick me out? I'm assuming you
wouldn't want to risk your mother seeing me when she
gets up in the morning."

A dull flush suffused his cheeks beneath the golden
stubble of his beard. "My landlady is a woman of dis-
cretion."

She fastened a button. "Your landlady is your mother.
Did you think I wouldn't see the photographs and por-
traits of you as a child when we came in? Did you think I
was so enamored of you, I wouldn't notice the note left on
your dresser reminding you to give her your soiled laun-
dry? She signed it 'Love, Mother' for heaven's sake."

He stared at her with a mixture of horror and hu-
miliation. "Get out."

"It's about damn time," she retorted and yanked

open the bedroom door. "And take that condom off. You look ridiculous."

"Bitch."

"Give your mother my best."

Evelyn closed the door behind her and made her way down the stairs, not caring if she was seen or not. She didn't care if by tomorrow afternoon Franz—and his mother—had told everyone in Germany what a whore she was. That would only make it easier to meet another man next time she traveled there on Warden business. Her reputation as a surgeon had nothing to do with her reputation as a woman. She would always be in demand because she was an expert at what she did, and she would always find a lover because she was an attractive, confident woman. Those few traits drew some people to her and repelled others at the same rate. Life was too short to worry about the ones who turned up their noses and looked down on her.

Mac had taught her that. The bastard.

She stepped outside into the waning hours of a beautiful September night. Perfect for a walk, even though there were plenty of steam hacks in the vicinity. This neighborhood wasn't far from the airfield where the dirigibles arrived and departed. Consequently, Evelyn's hotel was within close distance.

She paused on the walk, feeling eyes on her back. She glanced up and saw Franz in a window. She waved. He made a rude gesture that made her laugh. She truly was a bitch. She hadn't meant to hurt his pride, but if she was truthful, she'd really only been thinking of herself and her own wants and needs.

Regardless, she wouldn't see Franz again for a long time, if ever. His ambition meant he wouldn't be content to stay with the Ritters for long. She would enjoy telling this story to Claire and Arden when she returned to London. Perhaps it wouldn't be a good idea to share it with their husbands, though. Men were oddly sensitive about such things, the babies.

Her bootheels clicked on the walk, echoing softly among the sounds of passing carriages and noise from the nearby airfield. Evelyn kept a cautious gaze on her surroundings. She could still feel eyes on her. Surely Franz had left his window by now?

Footsteps behind her. Light, but there. She sped up, fingers slipping inside her coat for the weapon concealed there. It might be just another pedestrian, but years at W.O.R. had taught her that paranoia was a virtue.

Do not panic. What would Claire do in such a situation? Or Arden? Dhanya? They were smart, capable women, each of whom would keep her wits and be prepared just in case. She would do the same.

The footsteps behind her quickened, matching her own. No question now whether she was being followed or not. She clasped her blade, pulling it free of the sheath as fingers wrapped around her arm.

She whirled around, using her attacker's momentum to drive herself forward so that the edge of her knife came to settle at the base of a long, smooth throat.

"Jesus on the cross, Evie! Are you trying to kill me?"

Evelyn froze. "Nell?" She hadn't seen the woman in years, but there was no denying her braided gray hair and bright blue eyes, fanned by pale squint lines in her otherwise tanned face. She grinned, revealing unexpectedly straight white teeth.

"I knew you wouldn't forget me!" The tall, handsome woman came in to hug her, and Evelyn flipped her blade, moving it out of the way so Nell didn't slit her own throat. She hugged her back.

"Nell, what are you doing in Berlin?" She looked over the woman's shoulder, expecting to see another familiar face—one wearing a smirk—but there was no one there. That shouldn't be as disappointing as it was, damn it.

"Picking up," her old friend replied, releasing her. "You?"

"The usual." She wasn't at liberty to discuss her assignment with non-Wardens. Not even former ones.

"Understood." Nell adjusted the handkerchief that covered the top of her head and was anchored by her braids. "You all done or still working?"

That was something of an odd question, but Evelyn supposed her old friend asked because she had catching up on her mind. It was late—very late—but she wasn't tired, and it was good to see Nell.

And Nell could tell her all about Mac and rip those old wounds open again. Maybe throw a little salt in for good measure.

"I'm pretty much done. Just a lecture planned for tomorrow and then back to England. You?"

"We're to set sail before dawn." Nell began to walk, so Evelyn fell into step beside her. "I'll walk you back to your lodgings. Where are you staying?"

Evelyn told her. Her German was atrocious, but she attempted it regardless, "Der Lowe und Der Lamm." The Lion and the Lamb. It wasn't a W.O.R. hotel, or even one sanctioned by the Schatten Ritters. It was the hotel she and Mac once stayed in. The same room as well. She told herself she had requested it because of the view.

It truly was an astonishing view.

"Is that place still standing?" Nell chuckled. "No accounting for people's tastes, I suppose."

Evie didn't respond. The hotel was a beautiful old

stone thing and she loved it, but she wasn't about to say so in case her companion decided to share that information with her captain. Just the fact that she was staying there revealed more than she'd ever want him to know.

Instead she asked, "How is everyone? Did Barker get those new teeth he wanted?" The memory brought a smile to her lips.

Nell snorted and nodded. "He did. Can't get him to stop smiling now. McNamara's become a grandfather, and Esther and Dirty Joe finally jumped the anvil."

This was news indeed! "I thought he said he'd never marry her."

"He did. Then she decided that maybe she wouldn't marry him. That changed up his mind right quick."

"Yes, I imagine it would," Evie replied with a grin of her own.

"I suppose you wouldn't have heard that we lost Good Jock."

The grin slid from her face. Jock's real name had been Jacques le Bon, hence the foolish but suitable nickname. During their brief acquaintance he had taught her many of his grandmother's natural cures and remedies, some of which she often used. One had led to the discovery of the accelerated healing liquid she kept in the medical facility at Warden headquarters.

"No," she murmured. "I hadn't heard. How did it happen?"

"Garroted by one of those Bear Bastards." "Bears" was what most agents in Europe called their Russian counterparts.

"I'm so sorry. I know how much Ma . . . you all loved him."

Nell nodded, obviously ignoring her near slip. Mac would hear about that too, no doubt.

God, she couldn't seem to stop thinking about him—even before Nell found her. Maybe it was this city, where they'd made such bittersweet memories, or maybe it was the fact that every time she slept with a different man she was all the more aware that he was not the man she wanted. Nell's appearance was definitely a stick poking an infected wound.

Shouldn't it have healed by now? It had been years. She should be over him rather than pining for him like her grandmother had supposedly pined for her English lover.

Nell continued to talk about other crew members, but not the one Evelyn really wanted to hear about. She listened raptly, laughing and tearing up in tandem as she heard about their triumphs and sorrows.

She looked up and saw her hotel in the near distance. Soon this meeting would be at an end. It would have to be. If Nell came into the building with her, there was a good chance the older woman would be recognized and more than likely taken into Warden custody. The Wardens didn't much care for pirates, and after Evie left Mac, that was exactly what he and his crew had become, turning their backs on Crown and country.

"You'll tell Mac how sorry I am about Jock, won't you?" Evelyn asked, finally allowing herself to say his name.

Nell stopped walking, so she stopped as well. "You can tell him yourself."

Surely she hadn't heard that correctly. Her heart was beating so loud, it was hard to tell. "What did you say?"

The other woman's expression turned sympathetic. "I'm sorry, Evie. I need you to know I was against this from the start."

Cold settled in Evelyn's chest. Claire would have had a weapon in hand by now; so would've Arden. She just stood there, stupid. "Against what, Nell?"

Out of the dark alley just behind Nell emerged two more familiar faces—Barker and Wells. Barker with his leathery face and kind brown eyes. Wells with her hair so red, it looked to be on fire and eyes bluer than the waters around Jamaica. They didn't look happy.

Two more came up from behind her. She couldn't tell if she knew them or not. So someone had been watching her. It just hadn't been Franz.

Sloppy, Evie, she told herself.

"If it's ransom you want, you know the Wardens won't pay it."

"We don't want money, my girl."

Then what? Evelyn pulled her blade free once more. She couldn't take them all, but she could wound a couple of them badly enough that they'd feel it for the rest of their sorry lives. She'd start with Nell, her betrayer.

Evelyn lunged with her dagger but barely made it two steps before she felt a sharp sting in her side, followed by a jolt that dropped her to her knees on the cobblestones. They'd shocked her. She couldn't speak, couldn't really think. Couldn't do anything but twitch. At least she hadn't soiled herself.

Nell's face loomed over hers. "I'm really sorry, darlin'. I mean it." She pressed a white cloth over Evelyn's face.

Chloroform. Bloody brilliant. She'd have someone's head for this. Maybe his heart, too. Or his spleen. She'd remove them while he was still conscious. She'd—

She woke up with a mouth that felt as though it was lined with cotton wool and muscles that pinged as though they'd been denied blood. At least she was on a bed and her limbs weren't bound.

Evelyn moved her head on the soft pillow. It smelled delicious—vanilla and nutmeg. Some of her favorite memories involved a man with that exact scent. Often he'd join her in bed, his skin tanned yet smooth, hair damp from the bath, and she'd bury her face in the hollow between his neck and shoulder and take a deep, intoxicating breath.

She was in the middle of just such a breath when the reality of the situation struck her. She was on a bed that smelled of Mac. Beneath the pounding of her heart she could hear engines—a gentle *whump, whump* that never failed to lull her into slumber.

Bloody hell, she was on the *Queen V*!

Her attempt to launch herself off the bed ended with her strengthless carcass being dumped on the rug. Her muscles were still twitchy from being electrocuted. She spat out dog fur and managed not to be sentimental about it. She was the one who'd given him that overgrown mutt. Then she gathered all her willpower and pushed herself to her knees. Using the side of the bed helped her make it to her feet.

She grasped the edge of a window and peered out. The muscles in her thighs trembled, but held.

Clouds. Not fog but clouds. They were in the bloody sky. She knew it. She just knew it!

Closing her eyes, she swore silently until she ran out of foul words. It took three languages for her to pull herself together. She should have known that meeting Nell wasn't just a coincidence. It never was.

Why did they put her in this room, though? Of all the rooms about this vessel, why did she have to wake up on the bed she'd slept in for months during one of the happiest times of her life? Everywhere she turned there was something of his—a discarded shirt, a pair of shiny brown leather boots, a straight razor with a pearl handle she'd held in her own hand more times than she could remember.

That was a lie. If put to the test, she could probably recall every damn one.

Her knees trembled, but she'd be tarred and feathered if she'd touch that bed again. Slowly, she made her way to the desk. The room was large for one on a ship, but still small enough that there was a place for everything and everything in its place. The ship hit a pocket of wind and bucked, tossing Evie into the captain's chair with graceless ease. Thank God it was bolted to the floor.

No sooner had she righted herself than the door opened. No knock, no inquiry as to her state of decency. There was only one person it could be. She drew a deep breath.

Please let him be fat and pockmarked. And bald. His hair had always been his vanity.

God was obviously not in a mind to favor her today. The door swung open to reveal shoulders almost the same width as the frame in a cream linen shirt and narrow hips in snug brown trousers. She was on eye level with his crotch—not that she minded, but it wasn't very dignified.

She raised her gaze and wished she hadn't. The last few years had been kind to Gavin MacRae. He was a tall man with long legs. His back was as straight and proud as ever. His stubbled jaw was just as firm, and his chin still had that shallow cleft. His mouth was wide and slim, bracketed by smile lines. They fanned out from the corners of his eyes, too, like faint scars in the tan of his face. Only, those eyes didn't sparkle at the sight of her as they'd once done.

She dropped her gaze, chest pinching. It had to be because of the current still tormenting her body. His nose . . .

"Did you break that poor thing again?" she blurted.

He didn't have to ask. His hand went immediately to the center of his face. Even his hands were as she remembered—long and strong.

"No," he replied, quickly dropping his hand. "Someone else did it for me."

His mouth was as smart as ever as well. And he still possessed that drawl of a voice that sounded almost completely without accent except for a little Texas with a hint of Scotland—he'd grown up in both places and considered them equally as his home.

Or at least he had at one time.

Bloody hell but it was good to see him. Painful, too, like pressing on a bruise. He seemed healthy and hale— the lawless life obviously suited him. At least he was alive, which meant he'd survived a lot longer than she ever expected.

"You look good," he said, nodding his head in her direction as he crossed his arms over the width of his chest. His shirt strained at the shoulders.

Evelyn looked down at herself. Her clothes were dirty and she'd been wearing them for almost a full twenty-four hours, she calculated, given the look of the sky outside. If he thought this was good, then his taste certainly hadn't improved.

"So do you." How calm she sounded—like they were having tea. Like she hadn't broken his heart and her own in the process. "What Nell told me about Jock— was it true?"

His features tightened. "Yeah. It's true. We lost him two years ago."

Just a year after she'd walked out on him. "That must have been hard for you."

"Been through worse." The edge in his usually smooth voice said more than any words ever could. She hadn't been forgiven. Odd then that he'd had her brought aboard his ship unconscious.

"What's this all about, Mac?" she asked wearily. Despite a forced nap, she was tired. Exhausted even.

"Tired after your night of unbridled rutting?"

Under different circumstances she would have smiled at his jealousy. He rarely ever used coarse language in front of her. "Rutting" was as rude as he was going to get. She didn't smile, however; she rubbed her forehead and hoped the look she gave him was more disinterested than remorseful.

"If you wanted to talk, you could have come to my hotel. There was no need to grab me off the street." Wait. Was that her luggage in the corner by the armoire?

He flashed that smirk she remembered so well and leaned one shoulder against the doorframe, arms still folded over his chest. "Talk? I don't want to talk. Darlin', this is an abduction. Consider yourself my prisoner."

Perhaps he could have made the statement a little less gothic novel–style and a little more desperate, but Mac wasn't exactly in the frame of mind to give a damn how he sounded—especially not to Evelyn Stone.

She did look good, despite a little grime. More striking than he remembered. That was fate's way of buggering him good and hard. Long black hair spilled down her back in glossy waves, pins sticking out of it.

Large whiskey and chocolate eyes framed by long sooty lashes glared at him. And that mouth . . .

If he wanted to talk. Christ on a rudder, did she think so much of her own appeal? "You're here because of your skills as a surgeon, not because I care for your company," he told her roughly. A little too roughly to sound sincere, but she didn't seem to notice. Her shoulders pulled back as her spine snapped defiantly straight. She had strong shoulders for a woman. Her entire body was strong. He remembered times with her legs and arms around him, holding him to her like she'd never, ever let him go. He'd always admired the long, defined musculature beneath her soft café au lait skin. Always admired her.

And then she did let him go.

"Are you in need of some sort of . . . procedure?" she inquired, as though the thought of cutting into him gave her perverse pleasure. Obviously ripping out his heart three years ago hadn't been enough.

"Sorry to disappoint, Doc, but I'm not your patient."

"Pity. I warn you, I don't support piracy and I have no intention of stitching a pirate back together."

Yes, she despised pirates and all they stood for—it was part of the reason he'd taken on the profession. Every country in Europe that touched open water had heard of ballsy Captain Mac and his wily crew. "It's not a pirate, either." That was all he planned to tell her. "Get cleaned up and meet me on deck in fifteen minutes."

She arched a gently angled brow. "And if I don't?"

"It's a long way to the ground." It was an empty threat. He needed her too badly to let her go.

"Surely this wreck of a ship has swallows on board?"

Every smart captain made sure his flying girl had the small flying machines in case of emergency or necessity. "None that will be available to you. This isn't up for negotiating. Do what needs to be done and I'll deliver you safe and sound back to the Wardens' front door."

"And if I refuse?"

"Don't challenge me, Evie. And don't think for a minute our past makes one lick of difference. Twelve minutes." With that, he turned and closed the door behind him. He didn't lock it. At several thousand feet in the sky, it didn't seem necessary.

Plus, Evie wouldn't try to escape. She'd do what needed to be done and then try to kill him in his sleep, or give a detailed report to W.O.R. when he dropped her off. Regardless, she'd remain on board if for no other reason than to make his life miserable. She was good at that.

His right hand splayed over his chest. His fingers didn't have to search for the faint ridge of scar tissue; they went there instinctively. Evie might have saved his life, but she'd marked him forever with that cut, though the wound to his pride had cut much deeper. His heart was still raw and inflamed—the memory of her was like an infection that refused to respond to treatment.

And Mac tried to find "treatment" in the arms of every obliging woman he could.

He reached the end of the narrow corridor and the stairs where he could climb up or descend to the lower levels where the galley, hold and crew quarters were. This floor had his rooms, Nell's, and two cabins for passengers. Easiest money ever made was squiring people back and forth betwixt destinations they wanted to keep secret.

He climbed the stairs, the bright morning sunshine greeting him as he reached the deck. He blinked his watering eyes, squinted and stomped toward his first mate, who was at the wheel. Nell always had been the one who had the most common sense, and thus had a pair of tinted goggles over her eyes to protect them from the light.

His most trusted companion took her eye off the horizon long enough to shoot him an assessing glance. "You're still standing and in one piece, so I'll assume she didn't take it too badly."

Mac's own gaze went to the sky. He never got tired of the view. There were several ships like his soaring through the air over Leipzig—passenger vessels on their way north to Berlin, or perhaps southwest to Frankfurt. Germany produced some of the best airships in the world, which made the country a hub for dirigible traffic. People would transfer to other ships, and ships could often get serviced by some talented, mechanically minded buggers who always knew where a man like him could get some extra passengers or cargo.

"I haven't told her why she's here yet."

Nell snorted. "I don't know why you even have to tell her. Just get the gel patched up and we'll be on our way. Seems unnecessarily cruel to give her an explanation."

"I can't trust anyone, my friend. You know that." He turned his gaze to the ground far below them, partially obscured by low, wispy clouds. Everything looked small from this far up, including his life.

"You trust me."

"You're an exception." She'd only saved his arse six or a dozen times. He'd done the same for her.

"You telling me you don't trust Evie? Poseidon's hairy sac, Mac. She saved your life—twice."

"It takes saving my life five times for me to truly trust someone," he retorted with mock gravity.

"Don't you play that with me. I can still kick your skinny arse. Who broke your nose the first time?"

Mac tried not to smile. "You. I remember you got your arse slapped later by Ma."

"It was worth it," his sister shot back with absolutely no remorse. "I'm amazed you can even breathe through the damn thing now."

"You're just jealous because I'm so pretty. Have twelve minutes gone by yet?"

"You gave her a time limit? Good thing you're pretty, because there ain't a brain in your fool head."

"We don't have much time, Nelly. I'm already risking Imogen's safety giving Evie that long."

"It's been six minutes since you came up on deck."

"Damnation."

"Oh for pity's sake, just go get her."

"I can't appear too desperate."

"You are desperate, remember?"

Mac's teeth ground together. He loved his sister, but there were times he wanted to pitch her over the side of the *Queen V* without a volans canopy to slow her fall. "The longer I can keep her in the dark, the better. She may decide not to assist me on the principle of it." And that was something Mac couldn't risk.

"Are we still talking about Evie? Because I'm pretty sure that she is above those sorts of shenanigans."

"She used to be." He'd like to believe she hadn't changed, but he wasn't keen on thinking too highly of her either.

"I think she's still sweet on you."

He turned his head and locked his gaze with hers. "No, she's not. Even if she is, I'll be ruining all of that in a few minutes."

"She might understand."

"Are you sure we're talking about the same Evie? No matter how I play this, she won't understand it at all. It hardly matters."

"No," Nell agreed in that dry tone of hers. "I reckon not."

They stood in silence for a few moments. Finally, Mac consulted his pocket watch for the fourth time and said, "Bugger this. I'm going to get her." Three minutes shouldn't make much of a difference. Hopefully the extra minutes Imogen had to wait hadn't made much of a difference to her condition.

"If I hear screaming, I'll bring a bucket of water."

"Who are you going to throw it on? Me? Or Evie?"

"Not certain. Whichever one of you I think will be most entertaining, no doubt."

Nell was right—he was desperate. Imogen's life depended on Evie's skill, and here he was fretting and whining over a few moments. He shouldn't have given them to her to begin with. Damned stupid of him.

A few crew members passed him as he made his way below deck. They all smiled and acknowledged him with some form of respect. He wasn't much for standing on ceremony, but it was comforting knowing that his crew respected and trusted him.

Or at least most of them did. He had a sickening suspicion that at least one didn't share his crew mates' sentiment, but he wasn't going to think on that now, not when the only woman he'd ever die for—and almost had—was in his cabin. He didn't knock, the boy in him hoping for a glimpse of skin.

Alas, he was denied.

Evelyn had washed her face and, he assumed, the rest of her. She was clad in a fresh pair of trousers and a white shirt with a black corseted waistcoat, which was all the rage among ladies now. Her hair was twisted into a messy bun. Within an hour she would have little tendrils of curls slipping free around her face. He would have to watch that he didn't try to tuck them behind her ears like he always used to.

"You're early. I still have two minutes."

He didn't rise to the bait. "Come with me." When she didn't budge, he sighed in exasperation. "Please?"

"That's more like it. This life of debauchery has made sport of your manners."

"My manners are just fine. It's the people offended by them who are the problem." He stood sideways so she could slip through the door. Her hand brushed his thigh. He had steeled himself for contact, so he didn't jump three feet in the air and squeal like a little girl. He wasn't over her. He'd been aware of this for some time, but the realization of just how much power she had over him . . . well, it wasn't welcome.

"Second door on the left," he told her. Evelyn stood and waited for him to do the entering, which he did.

"They have this new thing now," she informed him—rather peevishly, he thought. "It's called knocking. Apparently it's all the rage. You should try it now and again."

"My ship. My doors." He held the heavy oak open with one arm. "After you." He wanted her where he could see her, and certainly not with access to his back. She'd already stabbed him there once.

The room was small but comfortable—as good as on any steamship. The shades had been opened to allow some sun into the room. The woman in the bed couldn't enjoy the sunshine—she was asleep. Sweat beaded her pale brow and pain furrowed it.

"Mac?" It was all Evie said when she discovered the woman.

"Her name's Imogen. She was shot yesterday. I thought it went right through, but I reckon it was scatter shot and some is still in her. She started running a fever a few hours ago." He didn't have to tell her how dangerous scatter shot could be, the tiny fragments breaking off to infiltrate organs and cause even more damage.

"This is why you shocked me and took me prisoner?" Evie turned a disbelieving gaze on him. "Bloody hell, Mac. You could have just asked."

Seriously? Yes, she meant it; there was none of the mockery she'd used before. She had to know he'd rather chew off his own arm than ask her for any favors. "I couldn't take the chance you might say no."

She placed her hand on Imogen's forehead. "I don't say no when someone is injured." She put her fingers at the base of the other woman's throat. "She's fevered and her pulse is erratic. I'm going to have to take a look at her wound and clean it. Fetch my bag, will you? I'm sure you made certain it was brought with the rest of my things."

He had, and he didn't care that she gave him that pointed look that said she knew him so well. "I'll get it." He'd put it someplace she couldn't get to it—he wasn't about to risk her injecting him or his crew with some sort of drug that would make escape easy. He would let her go, but not until he knew Imogen was safe.

"She must be important for you to come to me."

Mac paused at the door and turned his head to regard her over his shoulder. "She is."

"Who is she?" Did he imagine the tension in her features? The false disinterest in her tone?

Evie had walked out on him. There was no reason for him to feel any guilt over what he was about to say, but he did.

"She's my wife."